Murder on the Motu

A Sidney Blaise mystery

Valverde Maclean

Also by Valverde Maclean

The Disappearance of Merry

A young woman disappeared. Her brother was killed in a car crash. It's an old mystery but someone still doesn't want questions asked. Suzie and Peter must travel Australia to find the answer. All the while avoiding death as they relive their own pasts.

Magenta

In a remote region, a young woman's body vanishes, only to reappear fifteen hundred kilometres away. A road trip across the north and the west of Australia brings unexpected revelations, romance, danger and uncertainty that will change relationships forever.

The Letter

A search to understand the mystery behind a faded letter written a hundred and forty years earlier leads a woman to distant places, far from her home and family.

Her unexpected discoveries will change her life and the lives of those around her forever.

Visit **www.valverdemaclean.com**

This page intentionally left blank.

To

Art and Chris

Thank you for your companionship as we sailed the islands of French Polynesia.

Our past is what we have made of it.

Our future may not be what we dream it to be.

It is only the present, a precious time never to be reclaimed, that we may truly influence.

CONTENTS

ACKNOWLEDGMENTS

Thank you to all those readers who are interested in my novels.

I must especially thank Bryan Hughes. His wise suggestions and our many subsequent exchanges, sometimes over a word and other times over the personality of a character, have greatly improved my story and consequently the reader's pleasure. I appreciate his generosity and advice.

Also special thanks to Peter and June Rogers for their support, comments on the story and their encouragement.

Thanks also to Maria and Jack Carroll for allowing me to use them to test that the story is of interest to readers.

Thank you to Danielle and Alan Champness whose command of the French language and its idioms is far superior to my efforts. Also a 'Merci' to Patricia Barry. Her enthusiasm for the French language is infectious.

To Stacey Peterson, a "thank you" for her comments and advice on early chapters. It was appreciated, but understandably, a greater demand on her time precluded further assistance.

I must also acknowledge Marion Bull for her suggestions on the final cover design and wording.

Once again, a 'thank you' to Nahum Szumer for his advice and work in developing the cover design, and to Gemma Brown for her corrections of my many errors in the penultimate draft. Her comments, suggestions, editing and proofreading are greatly appreciated. Any errors remaining are due to my subsequent alterations.

And finally, thank you to my ever-patient wife, who tells me she at times felt like a writer's widow. However her wise remarks, and use of a pencil, made for a far more interesting story.

1   Paradise

True Paradise is a place we must find within ourselves.

The Paradise we are sometimes fortunate to see around us can be a mirage, perhaps even a dangerous place. Some travellers seek to leave their past and its traumas behind them, to find a new and better life, but our pasts have a way of catching up with us. Anyway, at midnight, no airport is a paradise, not even one in Tahiti.

It was midnight in the Arrivals Hall at Faaa Airport. A young Tahitian man in a colourful hibiscus-patterned shirt and white shorts stood in the waiting bustle of tour guides. In one hand leis of frangipani, and in the other a tablet bearing two names, Parker/Gordon. Even in Papeete handwritten signs had long been replaced by technology. Outside the terminal the white minibus was waiting ready to transport the new arrivals from LAX to their hotel. After a two-hour delay in departure and nine hours in an aircraft all that the four travellers wanted was to get away from the airport, a quick hotel check-in, their room key and a comfortable bed.

The tallest of the arrivals was middle aged, possibly in his late fifties, a touch of grey just starting to appear on his temples. Dressed in slacks and a polo shirt with a tiny logo on the breast he wore the look of success. Trimly built and quietly spoken, he was unfazed by the bustle of the airport terminal. His luggage bore the scars of many luggage conveyors and carousels. It was obvious to an astute observer that airports were a familiar part of his life. Perhaps a much travelled businessman or lawyer. While he had the appearance of hours spent in offices he still looked as if he had time enough for a golf course tan.

The woman standing beside him showed the benefit of regular visits to a hair stylist, a careful diet, and clothes purchased without concern of the cost. Her jewellery was expensive but modest, displaying a preference for quality rather than quantity. She gave the impression of being financially free to live life as she wished without the need to advertise it. While no longer young, she was perhaps a few years younger than her husband, she carried her age well. They shared an easy and comfortable familiarity that came from many years of being together.

The second couple lacked that ease. The two men obviously knew each other and were chatting freely, however it was apparent that the two women had never met. The second man was younger, perhaps late forties and more solidly built, a shaven head to cover the already thinning hair and a deeper tan that came from careful tanning beside a pool. His partner was younger again, maybe late twenties, or at most early thirties, and very attractive. She was expensively dressed, her clothes displaying her current label of choice, though her high-heeled shoes were out of place amongst the loafers, sandals and thongs of the milling travellers and locals crowding the terminal exit. Her jewellery was not so much discreet as ostentatious—the gifts of an indulgent partner on display. One suspected a woman for whom age, when it became noticeable, would be put on hold no matter what the cost. From the manner of the two women an astute observer would suspect possible tensions could eventually arise if they had to spend too much time together in close quarters. A tension that would be politely suppressed by the older woman but loudly voiced by the younger.

While both couples had arrived on the same flight, from their greetings it was obvious they had not shared time together on the aircraft.

Soon the four were in the van and away to their hotel. The morning would be the real start of their reunion in Paradise.

2 The Gathering

The two men met for a morning coffee beside the hotel pool. The blue water of the infinity pool seamlessly merged into the varied blues of the lagoon beyond. Then, further out past the white breakers on the coral reef, into the even darker blues of the deeper waters. In the distance the green peaks of the island of Moorea rose from the sea. All were set under a cloudless blue Polynesian sky. Already, yesterday's clothes for travelling had been discarded for cooler holiday attire.

The men were part of an international group that was assembling. They had come from the States, Dubai, from England and from Hong Kong. Men and women, some known to each other and some known only to their partners. Like any such group coming together and spending time in close confinement, understanding and tolerance might be called upon. This trip was to be a celebration. A celebration of a time past. Of when they were younger, and of a time when they were more eager to challenge the world and to enjoy all the delights it had to offer. But that was twenty-five years ago. Much had changed in their lives, and in their souls. How much, and what they had left behind in the past, would be discovered in the warm sunlight and gentle breezes of the Society Islands.

"Who else is coming on the cruise?" It was the younger man, Mike Gordon, who asked the question.

"I think there are nine of us. Casey and me, you and your friend Nikki. Annette, of course, and James and his girlfriend from Hong Kong, and Peter and his wife from Dubai."

"What do you know about the plans?"

Ed Parker shook his head. "Nothing really. Annette contacted me about three months ago. She thought it might be interesting to catch up with the group involved in Project Dynasty and suggested a cruise in the South Pacific could be fun. She said she knew someone who could arrange a charter on a fancy boat at the right price. That would be Annette, she always knows the right person."

"That hasn't changed since the Dynasty days. Even twenty-five years ago she always seemed to know the right person."

"I think that has been her main attribute. Her sense of the law was more doubtful."

"You're still speaking like the lawyer you were then. Nothing's changed?"

"I'm still a lawyer, only some of the laws have changed. I'm still doing takeover law but the people I work with have changed. It's been good to me. What about you?"

"Those days in Hong Kong really gave me my start. I'm based on the West Coast. Nowadays most of my work is with arranging investments in new IT start-ups. It's a bit different to arranging finance for a small Asian investment fund involved in takeovers and buyouts of local businesses."

"It's going well?"

"Yes. It's a great place to be now, although there were a few lean years at first. Some of the people I'm working with these days are very conservative. Not like the old days."

"I thought the IT industry would be very free-wheeling."

"For some it is but I seem to accumulate very old-fashioned, no-nonsense clients. They may be into innovation, but they can also have very definite views of what's right or wrong."

"I see you have a new friend. What happened to Stacey?"

"It didn't last. I guess it didn't help when she moved back to the States and I stayed in Hong Kong. Once we got back together in California it fell apart. Common problem. Too much had happened—with each of us."

"I'm sorry. She was a nice girl."

"Too nice. I wasn't nice enough."

"How long have you been with Nikki?"

"Two years now. She's great fun. Can be a bit demanding at times but everything comes at a cost."

The older man said nothing but his eyes showed agreement. Mike Gordon's new girlfriend Nikki Olson looked as if she would come at considerable cost, and not just financial but also emotional. He hoped for Mike's sake she was worth it. Turning his head he saw his wife approach.

"Good morning Michael. I've just left Nikki. She's looking for you. She's in the foyer. I think she's found a shop."

The younger man grimaced and left and the older woman took his place on the lounge beside her husband. "It's beautiful here. I'm so glad we decided to come."

"I hope the rest of the trip will be as beautiful."

"Why won't it be Darling? Two weeks on a boat cruising the Pacific. The weather is wonderful. We can revisit old times. Those days on Project Dynasty were very special and it was an interesting group of people."

"I know. It's just whenever Annette is involved there is always something going on. It is always for her benefit and I just don't see what it could be now."

"Do you often see her?"

"No. Well rarely, but I keep hearing reports of her activities. Every now and again I might run into her at an airport. I think these days she's based in Houston but she seems to move around quite a bit."

"She's done well for herself?"

"She's very good at what she does. It always seems to be very profitable for her, and the businesses she works with. At least that's in her favour."

"Do you know anything about this boat?"

"No more than I told you. I will be interested to see it myself. Knowing Annette it will be comfortable. I can't see her settling for anything less."

It was the van and driver from the previous night who returned to take the four travellers to the boat.

"Are you sure this is the right place?"

"Sure is," the driver replied. "Marina Taina. The visiting boat quay. The *Ocean Rover*. That's what I was given and there's the boat."

Ed's comment about Annette not settling for less was prescient but not even he had imagined the boat in front of them. It looked massive for just nine guests.

"Wow. I like it. Way to go. This is me!" Nikki's enthusiasm was honest.

"Where's Annette?" asked Mike.

Casey smiled. "You should know Annette. She'll be the last to arrive. She'll wait until everyone's here and then she will make a grand entrance."

Two men came over from the boat. The first was dressed in white shorts and a neatly pressed short-sleeved white shirt with epaulettes and gold braid. The second was a young Tahitian man in white shorts and a white t-shirt.

"Welcome, I'm Claude Durand. I'm your captain for the cruise. You must be Edward Parker."

"Yes. Please, my friends call me Ed. It is only my wife who calls me Ted, or Teddy. When she does that I know she is either being affectionate, or wants something, or else I have done something very wrong."

"Ah, I understand, my wife Matilde, it is the same."

"My wife Casey."

"Enchanté Madame. And you must be Michael Gordon?"

"Please call me Mike. My partner Nikki Olson."

"Welcome to the *Ocean Rover* Ms Olson."

"Thank you Captain, your boat sure looks wonderful."

"I hope you will enjoy your travels. This is Tamahere, just call him Tama, he's one of our crewmen. He and our other deckhand, Amura, will take care of your luggage. He knows which staterooms you will have, so please, just tell him your name and which are your bags and he will take care of them for you. Come on up to the aft deck, we can offer you a welcome drink, whatever you prefer. We are still waiting for five more passengers. Two are already on their way and the last three should be here later this afternoon."

The group, led by Nikki, took the captain's invitation and walked up the short gangplank onto the deck at the rear of the boat. Waiting for them was a young Tahitian woman bearing a tray of hot moist towels. Another young woman moved around the group carrying a tray with glasses and a bottle of champagne. "If you prefer I can get you something else?" The Captain smiled at the young woman. "This charming young lady is Ana". Just then an older woman came from the cabin with a plate of canapés. The captain introduced her. "My wife, Matilde, she is the chef and will take care of your needs on board and it is Eeva with the towels. She and Ana will assist and take care of your cabins."

The four arrivals took glasses and wandered the deck. The boat was certainly spacious; huge was an even better description. Sun lounges complete with pillows and towels were scattered around the deck and at the stern of the boat more lounges and chairs were positioned around a table. No matter how you wanted to relax, there was a place to meet your needs.

"Please, feel free to wander and get to know the boat. Above on the sun deck there is a spa bath if you wish. When we are at anchor you can swim from the sports deck at the stern of the boat. In the saloon you will see steps down to your cabins. Ana will show you which one is yours. Excuse me, I must go, another taxi has arrived. More of our guests I think."

"Captain. Can I get my Facebook posts and use Instagram while I'm on the boat?"

"Ms Olson, that may depend on where we are. If we are near an island I believe you will have a service. When we are at sea it may not be possible at certain positions. It may also depend on your service provider and your cell phone. Please speak with Ana, she is much better with such things than I. However if you have an emergency we can provide satellite communications for you."

On the quay a man and a woman were exiting a small yellow taxi. The man looked up at the group on the boat and waved.

"Well that's Pete and that must be his new wife."

"Have you met her Mike?"

"No Casey I haven't. I haven't seen Pete Metcalfe for years. Not since he went to Dubai. I get a card each Christmas and I knew he and Julianne had divorced and that he'd remarried about eight years ago but I've never met his new wife. Her name is Marlene. I think she's English."

"She looks lovely."

The newcomers came up the gangplank and joined the group. Introductions were made and more champagne offered.

Of the six present, Casey Parker was the only woman to have been part of the group from those earlier days in Hong Kong. Her and Ed's marriage had survived. All the other wives or girlfriends from those years had vanished—replaced by new partners. It was a sign of the changing times. Marriages were now no longer forever, for better or for worse, for richer or poorer. To love and honour might still be used, if people did marry, but obedience was now no longer mentioned.

The latest arrivals had flown in from a nearby island resort. Their trip from Dubai via the States was long and they had decided to add days to their holiday and recover from their flights across the world by having five lazy days beside a warm pool with attentive waiters on hand to meet every request.

Another taxi arrived and a sandy-headed man and a young Asian woman stepped out.

Mike waved to the new arrivals. "Well that's James. A bit thinner in the hair than I remember him. Who's the woman?"

It was Casey who replied with an answer. "Annette said James was bringing his girlfriend Gabrielle Secombe. That's not a Chinese name. I guess we'll find out soon enough."

The latest arrivals had come from Hong Kong but it had also been an extended trip via Australia and New Zealand, and Annette had been correct. The Chinese woman's name was Gabrielle Secombe.

At last a large black car pulled onto the quay. On Tahiti, where most cars were small European or Japanese makes, and usually white or coloured, Annette must have found the biggest, blackest car on the island and chosen the reddest dress she could find. She was making her entrance.

3 Departure

Dusk was falling as Tama and Amura cast off the lines and the yacht pulled away from the quay. On the rear deck the nine guests watched as Claude threaded the boat through the yachts moored around the marina and steered the *Ocean Rover* towards the buoys marking the channel leading to the opening in the reef. Soon the boat would commence the brief passage to the high green island that always seemed to beckon mysteriously to anyone who visited Papeete.

On shore, the lights of the town became brighter as darkness slowly fell. The lights rose away from the shoreline and the busy coastal road up onto the slopes of the hills, revealing habitations that had been hidden in daylight by the green trees and palms blanketing the steeply rising slope. In the distance the lights on Faaa airport runway blazed as an aircraft approached. Ana and Matilde moved among the group with drinks and canapés. Already Nikki had changed from champagne to her favorite cocktail. Ana, the young blonde waitress who served her had obviously acquired skills as a bartender somewhere in her travels. Some of the men had changed to beer but the four other women still held glasses of champagne in their hands.

The voyagers stood on the deck admiring the sights and

enjoying the warmth and the sound of the sea breaking on the reef as the boat passed though the opening and out into the open sea. The waters were calm and the boat appeared to glide across the now dark ocean without even a slight roll or rock to disturb the glasses they held in their hands. From somewhere on the boat soft music played.

Casey stood watching the lights of the airport as another aircraft landed. She turned to her husband. "It was only last night when we landed there." Ed corrected his wife. "It was actually early this morning when we left the airport."

"I hate late-night arrivals. I always try to plan to arrive at a reasonable hour. As long as I can get a lay-flat bed in business class I'm happy to sleep on the aircraft, and the wine and food on the flight was so much better than the usual airline crap. Real bubbles from Champagne and food by Michelin-starred chefs, and I loved their travel kits. So glamorous." Unlike the other arrivals from the States Annette Freidman had taken an overnight flight from Los Angeles. It had arrived that morning but she had still taken a hotel room to catch a few extra hours of sleep and to be fresh to make her appearance at the *Ocean Rover*.

Matilde called them to the dining room. "My husband apologises but he must remain on the bridge. There is so much traffic here. Small boats. They do not always show the lights they should. Tama remains with him on watch, but Ana and I, and Eeva, we will serve your meal."

"Wow, look at this room." It wasn't just Nikki who was impressed by the stately, slightly old-fashioned timber-panelled dining room. Apart from the view out the windows it could have been the dining room of a fancy New York apartment. "Guys, this boat is so classy." It was an opinion that none of the guests could disagree with. It was almost unreal, surreal even, to be sitting in such a room on a boat somewhere in the South Pacific.

This was the first time all the travellers were together around one table. The talk was of the present rather than the past they had come to celebrate. It became apparent that while they had kept in touch, some more than others, generally they knew little of the details of their present day lives. There would be lots of catching up to do. Since Hong Kong they had taken different directions. Ed, the lawyer, and Casey, had returned to the States and he had continued working on international mergers and take-overs. Mike had also returned to the States, but to the West coast; his wife from the Hong Kong days replaced by a new young pretty girlfriend, Nikki. Unlike the others, the sandy-haired Englishman, James, had remained in Hong Kong, but he also had a new partner. That was hardly surprising as he and his wife had already separated before the group had gone their different ways. His new companion, the Chinese girl, was Gabrielle, or Gaby as she preferred to be known. Pete, the Australian of the group, had divorced his wife of those days, or perhaps she had divorced him. His new wife, Marlene, or Marly as she introduced herself, was English and they now lived in Dubai. The ninth member was Annette. She preferred to describe herself as "a citizen of the world" although her life was mostly in the USA.

Matilde had arranged a variety of courses to allow each to choose as they preferred. During the meal she and Ana were attentive to their needs, and then would discreetly withdraw to give the guests privacy.

Gradually more stories emerged of their activities over the

last twenty-five years. For some, times had been good, for others there had been lean years and better years. For a few, lives had been reinvented through necessity and new careers started. Over dinner more memories of those earlier days returned, some happily embraced, others tactfully avoided. Old relationships were resumed, yet life had moved on and the relationships would never be as they once were. Already the deference that had once existed between some people was being renegotiated and a silent struggle for power and status had begun to unfold. The hierarchy that had once existed in Hong Kong would be replaced and a new and different one established.

As Matilde and Ana served coffee Annette took the hand of the cook. "Matilde, I must congratulate you on your meal. It was excellent. Where did you learn to cook like that?"

"My maman. She was a wonderful cook and insisted that my sister and I learn to cook like her. She believed it was most important. For us French people, the food is important. I was a good child and did as I was told but my sister, she would always disagree and run away. But she learnt also."

"And the dessert. It was superb but the flavour was a little different to what I expected. A touch bolder perhaps."

Matilde smiled. "Yes, all guests comment. It was something I learnt when the boat was in the Caribbean. I use muscovado instead of white sugar."

The term 'muscovado' meant nothing to those seated around the table and Matilde explained it was an earlier, less processed form of sugar than commonly used. It carried a stronger flavour from retaining a little of the molasses from the cane juice.

Annette continued. "Perhaps I should have paid more attention to my mother but I doubt I would have learnt to cook like you. Her cooking was...well, I need to be near restaurants and coffee shops. My husband was very disappointed in my cooking. He used to do most of it."

The mention of Annette's husband caused a momentary pause in the murmur of thanks being voiced around the table. For those who had been in Hong Kong it brought back memories. For the others it was news. A husband? Where was he? Was he still around? Why wasn't he here with them? She didn't look like a woman who would have a husband. The pause ended and the conversation moved on.

"I have a question for you Annette. How did you find this boat?"

"I know the man who owns it, Mike. Over the years I've done a few favors for him. He spends a few months each year on it. Sometimes here in the South Pacific and sometimes in the Caribbean. When he's not using it he makes it available for charter. He offered it to me, and don't worry, he gave us a discount on the usual price. He flies out here not long after we leave."

"I'd like to know a man with a boat like this. I could get used to this life."

"Don't worry Nikki, your life isn't too bad. Enjoy what you have."

Heads turned towards Mike who had made the comment.

Nikki was about to reply to Mike's comment but paused.

After a moment she spoke. "Well, we're very fortunate that Annette has friends. Let's just enjoy our cruise."

They were still sitting at the table when there was a long rattle and then the noise of the engines died. Matilde explained. "We have arrived. We are anchored in the Lagoon of Moorea, it is the Bay of Cook. The Captain Cook, the explorer and seaman. It is very beautiful, you will see in the morning."

The group walked out onto the deck but there was little to see. A distant patchy ribbon of lights circled the boat on three sides but apart from that there was nothing to see in the darkness. A solitary car appeared and could be followed as it moved in and out of the streetlights. Then it too disappeared into the darkness. Even the boat lay in silence in the darkness of the black night.

4 Moorea

As the first of the travellers walked into the saloon seeking an early breakfast he was met by a sharp, angry voice from the galley. Moments later Ana appeared and greeted him politely. She didn't look happy, but there was no acknowledgement of the cause of the outburst as she disappeared towards the crew's quarters.

Daylight had revealed the boat nestled in a small inlet. The ribbon of lights from the previous night was now shown to be a road around the inlet. Often it ran close to the water's edge and in places was lined by houses and gardens. At other times it moved away from the shoreline and was hidden from sight beyond trees. Near the small marina stood an empty aging resort, its once stylish rooms replaced by a nearby new, more fashionable, resort of bures built out over the water. Beyond the road the vegetation rose up to bare rocky peaks: the remains of old volcanoes. In places, small patches of land had been cleared of trees and gardens created. Not far from the *Ocean Rover* seven or eight yachts lay anchored. Closer to the shore small runabouts were tied to buoys while others had been pulled from the water onto dry land.

Gradually the group assembled. Already a pattern was

forming. The early risers settling on lounges surveying the scenery and eager for food and their second coffee as the late risers slowly drifted from their cabins to join them.

Matilde and Eeva had arranged a buffet breakfast on the aft deck. "My husband will join us soon to explain where we are. Please, help yourselves. If you need more just ask."

Today the all-white uniform had gone and Matilde Durand and Eeva, the Polynesian stewardess, were wearing colourful dresses patterned with flowers and tropical leaves. Eeva, in keeping with the local fashion, wore a pink frangipani flower behind her ear. There was no sign of the two crewmen, Tama and Amura, or of Ana, the young Polish woman.

When Claude Durand appeared he was wearing a similar patterned shirt with his white shorts. He explained "We are in the lagoon of Moorea Island. Where we are anchored is called Cook's Bay. It is named for the famous English sailor and explorer. In truth it was named in honour of him as Cook did not anchor here but in the next bay. Although perhaps as a Frenchman I should support my compatriot Bougainville. He came to Tahiti earlier. However I think this is one of the prettiest bays in French Polynesia."

Over breakfast the group had discussed the plans for the cruise but no one, not even Annette, had any knowledge of what the cruise would entail or where it would go. James broached the subject with the captain.

"Please call me Claude. The boat is at your command. You can go where you wish and when you wish. Or not go anywhere. It is up to you. However I would suggest that we perhaps go tonight to Huahine. It is a small island not much touched by tourism, and then to Bora Bora. It is very famous."

Bora Bora had been discussed at dinner the previous evening. The Australian of the group, Peter Metcalfe, and his wife had spent five days at one of the glamorous resorts on the island. They had told of being met at the airport on the island and whisked away by launch to their romantic bure on stilts over the water. Nikki had been captivated by their description and was already suggesting to her partner to extend their stay and visit the resort.

The captain continued. "I would also suggest we go to Taha'a and the island of Raiatea. They are very pretty and beyond the usual tourist throng. Perhaps you just want to laze, so there are lounges and the spa pool. You can also swim in the water from the sports deck at the stern of the boat. We can put out floating mats for you if you wish to swim and lie in the sun. But please, tell Ana or Tama or myself if you wish to leave the boat, even for a swim. We don't want to lose you. That is important. If you want activity then we have kayaks and stand-up paddleboards. Tama can also take you water skiing behind the Zodiac. If you wish he can also take you snorkelling. The corals are very beautiful but you must be aware of the currents. They can be very powerful at times. These waters are also very beautiful for fish and rays and sharks. We do have scuba gear on board but by law you can only use it if you have the appropriate certificates. It is not dangerous for those with experience but still you must take care. Please decide among yourselves what you wish to do."

"When do we go ashore?"

"Whenever you wish James. Tama or Amura will take you ashore in the Zodiac. They will shuttle back and forward.

Just ask them and they will look out for your return. They will give you radios so you can call us and they will come and get you. On the shore there are travel agents and you can hire cars or arrange tours. Please, just let one of us know of your plans. We also have some electric bikes on board that we can put on shore for you to use but, I regret, not enough for everyone."

"You certainly have all the toys."

"Yes Edward. The boat is well supplied. One more thing. Matilde asks that if you have any special needs for your food that you speak with her. We have good supplies but perhaps she will need to get something special for you and once we sail further it can become more difficult."

An hour later six people went ashore.

Of the three guests left on board Annette had disappeared to her cabin but Ed and Casey were soaking up the sun on the foredeck.

"What do you think of the plans for the cruise?"

Casey replied to her husband's question. "It all sounds fine to me. I'm quite happy lying here in the sun, soaking up its rays and listening to the lap of water on the boat. I don't want to go racing away exploring like some of the others. I guess we must be getting older."

"Well, we certainly are the senior citizens of this lot but I won't accept 'old'. We are also the only couple still together since those early days."

"Did you pick up the silence when Annette mentioned her

husband? Have you ever heard any more about what happened to him?"

"No. Only what we knew in Hong Kong. Paul disappeared. Police enquiries came up with nothing. As far as I know nobody has ever heard of him again."

"Do you really believe he was killed like some of the rumours said?"

"It's impossible to know. There was no body, but then there was no activity on his bank accounts or his cards. The police found nothing. No one knew of any reason why he should vanish."

"Except perhaps Annette. I think life with her could be trying at times."

"You still don't warm to her, do you Darling?"

"I will never forgive her for when she tried to come onto you Ted."

"You needn't worry. She's not my type."

"She was once."

"That was a long time ago."

"I've seen her at work. She could turn on the charm, and sex appeal, when she wanted to. I expect she still can."

"Talking of sex. What do you think of Mike's new girl?"

"Nikki's a girl making the most of her attributes. Mike's happy."

"Speaking as a man I think she needs to be careful. Mike might tire of her demands. Even when we first knew him he liked variety."

Casey laughed. "I'm sure Nikki would find another friend. I think she would like to meet the owner of this boat."

"I'm not sure Annette told us the full story about him. I was talking to Claude. The boat is owned by a company in the Cayman Islands. He reports to a management company in George Town and they tell him where to be and when he will have guests. The boat shifts from the Pacific to the Caribbean depending on the season. He told me that some years it goes to the Mediterranean. He is very discreet and never mentions the names of any guests who use it. I expect that's a condition of a job like his. If he knows who actually owns the boat he certainly won't tell us, although I gather some people keep returning each year, perhaps that's the owner."

"I wonder if he will have the same crew in the Mediterranean. It would be very different for Tama and Amura and Eeva to be in Europe. So different to Tahiti."

"Perhaps they'll stay here and he'll find a new crew. I expect there would be plenty of young people like Ana prepared to work a passage to the Mediterranean on a yacht like this."

The sound of a boat approaching caused the couple to rise and walk to the side rail to watch its arrival. It was Tama returning with the six who had gone ashore. They were in a lively mood as they came up onto the deck where Eeva was waiting with moist scented towels. Soon all six were settled in lounges, a cold glass of their favored drink in their hand, discussing their adventures. Above them the high bare peaks were vanishing and reappearing through grey scudding clouds and a rainbow hung low over the shoreline where a gentle rain was falling, but none of it reached the group on the boat.

"I loved the kids. They're so sweet."

"Nikki that was obvious. They loved you too because you were always offering them lollies. I think they also wanted to practise their English with you."

"There's no harm in that James. You should be nice to people. Maybe we should learn a few words in Tahitian."

"Did you find a black pearl?"

It was Mike, not Nikki, who answered Casey's question. "She found a pearl shop and she had fun looking but there was no buying. Not yet anyway but I reckon watch this space. I doubt if she can resist for long."

"Darling, I was very good. There were some beautiful necklaces."

"Marly and I liked the gardens. There were so many different fruits and plants. What about you stay-at-homes? What did you get up to?"

"Nothing. Ted and I just lay here in the sun, reading, talking. We're on holidays. A holiday of doing nothing. You others can run yourselves ragged while we relax and chill out."

"Where's Annette?"

"Don't know, neither Ted nor I have seen her all day. I think she's been in her cabin."

At the mention of her name Annette appeared. "No Darlings, I've been up in the saloon and down the stern. That's the correct word for the rear end of a boat, isn't it? I had to catch up on some messages and make some calls while I have a signal. Besides I've been chatting with Claude. He's a lovely man."

"Are you still working Annette? You told us you were on holiday."

"Sort of. There were a few things that needed attending to, but hopefully it's sorted now."

That night around the dinner table the conversation was not of the past but of the present, and not of their lives but the world in general. It was an interesting time to be alive. The growth of a China that was now so different to the country they had first known twenty-five years earlier. A President in the USA who was so different to previous Presidents. A Europe that had also changed. Brexit in Great Britain, separatists on the rise in Spain, a youthful new president in France and so many changes in central Europe. Russia was no longer communist but once again exercising its influence. Then there was the Middle East and Africa with the flood of people leaving war-torn or economically troubled countries in search of better lives. Opinions and politics among the nine varied. It was fortunate that the evening drew to a close before the wine and strongly held views caused politeness to be discarded.

It was midnight when they finally left the table accompanied by the rattling sound of the anchor being raised. A full moon shone above Tama and Amura as they stood stationed at the bow watching the heavy chain being winched on board and slide down into the chain locker. Some of the guests remained on deck watching as Claude piloted the white yacht between the red and green buoys marking the narrow passage through the reef and turned the boat towards their next island, and their next discovery.

5 Huahini

Morning found the *Ocean Rover* at anchor in another small inlet. Unlike Moorea, today there were no other yachts to be seen. Once again a few local runabouts, barely moving in the early morning slack tide, were tied to buoys. Others had been pulled from the water up onto a beach. From the island came the sound of a rooster crowing, to be answered by another from a garden further along the roadway running beside the water's edge. The houses were still and quiet, not a person could be seen on shore. From one house a wisp of smoke rose into the blue sky.

After breakfast the inflatable made two trips to the little jetty. The first with four electric bikes and the second with Mike and Nikki, and Pete and Marly, then Tama returned to the boat. In the distance two out-rigger canoes appeared to be having a race to the boat. As they drew level the young paddlers waved and continued their race towards some unknown finish line.

"Tama, your outrigger canoes are very smart. You Tahitians seem to love the water."

"We grow up in the water, Mister Edward. For fishing and to go to places. It is also play."

"I believe you Tahitians are great sailors."

"It is not just from Tahiti. The other islands as well. My island is a long way away. I come from Rangiroa."

"I've been reading about your forebears' settlement of Hawaii and Easter Island. Those canoes must have been very large but I understand they had sails as well."

"Yes. And we sailed to New Zealand also."

"Our yachts have keels that enable the sails to gather more power from the wind. How do you manage with an outrigger? Won't a strong wind capsize the canoe?"

"Sometimes if it had an outrigger then a man would move out to add his weight. Our big war canoes and voyaging canoes would be two canoes joined like a catamaran and have one or two sails. The old men tell stories of them carrying three hundred men."

"That would be a fearsome sight. Three hundred warriors ready for a fight. I don't envy the enemy."

"Nowadays we prefer our canoes made out of fibreglass and plastic. They are so much easier."

The two couples remaining on the boat had moved to the sun deck where James and Gaby were enjoying the warmth and bubbles of the Jacuzzi. Ed and Casey sat close by with coffees and chatted to them. Annette had still not appeared. The talk moved on from the past to the present and turned to James and Gaby's life in the Colony.

James and Gaby told of the changes that had taken place in Hong Kong since Casey and Ed had left all those years earlier. Not only had there been a building boom, but more land had been reclaimed from the sea and was now covered in new high-rise offices, hotels, shops and even more apartments. The old Kai Tak airport that Ed and Casey remembered had been replaced by a huge new airport on the island of Chek Lap Kok. No longer was arriving in Hong Kong by air as dramatic as it had once been. Businesses had changed as well. Now most of the international trade was direct with mainland companies. Once the British had left the way of life had gradually changed and it was now obvious that the mainland government was in control.

"I think the day is not far away when Gaby and I will leave."

"Where will you go?"

James shrugged his shoulders as he answered Casey's question. "We are still trying to decide. I think Singapore, perhaps. Gaby would like to return to Australia but she also has a link to Singapore. It will depend on what we can find. On a job, the pay, and housing."

"Ted and I were talking yesterday. About Annette's husband. James, you stayed in Hong Kong. Did you ever learn anymore about what happened to Paul?"

"No. Nothing. There was no news after you left. Annette left. The police just dropped the case. Another missing person. I don't think she ever came back. She certainly never contacted me if she did."

"So what do you think happened?"

"I don't know. There were rumours. You would have

heard them but I don't know how much truth was in them."

"You mean about the drugs?"

"Yes."

"James, you were the person who knew everybody in town and what was happening. That was why you were part of the team. If anyone would have known it would have been you. I remember you had lots of contacts, not all of them respectable."

"There are always lots of stories in Hong Kong but most of them are fantasies."

"But James, Casey is right. You knew some very dubious characters. Did you ever get any clues from them? I was always suspicious of Paul's activities. Could he have been on the wrong side of some drug deal?"

"Ed, I just don't know. I never really understood exactly what Paul's business was. As far as I could make out, he sometimes acted as an agent for American businessmen importing goods out of China. He would talk with the contacts in Hong Kong who would arrange the supply. It was cheap clothing and toys. There were a number of people trying to do that, most of it was legitimate, but for some it might have been a cover. I never saw anything to say Paul wasn't legit, although he did know some people who could have been on both sides of the law."

"Would he have made much money from that?"

"I doubt it. I think he mostly lived on Annette's income."

"Have you seen Annette since she left Hong Kong?"

James shook his head. "No. I've no idea what she has

been doing. Has she remarried or does she have a partner?"

Casey answered. "Not that we know about! Ted tells me there have been a few possible men. But at present there doesn't seem to be any man, or woman, that she mentions. I don't even know if she still uses an English passport or if she's become an American citizen."

The information surprised Gaby. "I didn't think she was British. I thought from her accent she was from somewhere in the States. James never mentioned she was from England."

Ed answered. "She was from the UK, somewhere down south, Cornwell I think. She has worked very hard to lose her accent and sound American."

"That explains it. I couldn't place what her accent was. It wasn't New York or the South. Definitely not Texan or West Coast. I thought perhaps the North East, Boston, but even that didn't really fit."

"You are interested in accents?"

"Yes. Language is a pet interest of mine, Casey. For me it's a game to try to place people from the way they speak. Unfortunately it is not always a very accurate way of discerning their character."

Annette appeared just in time for lunch. Before even greeting the four sitting around the table set out on the rear deck she ordered a glass of champagne. "I'm enjoying this cruise. The freedom. The escape. The opportunity."

"Well you are certainly free. We've hardly seen you."

"You and Ted are so lucky. No problems, no hassles. I envy you."

"Surely your life can't be that difficult. You've always been so in charge. Look at this trip. It was your idea."

"You have no idea what this is all about do you? Well, you will find out soon." Annette continued with a long rambling discourse about how it was important to work together or they would all suffer. None of it made any sense to those listening.

"What do you mean we must work together or suffer? We no longer have any mutual connections apart from being on this boat."

"You wait and see Teddy darling. All of you!"

With that she fell silent.

It was Gaby who changed the subject. "Ana is different today, she isn't as bright and bubbly as she has been. At lunch she was very formal and polite."

"Something happened yesterday before breakfast. I heard angry words and Ana walked off. I didn't see her again until the afternoon."

"I think Ted might be right. There's been some tension in the staff quarters. Last night I saw the Captain and Ana together and they were laughing. Then Matilde walked in and Claude left. Matilde was not happy from the tone of her voice, although I didn't hear what she said."

"A bit of jealousy perhaps?"

"Who knows? At least Amura is always smiling."

"Yes, he's a lovely lad. I was talking with Tama and mentioned Amura's smile and he told me Amura means 'big smile' in Tahitian."

"Did Tama say what his name means?"

"Yes. He went very quiet and said his mother named him. It means 'the loved one'."

"What about Eeva? That's an unusual name."

"It's lovely. It means 'the star that rises in the sky'. The Polynesian names are beautiful."

The chat around the table was broken by the noisy arrival of the four bike riders returning from their visit to the island.

Nikki was full of news of their travels. "I've learnt some Tahitian. 'Nui' means big, 'iti' means little, itti-bitty, how cute. Huahine is actually two islands, there's a bridge that connects them, and a sand bar at low tide. We were going to ride up to a lookout but Mike and Pete were worried whether the bikes would have enough charge. You still have to pedal as well, they're not just a motor but I'm used to riding bikes. I do it all the time at the gym."

"Nikki had a wonderful time. I wasn't as fit as I thought. We had a break at a little village."

"You were fine Pete. Pete told us all about Dubai. It sounds really interesting. I'd love to go there one day. Their life is so different from LA. Especially when you can go skiing at a mall in the desert. And it has penguins. That's unreal."

"Perhaps one day you will get there Nikki, if Mike is good to you."

"I hope so. He's a good guy. Then the guys started talking about the old days. I think they were naughty boys in those days. Mike still is. Perhaps that's why they like naughty women. What do you think Marly?"

Marly's expression suggested that she wasn't happy with being considered 'naughty'. Whether it was her own behaviour, or the thought of her husband's possible naughtiness, that concerned her was not to be discovered as Nikki continued without waiting for Marly's reply. "I loved all the little gardens and the water was just so beautiful. So many blues, but it was brown in places and all the little beaches. It was so gorgeous, and the boat looks so beautiful sitting in the lagoon. Thank you Annette. This is going to be such a wonderful holiday."

6 Nikki

The men and Marly went off to their cabins but Nikki stayed and sat with Casey. She continued her enthusiastic chatter about their bike ride around the island. It was the first time Casey had been alone with the girl and she took the opportunity to learn more of Mike's latest partner.

"Where did you meet Mike?"

"In California. I met him at a club."

"You look like LA but there is something different. You're not really a Californian girl?"

"Sure am not. I'm from Walker, Minnesota. It's a small town near Duluth. Well, that's the biggest place near Walker and it's a distance. It's cold there in winter when the lakes ice up. I hate the cold winds. I wanted to be warm."

"So you moved to California?"

"Not at first. I went down to Florida. To Miami. I thought that was where you went. Old rich folk from around us used to go there for winter, but I didn't like it there. Then I came home but I didn't want to stay there either. The town's getting smaller, people are getting old. Life's pretty hard there if you're young. As soon as I had enough money I left for Los Angeles. I like LA better than Miami."

"That must have been a big change to Walker?"

"At first people used to make fun of the way I spoke and my clothes so I had to change. Be more like the locals."

"How did you find your new life?"

"It was lonely at first, but I met a girl, Sally, and we became great friends. We found some work, we had to, and then we got a little apartment."

"What sort of work were you doing?"

"Whatever we could find. Coffee places. Waitressing. I got some work in an office. Doing messages and greeting people. Meeting people at the airport, taking them places. Bit of anything they wanted. My Pa made sure I could do typing and use computers and was polite, so that was good. My Ma was different. She reckoned a girl had to be able to sew and cook and understand men. That was useful too when we didn't have much money. I used to make my own clothes for when we wanted to go to clubs. Then we both got a job working at a club. Sally and I were security. We had to talk the guys out of causing trouble. Sweet talk 'em. We could settle things down better than the guys. The troublemakers just wanted to fight other guys but they would be nice to us girls."

"You didn't want to become an actress? So many girls dream of movies and television or being in a music video."

"I see them all the time in the clubs. I'm not pretty enough and I can't sing. Even in the shower I'm bad. But I do love dancing."

Nikki had sounded genuine in her self-appraisal about not being pretty. Yet many would have disagreed with her harsh opinion. She was friendly and warm with an open charm. Even without the attention she lavished on her make-up and hairstyle her looks would still have attracted attention from men and women.

"So you met Mike in a club?"

"Yes. He was sweet. He used to come some nights and we sort of hit it off, not that I ever had to sort out any problems with him. Then we decided to get together. We've been together for two years now."

"Are you still working at the club?"

"No, he wanted me to stop. So I did. He's so sweet and kind."

Later, changing for dinner, Casey recounted her conversation with Nikki to her husband.

"What do you think will happen to her when Mike tires of her? And he will, knowing his past."

Ed was unconcerned. "I wouldn't worry about Nikki. She's tough, she's a survivor. When Mike moves on she'll find someone else. There will be plenty of men who would like to have her on their arm, or in their bed."

"Does that include you?"

"No, my love. I'm old enough to be her father. But I do have some respect for her sort. She's out there making a life for herself the best way she knows how. She might be an expensive ornament but I think she is genuine. I would trust her more than Annette."

Like the first evening Matilde's dinner was worthy of an expensive restaurant. Ana was still very correct and formal in her manner, her natural vivacity remaining suppressed. It was only Eeva who smiled as she moved around the guests with plates and drinks.

Unlike the previous night, when the talk had been of the present, the talk around the table at dinner returned to the days and nights in Hong Kong. For Nikki, Gaby and Marly the stories were often new and informative about the earlier lives of their partners. As the alcohol flowed Annette's talk became less inhibited and the memories more embarrassing. The attempt by Ed to change the subject was ignored. Mike's effort was even less successful. James' introduction into the conversation of stories about their yachting experiences in the South China Sea was a failure. It was as if Annette realised what the men were attempting and chose to deliberately ignore them.

At last she said, "We all have secrets. You Ted, James, Pete, Mike. I don't know about you girls because I've just met you but I know these guys. We all have things we would rather the world not know. The past has a way of finding you, and you have to pay for your past. I'm going to bed. Goodnight." And with that she left the room.

7 Bora Bora

When the early morning risers came on deck they found the boat at anchor in the lagoon of the island of Bora Bora. The island where Marly and Pete had spent time at a resort before joining the cruise. Over breakfast it was decided that four of the group would go ashore, hire a car and circumnavigate the island.

As they travelled around the island Marly had pointed to the airport where they had been met and whisked away to the glamorous resort. Marly had told Nikki and Mike of her and Pete's stay in a bungalow over the water, the huge swimming lagoon, the pools and beautiful restaurants available to guests, and of romantic breakfasts watching the colourful fish swimming in the clear waters around the bungalow. She also told of how they had access to a private lounge at LAX as they waited for their flight to Tahiti, and the seamless transfer at the airport for the flight to Bora Bora where a waiting launch transferred them to the resort.

Nikki was already suggesting to Mike that they change their return flight to the States to allow three, or even better, four days to visit one of the luxury resorts Marly had pointed out on the atoll on the far side of the lagoon. The more

Marly talked of their island interlude, the keener Nikki became for Mike to change their plans when the cruise was over.

It was Pete who pointed out that the smaller resorts they had driven past that morning were also beautiful, and the amazing colours of the waters lapping their private sandy beaches. He'd also remarked how different the lifestyle at the resort where he and Marly had stayed was to the villages they had passed through on their drive. Nikki had been unimpressed. For her the distant, unreachable resorts across the lagoon were a dream she wanted to fulfil.

Pete continued. "I think the villagers and their kids looked happier than some of the guests I saw at the resort. There were a couple of obnoxious kids and teenagers there, and some of the other guests were more concerned about how they looked, or with trying to impress others, than enjoying life. Happiness comes from inside, not where you are or how you look."

Marly had encouraged Nikki's dreams. "I can be happier in some gorgeous resort than a ramshackle village of huts. Keep at him girl!"

That night, when the nine gathered around the table in the formal wood-panelled dining room, the talk was of the day's activities and not of the past. Tama had taken Pete, Marly, Mike and Nikki ashore to the pier at Viatape where they had hired a car to drive around the island. He'd returned to the boat and then taken James and Gaby and two of the electric bikes to the shore with directions for a shorter path to a famous local restaurant and bar where Claude Duval had suggested the entire group should meet for lunch. Tamu and his Zodiac had then made another trip and taken Ed, Casey and Annette to the pier in front of the restaurant at midday. He'd returned the bikes to the boat and had come back to the bar when called. Finally, he had returned to Viatape pier to pick up those travelling by car.

The four in the car were already waiting outside *Bloody Mary's* when the bike riders arrived.

After the group moved inside Gaby had tried to temper Nikki's enthusiasm by pointing out how the resort lifestyle was really just an artificial bubble, a fantasy world for those with lots of money, and not real. It was of little use. For Nikki, the fantasy had become the reality of her dreams.

The six were already on the second cocktail of the lunch when Tama dropped off the last three arrivals.

"I loved the names of all the celebrities who have been here. There are some very famous names. Film stars, politicians, a whole range of people."

Ed had also seen the boards at the entrance bearing names of visitors to the bar. Unlike his wife he was unimpressed. "I saw you and Annette checking them out. There are names there that mean nothing to me. I've no idea who some of them are but they must have been well known once. I guess fame can be so fleeting."

"Ted you just don't follow popular culture. How did this place get its name?"

Gaby had the answer. "It was the movie *South Pacific*. It was a big hit in the early sixties. One of the characters was called Bloody Mary. She was a native who did deals with the

American servicemen."

"You seem to know a lot about it Gaby. How true is the story?"

"I don't know Mike. Movies take a lot of latitude with the truth. Look at *Casablanca*. There was never a 'Rick's Bar' until it was set up for tourists to visit. My dad loved *South Pacific* and took me to see it when I was a little girl. Not when it first came out Mike. I saw that look! I was so in awe of the film I read the book. The movie was based on stories from 'Tales of the South Pacific' by a very popular author of the period, James A Michener."

"Your dad must have been good to you Gaby."

"He was Nikki. I had a great dad."

It was Casey who added more information. "There was some truth in the story. I remember hearing Ted's dad talking about the Second World War. He was in the Pacific. One day he and some old mates were talking and one of them mentioned building an airstrip on Bora Bora."

Gaby continued. "Michener's book was about the war in the Pacific. It was very popular when it came out. He even won a Pulitzer Prize for it, but it was set in the Coral Sea and the Solomon Islands. Then when they made the film the locations used were actually in Hawaii and Ibiza in the Balearic Islands. Actually the airstrip in the book was on Norfolk Island between Australia and New Zealand, not on Bora Bora."

"So where does French Polynesia come into the story?"

"The romantic lead in the film was a handsome French planter, and the island with all the beautiful native girls that the sailors weren't allowed to visit was just across the water, a bit like Moorea and Tahiti. I guess fantasy is more exotic and exciting than reality."

"You seem to know a lot about the story Gaby."

"Yes, when I first saw the movie it was so big, and the music was so great I fell in love with the story."

"So who was Bloody Mary?"

"In the film she was a Tonkinese woman. That's from North Vietnam. She was quite a character with a very beautiful daughter."

"Well, here's to Bloody Mary and our travels."

As they raised their glasses to Pete's toast a short stocky man with a bushy beard walked into the bar. He was wearing crumpled shorts and a shirt that looked equally crumpled. He was deeply tanned and his face was wrinkled from the sun. His uncombed hair was bleached by exposure and he was barefooted, but he was not a native Polynesian.

"Here comes a local," was the comment from Pete. "He looks like he's gone 'islander'."

The man strode to the bar and ordered a Hinano. There was no recognition by the barman to indicate he was a regular. However Annette gave a start and moved closer to Ted. The stranger sat alone drinking his beer, ordered a second and sat watching the group.

He was on his third beer when Annette went to the man and spoke to him. From where the others sat they could see the anger in her expression. She exchanged a few terse words with the man and while they couldn't hear the words it was obvious she was not pleased. When she had finished she walked out of the bar to sit alone at the end of the pier waiting for Tama's return. The man also left as quietly as he had arrived. Discussing the event no one could recall him speaking at all. Yet, somehow the man and Annette had affected the mood of the group. It was a quiet passage in the Zodiac back to the *Ocean Rover*.

That night as they sat around the table discussing the day's activities the mood was different. There was a tenseness in the air. Annette was withdrawn, Nikki sullen, and Marly subdued. The feeling affected the men as well. It was only Casey and Gaby who kept the mealtime conversation bubbling along.

The subject of the scruffy man was raised with Annette, but all she would say was "He was so rude. I don't want to talk about him." But then later in the evening when asked a question she had answered with "The past has a way of finding you." It was an answer that had no connection with the subject under discussion, and it was obvious that she had not been listening and her thoughts were somewhere else. Those who heard the remark were puzzled, but by then Annette had enjoyed many refills of her wine glass.

It was late in the evening when the four men and five women rose from the table and moved to the aft deck. Above them, a myriad of stars twinkled, some reflecting as tiny points of light in the gently ruffled waters of the bay. Matilde and Ana were already waiting with coffees, or something stronger if preferred. Some took the offered coffee, a few of the men continued with their wine but Nikki returned to her favourite cocktail and Annette joined her. After her unexpected comment at the meal-table she had become strangely quiet, apart from her frequent demands to Ana for another cocktail. To an observer it was obvious that both Matilde and Ana were trying to slow the number she was consuming. Their efforts were in vain.

"Ana, you're such a sweet girl, bring me another cocktail. Make it a martini this time! Not one of those fruity things Nikki is drinking."

Ana exchanged a look with Matilde and left to fill the command. James moved to Annette and attempted to start a conversation about the day's activities. He was quickly rebuffed as she moved away and joined the women. He was left standing alone. He turned and rejoined the men. "Amura will be happy tomorrow. Taha'a is his island. He tells me it has the most beautiful smell in the world."

"I've never heard Amura speak?"

"He says that his island is famous for the vanilla that grows there. He says you can tell from far away when you are coming close."

"How?"

"By the smell of the vanilla."

"Those little black stringy things that are so expensive. Casey usually uses the essence."

"You are certainly right about the cost Ed. Apparently it's a vine, a type of orchid, that has a bean. Amura says it is very difficult to grow. The flower must be pollinated by hand only on certain days. Then when it has the bean they must be picked and dried carefully. That's why it is so expensive."

"And you can smell the island from a distance?"

"So he says, Pete."

"Well we will see if he is correct in the morning."

The women had started to discuss a book that Casey had found on a shelf in her cabin. The cover had a vivid scene of a well-endowed young blonde woman, dishevelled and wearing a blouse and skirt that had been strategically slashed to display her charms. It appeared she was fleeing from some unseen horror.

"That looks like Ana."

"Shush Nikki. She might hear you." The murmur among the women agreed with Casey's reprimand although not disagreeing with Nikki's comment.

Beneath their feet a vibration began as the motors came to life, and soon the boat was moving through the calm water. The group stood watching as it slowly passed through the opening in the atoll and commenced the nighttime passage to their next destination: a beautiful spice island with the sweet aroma of caramel and anise.

8 Who is Sidney Blaise?

In comparison to the often thick and weighty books bought by travellers at airports, the Sidney Blaise novel was thin. It would certainly have failed the test of a reader seeking value in hours of reading per dollar spent. Yet the book had been quickly passed from reader to reader on the Ocean *Rover*, not that it took a great deal of time to read.

Mention of the book had arisen during the late night drinks under the stars. The last to finish the book was Marly. "I'm not sure whether this is a great book, or if it's so bad that it's enjoyable in a strange way." Her comment started a discussion among the other women who had already read it.

James joined the women. "Gaby read parts of it to me. I couldn't work out if it was for real or not. Still, she wouldn't put it down and turn off the bedside light until she'd finished it. Then she gave it to Nikki." It was apparent that James had not been given the opportunity to read the book in full.

"I've never heard of Sidney Blaise. Has anyone read anything else by her?"

"I don't think it's a her, Marly. I think he's a man."

"Why do you think that Casey?"

"Just the way it is written, and I think he's American."

Gaby, who was holding the book flipped to the imprint page and discovered the book had been first published in Great Britain.

Annette had also read the book and gave her opinion. "English, and she's a woman. There's a feeling for women in the way it's written."

The enthusiasm of the conversation between the women had attracted the attention of Ed and Pete.

Mike also joined the conversation. "Nikki read some of it to me. You women must have a great feeling for murder. There were bodies everywhere."

"Why do you say an English woman, Annette?"

"Teddy, American writers are male. Dan Brown, John Grisham, James Patterson. English writers are female. JK Rowling, EL James, Agatha Christie, Emily Bronte."

James objected to her list. "I don't think you should include Emily Bronte in that group. She died years ago. So did Agatha Christie, and EL James' bodies are very much alive."

Casey also objected. "What about Nora Roberts, she's American. So is Danielle Steel, and Janet Evanovich."

"What about Alexander McCall Smith?" asked Pete.

It was Marly who answered. "McCall Smith's not English, he's Scottish!"

"Nikki told me the story. At least the murderer was caught in the last chapter. From what she told me I don't think I will ever look at another woman again."

"It wasn't that bad Mike."

"I loved the way it ended. It was a very complicated plot with lots of twists and turns but Blaise made it all so obvious with his explanation, and you realised all the clues were there all the time. It was very clever, and I don't usually like 'who dunnits'."

"I agree with you Marly but I don't think she's American or English. I suspect she might be African. White African, South Africa or Rhodesia, Zimbabwe."

"Why do you think that, Gaby?"

"I've met people from southern Africa. There are lots leaving that part of the world looking for security and to make a new, safer life. Quite a few come to Australia. You can pick them by their accent, but it's more than that. The way they phrase their sentences, the words they use. I think I detected a glimmer of that in the book. And I think it is a woman. The men are much more direct and used to giving orders, and it's definitely not by an Afrikaner. They are even more obvious in their speech patterns."

"There is an easy way to answer the question. I'll google it." Annette reached into a pocket of her red dress for her cell phone and tapped on the screen. "No signal. I'll have to wait until we reach Taha'a tomorrow. Hopefully I should get a signal there."

By the time the boat would be anchored off the island of Taha'a, and the travellers were again gathered together in the saloon, the question of the nationality and gender of Sidney Blaise would be the least of their concerns.

9 Ana

Something in the chatter around the meal table, or perhaps the later talk around the aft deck where Matilde and Ana served coffee and refilled the glasses of those who chose water or something stronger, had disturbed Ed. Neither he nor Casey had settled when they went to bed. They'd discussed the conversations, yet neither could find a reason for his unease. At last they decided to take a walk around the boat in the hope that when they returned to their cabin the unsettled feeling would have vanished.

The boat was in darkness with only the navigation lights reflecting in the broken water. There was only the quiet hum of the engines, and an occasional splash of water against the hull, otherwise all was in silence as the boat made its way to the next destination. It was a moonless night and the stars, with little competition from town or city lights, were bright in the sky. In the dimness a figure emerged from the plunge pool.

"Oh, I am sorry. I thought all were asleep. Staff are not supposed to use the pool but Claude lets me if all have gone to bed." In the light of the stars the bikini-clad figure of Ana wrapped herself in a pareo, the light fabric clinging to her still wet body. "Please don't mention to anyone I use the pool. It will get Claude in trouble." With that she disappeared down a stairway to the staff quarters.

"Ana's a very attractive girl."

"Especially in a bikini like that. Not that there was much of it. It would certainly attract you men."

"I noticed Mike checking her out when she was serving drinks tonight. I think Nikki had better watch out."

"Do you think he would try anything?" Memories of Mike's life in Hong Kong returned to Casey.

"She is very attractive. Mike has always had an interest in ladies. I expect Nikki's had a good run. She will need to be special to hold him forever."

"I was talking with Ana tonight when she was serving drinks. She comes from a small town in Poland. She is backpacking and working her way around the world. Although being on a boat like this is hardly the backpacking you and I did when we were her age."

"Those two girls probably have a lot in common. Mike told me that Nikki comes from a small town in Minnesota. Apparently life at home was hard and she just wanted to get away and find a better life."

"Do you really think the two girls are alike Ted? I thought there was some sort of tension between them. I was watching this evening and they were very polite with each other but quite cool."

"Perhaps Nikki had noticed the attention Mike was paying Ana. There's nothing like rivalry to bring out the claws."

"Maybe that's it?" Casey's answer showed an uncertainty

that Ed's conclusion was the only reason, but she made no comment and moved on. "Ana seems very capable."

"Probably is, and I suspect like Nikki she knows her looks can open doors. I don't know if she is as high maintenance as Nikki."

"Talking of high maintenance. What about Annette?"

Ed frowned and shook his head. "I'm surprised. For someone who organised this trip she keeps disappearing into her cabin. I don't know why. We never see her until late in the morning, then she disappears after lunch and only reappears when it's drinks time."

"Just as long as she stays away from you. I don't want a repeat of what happened before."

"Relax, darling. I have no intention of any involvement with her. Besides, nothing happened!"

"So you say. Well, you just keep your distance and make sure she keeps her distance."

"Trying to get Annette to do what you want is impossible. You know that. Look at tonight. She was really giving Ana a hard time. Always demanding more wine and then cocktails. It was obvious she was drinking too much but that didn't stop her. It was strange. I've never seen her like that before."

"Do you see her often?"

"No. Rarely. Sometimes we pass at airports or have meetings with the same people. It's years since we were anywhere together."

"At dinner she said something about 'the past has a way of

finding you.' Do know what that might be?"

"I expect she could have a lot in her past. Probably we all have. I do. Things I shouldn't have done and things I should have. I expect Annette's the same. With her, it was always about her, she was never concerned about anyone else. I don't know about anything in particular. Besides she was the one who organised us to come on this cruise. She found us. That's hardly the past finding her."

"What about that man at *Bloody Mary's*?"

"Annette's mystery man."

"I don't know if he even said anything to her, but she was very upset and walked off."

"She can get upset very easily if it suits her. I've seen her pull that stunt on some people. Then they'll try to calm her and end up doing exactly what she wants."

"That hardly applied at lunch. She said she had never seen him before and she certainly didn't talk to him again. She went for a walk on the pier on her own. Have you ever seen the man before?"

"No. Never. None of the other boys seemed to recognise him so I don't think he was in our joint past. Was he familiar to you?"

Casey shook her head. "No, but it could have been anyone behind that beard. He looked like a local with his shorts and open shirt and bare feet."

"I've had enough. The hum of the motors and the roll of the boat is getting to me. I'm ready for bed. Come with me gorgeous."

As they entered the saloon and headed down the stairs to their cabin, another figure emerged from the shadows.

10 Taha'a

It was another beautiful day in Paradise.

The *Ocean Rover* lay at anchor close to a small tropical islet of white sandy beaches and palm trees: the classic tropic island of tourist brochures and dreams. Close by, on the starboard side, the green hills of the island of Taha'a rose up from the sea. A gentle breeze floated the faint smell of vanilla across the water to the boat.

Beneath the overarching blue of the sky the waters of the atoll sparked with varied hues of blue. In places a darker blue marked the deeper channels, in other places a lighter blue the shallow waters. A multitude of different shades showed the ever-changing depth of the clear, clean, pristine water. In the distance waves breaking on the coral reef traced a narrow line of white. A solitary dark cloud hung low on the far horizon.

Just like previous days the couples drifted together in their own time to take their breakfasts on the open deck beneath a warm sun. As they sat around the table they planned their day. Gaby's great interest was to visit a vanilla plantation and James, Pete and Marly agreed to join her. Soon the four, with Amura, were in the inflatable heading to the jetty at Patio. There they hoped to find a local who could guide them in their search for the source of the aroma. Next Mike and Nikki decided to go ashore for a walk and again the Zodiac returned to the jetty. Ed and Casey remained on board: Casey to improve her tan with some morning sun and Ed to finally read the Blaise book that had been discussed the previous night.

It was almost eleven o'clock when Mike and Nikki returned and joined Ed and Casey. Nikki was full of news.

"There was some excitement in town. A fisherman found a body on a little island, a motu, not far from our boat."

"That would explain the boats coming and going from that little island over there. Casey was wondering what the activity was. It seemed unusual. Do you know what happened?"

"No one seemed to know very much. The police and medics went to the island. Apparently a fisherman found the body washed up on the sand. That's all we heard."

It was the returnees from the vanilla plantation who brought more news.

"The body was a woman. The word is it must be a tourist. It's definitely not a local."

"Do they know anything else?

James shook his head. "No. Nothing. They haven't made any identification."

Matilde and Ana appeared with lunch and the group settled around the table.

"Ana, could you tell Annette that lunch is being served. She must be in her cabin."

On Casey's request Ana disappeared down the stairs. Within a minute she had returned. "Excuse me mam, but I knock on the door but there is no answer, so I knock again very loudly but again no answer. Eeva tells that her room was empty when she make up the cabin thirty minutes ago. Perhaps she is somewhere else, or went on shore."

Ed went off to find Tama to see if he or Amura had taken Annette to the shore, but came back with the news that only two trips had been made to the jetty with passengers. "She must be somewhere. Ana, please have a look on the foredeck and see if she is there."

Again Ana went off, and again she returned without finding the missing woman. Suddenly the mood of the group changed; an unspoken concern spread around the table.

It was Ed who took charge of the situation. "Please ask Claude to join us?" Matilde left to find her husband. Soon the crew were searching the entire boat.

As they waited for the Captain to return the fear around the table grew.

"It couldn't be Annette. How could she be washed up on the motu?"

No one could answer Casey's question but the fear remained.

A fear that increased with Claude's report that no sign had

been found of the missing woman. A silence fell over the group.

It was Claude who broke the silence. "I'm sure it cannot be your friend, but perhaps we should go ashore and make enquiries. It is a woman and a tourist. But I cannot see how it can be Madame Freidman. But, she is not here."

Once again Tama and the inflatable returned to the jetty at Patio. This time with Ed and Claude, not in search of vanilla plantations but the local police station. Meanwhile, a second search commenced on the boat.

It was only a short walk from the jetty to the police station. One glance was sufficient. The body in the red dress was Annette.

11 The News

From the local gendarme the story of the discovery emerged. It was just after sunrise when a fisherman passing close by the little islet on his way to a favoured fishing ground noticed a red bundle on the sand. At first he was annoyed thinking it to be garbage, cast overboard by some travelling foreign yacht, that had been washed up on the beach of the motu, but his curiosity was awakened and he had gone closer to investigate. It was then that he realised the bundle was a woman in a red dress. It was too late. The woman was dead.

There were four men in the tender when it returned to the *Ocean Rover*. The fourth man was a solidly built Polynesian gendarme with instructions to let no one leave the boat. Nor was the boat to move without permission until his sergeant arrived to interview all passengers and crew.

Fourteen people gathered in the saloon to hear the news from Ed and the Captain.

A second search of the boat had been made after Ed and Claude had gone ashore. But, like the first, it had proved fruitless and the group were already concerned. Concern that changed to horror with the news of the death.

"What happened?"

Although it was Casey who asked the question, it was the question in everyone's thoughts.

"The police haven't said but Claude and I think they believe she must have fallen overboard and drowned. The senior gendarme on Taha'a will come and interview us as soon as he has arranged the transport of the body to the hospital in Raiatea for examination."

The groups drifted away, some to their cabins, some to comfort each other and to try to make sense of the news. Casey and Nikki sat together on a lounge near the stern of the boat. Both were subdued. Nikki had none of her usual vivacity.

"It's too horrible. I had an auntie who drowned. She committed suicide. She planned it and drowned herself in the lake near our house. I was only a small kid when it happened. I didn't understand. But my mom was so sad, and my pa so worried. I knew that. They never spoke of it when I grew up. Sometimes I'm frightened I might be the same."

"Don't worry Nikki. You're a survivor, you will be OK."

"Do you think so Casey? It still frightens me."

The older woman reached out and took her hand. "It was an accident. Annette must have fallen over the side. There is no other logical reason. She was... Well she wasn't really herself last night."

"Do you really think that?"

"Yes. What other explanation is there?"

Mike, who had been standing nearby looking towards the small sandy beach of the motu where the body had been found, turned and joined them. "It will be OK Nikki. It was an accident. Annette is not the sort of person to commit suicide. She causes problems, not has them. She was really hitting the booze last night and she must have come back on deck and stumbled and fallen into the water."

"But wouldn't she call out for help or something? Swim? All she had to do is get to the steps at the back of the boat."

"I don't know that Annette could swim. The closest I've ever seen her near water was at a hotel pool with a drink in her hand. I doubt if her swimsuit ever got wet."

"What about calling for help?"

"We were all in our cabin, Nikki. I doubt if we would have heard any calls."

"It's so horrible."

"I know Baby, but we have to be strong."

James and Gaby had moved apart from the group on the aft deck but their thoughts were on the same subject. How could it have happened? Even if you were drunk? And they had agreed that Annette was very definitely drunk last night. "You would still have to topple over the side rails of the boat." James leant against the rail and leant over. "I doubt if you would fall unless you really tried. Maybe if you were stumbling backwards?" He turned and backed up to the rail.

"Stop! Don't do that!" Gaby reached out her hand and led her partner away from the rail. "Don't frighten me like that.

I don't care if that's what happened to Annette. I don't want it happening to you."

James was puzzled. "I can understand walking, even stumbling if you were drunk, towards the rail but not stumbling backwards. Unless you were trying to get away from something."

"What would Annette be trying to get away from at whatever time it was? We would have all been in bed."

"I agree, it doesn't make sense."

"Do you think she jumped?"

"Gaby, I just don't see Annette standing here and then doing a swan dive into the water. Not without an audience."

It was an hour later when the greyish-blue outboard pulled alongside the *Ocean Rover*. A gendarme standing at the bow of the outboard threw the painter to Tama. Once the rope had been securely fastened three gendarmes boarded the luxury yacht and joined the gendarme who had come to the boat with Claude and Ed. One, the most senior of the group, went to Claude and introduced himself and they chatted for several minutes. Then they joined the waiting group and Claude spoke.

"This is Sous-Lieutenant Leo Joubert. At this moment he is the senior officer on Taha'a and is to make preliminary enquiries. He does speak English but he has asked me to translate as he understands I am much better at the language. Matilde will also help if necessary."

The two men spoke again and Claude passed on the

question. "At what time was the lady last seen?"

There was some discussion around lounges and Ed explained that they had all been at this very same place when Annette had announced her decision to retire.

"The Lieutenant wishes to know at what hour that was."

"It was twelve-seventeen." All heads turned to Mike who had made the comment. "I looked at my watch. I was ready to go down to the cabin but Nikki was talking to Marly. It was probably five minutes after that when we went down."

"Leo, Lieutenant Leo, asks where you all were?"

Ed answered the question. "We were all here on deck. The last we saw of her was when she left us."

Claude spoke. "That is not quite correct. Matilde and I were in our cabin. Also Eeva who was on early breakfast duty, she was to start work at six-thirty in the morning. Ana was still on duty with the guests. I think Tama was on the bridge. He was on watch, and Amura would be in the cabin. They would change at six in the morning."

Again the gendarme and Claude spoke. "Leo wished to know who was the last person to see her?"

There was silence around the group and finally Ana spoke. "I was coming from the bar when she went past me. I am sure she went down the stairs to her cabin."

"Did anyone see her after that time?" Heads were shaken around the deck.

"Did anyone see her in the morning?" Again all heads were shaken.

This time Claude asked the question without waiting for the policeman. "Tama and Amura. Did you see the lady when you were on watch?"

Neither of the Polynesian men had seen her on the deck after the group had gone down to their cabins.

"You didn't see her in the morning?" Again both men answered in the negative.

"The Lieutenant wishes to inspect the lady's room. He asks if you will be so kind to wait here. He may have more questions."

It was only ten minutes before the gendarme and Claude returned. There was a quiet conversation between the two, after which they climbed the steps to the sun deck. In a few minutes they returned.

"The Lieutenant has asked me who was the last to leave from here?"

Casey answered. "That would be Ted and me, and Gaby and James. Nikki and Mike had left earlier and Pete and Marly weren't far behind them. We chatted on for, maybe, ten minutes."

"The Lieutenant asks what lights were on when you left? How dark was it?"

"There was no light out here on the deck but there were dim lights on in the saloon. There was no moon but the stars were wonderful."

Claude explained to the Lieutenant that it was normal practice to dim the lights when guests were enjoying the evening on the decks. That way they could appreciate the immense number of stars in the sky. It was something that people who lived in large cities rarely saw and they were always amazed. Only the lights on the steps of the stairways and the night-light in the spa pool were kept on for safety reasons. All other lights would be turned off when the guests went to their cabins.

"Qui fait ça, Claude?"

"Tama surveillait. Il est très compétent." Claude and the officer exchanged a few more words then Claude passed on the question. "The officer wishes to know what state the deceased was in when she retired?"

There was silence that seemed to last for a minute before Ed spoke. "I think you would have to say she was probably intoxicated."

Claude passed the message to the policeman who appeared to have already understood the reply.

"The Lieutenant wishes to know how intoxicated?"

Again a pause before Ed spoke. "I think you would have to say very. Her behaviour was unusual."

Once more Claude and the gendarme spoke together. "And what of her behaviour on this voyage?"

No one spoke until finally Casey broke the silence and answered the question. "She spent a lot of time in her cabin. I thought that was surprising since this holiday was her idea. She didn't spend a lot of time with any of us. Mostly just showed up for meals and drinks."

"And she spent a lot of time on her cell phone." added Nikki.

"Il y a quelqu'un qui connait avec qui elle parlait ?"

"The Lieutenant wishes to know if anyone knows with whom she was speaking?"

Heads were shaken. Annette had often been seen speaking on her cell phone, but no one had any knowledge of who was on the other end of the call.

Casey recalled "She did say something about attending to some matter but I don't know what it was."

Again the gendarme spoke with Claude who passed on his next enquiry. "What was the condition of her health?"

The unexpected question took the assembled group by surprise. Finally Ed answered. "I have no idea. She seemed fine to me. Probably drinking too much, but she had never mentioned any problems to me. I don't know about the others."

No one else in the group offered any knowledge of Annette ever speaking of a health issue.

"And what about drugs?"

If the previous question had caused a surprise, the next caused an even greater one. Claude explained. "We found opiate drugs in the cabin. They have been prescribed by a doctor but they are very strong. The police will need to check the deceased lady to see if she may have been affected unduly."

Again Claude and the policeman chatted and then Claude informed all those on the boat of what would happen. "We must wait here on the boat until further enquiries have been made. A more senior officer will come from Uturoa to investigate. Until then the boat must remain here. A gendarme will remain with us. The Lieutenant says no doubt his superior from Uturoa will also want to ask questions. The same questions. Leo apologises but that is the police way."

Three gendarmes boarded the outboard to return to the island. Two of them carried black plastic bags. One was the burly gendarme who had come to the *Ocean Rover* with Ed and Claude. In his place, remaining as a guard on the boat, was a younger officer. Below his short-sleeved shirt tattoos in a traditional style showed on both his arms. While he wasn't as heavily built as the older man he looked fit and strong – the type of young man that you would be unwise to argue with. Stripped of his gendarme uniform it was easy to imagine him three hundred years earlier as a warrior, spear and club in hand, in a war canoe on the way to raid a neighbouring island in search of territory, wives or human victims.

As Claude waved the small boat away Casey approached him. "Claude. What does the policeman think happened?"

"The last time anyone saw your friend was Ana at twelve-seventeen. The fisherman found her on the motu around six-thirty. Leo thinks she must have fallen overboard, sometime before then, drowned and floated to the motu. It is possible that as well as alcohol she had taken some of her medication. They are waiting for a report from a doctor and laboratory."

"I overheard your conversation with the police officer. He said 'Une deuxième touriste morte. C'est une catastrophe pour Taha'a.' What is happening?"

12 Gendarmes

"It's true. I didn't know you spoke French, Casey. The lieutenant is most concerned. This is the second death of a tourist on the island in the last month. He worries it will give the island a bad name and tourists will not come. They are so important to the people for the economy. But you should not be concerned."

"Two dead tourists is a concern."

"It is different. The first was a young woman. She was drift snorkelling in the corals. She was not very experienced but she ignored the guide's advice. She was in a pass with a fast flow. It pushed her against the sharp coral in the reef and she panicked. She drowned. She fought against her guide and he could not save her. It was an accident but tragic. I think your friend is also an accident."

"What happens next Claude?"

"We must wait. Leo waits for orders from his superior on Raiatea. Until then we cannot move."

It was several hours later and darkness was settling over

the boat when Claude again called the group together. "I have a message from the gendarmes. A Capitaine from Raiatea is coming to inspect the motu and to speak with us. He will leave Uturoa early in the morning and should be here by breakfast time. Your friend's body has been taken to the hospital there for an inspection. Until he comes we must wait, but it will not be long."

Later that night, as the group once again sat around on the lounges on the aft deck, the talk was of that afternoon's visit from the police. Pete also had some more news regarding the nearby island. "Amura said his people are sad. There has been a murder on the island."

"The scuba diver? I thought it was an accident?"

"She was a snorkeler. Apparently this was a different case, Mike. Amura says the gossip on the island is about a man who was found hanged. This is Amura's home island."

"Have they found the murderer? What's the story?"

"It was in the news before we left Papeete but I didn't link it to where we were going. Some domestic problem. It appears three sisters are suspected of murdering a partner of one of them. They have been taken to Papeete. I don't know the outcome. But it has nothing to do with the death of Annette or the other tourist. It seems it is a local matter of lust. Or hate."

Marly added some more local news. "Amura told me the gendarmes have arrested five people for drugs. Paka, whatever that is, and Ice."

It was James who supplied the answer. "I don't know

about that story but paka is cannabis. Drugs are everywhere unfortunately. Even on a tiny island in a Paradise like this. That hardly affects Annette, she had nothing to do with any locals."

The consensus around the table agreed with the police view that Annette had been drunk and fallen overboard and drowned. Then her body had floated onto the motu. It was impossible for any who knew her to believe that it could have been intentional. Still there were some troubling factors. She had gone down to her cabin after making her departure so obvious. Why did she come back up on deck? It was likely a good night's sleep would have been of more benefit than coming back on deck after everyone else had left. Then there were her comments on Huahine, her talk about 'working together or all suffering' and 'everyone having secrets we would rather the world not know.' There was something on her mind. Something that she must have intended to raise at a later stage, yet none of those who knew her gave any inclination of knowing what it may have been. Now it would never be known. And, another question: what was in the plastic bags the gendarmes had taken away?

13 Capitaine Broussard

It was a little after eight in the morning when the boat bearing the markings of the gendarmerie was sighted at the jetty of the motu where Annette's body had been discovered.

Watching from the deck, those gathered on the *Ocean Rover* could see six gendarmes searching the tiny island. It appeared to be a thorough search: as though there was something in particular that they were seeking. There was curiosity amongst the watchers over what it could be. Two gendarmes separated from the searchers and walked to the small jetty on the motu and stood talking.

"I wonder if that was where the body was discovered? That's the place where the police were yesterday."

Marly's question was answered with a "Probably. It looks like the same area" from Ed. "I wonder what the others are looking for? If her body was washed up I don't expect there would be anything to find away from the edge of the water."

The search on the motu continued even after three of the gendarmes boarded their boat and motored across to the *Ocean Rover*. Claude and Amura were waiting for them and took the ropes cast from the large inflatable, lashing it to the

Ocean Rover. Two gendarmes stepped aboard.

After a brief conversation with the captain of the *Ocean Rover* the officer in charge joined those gathered on deck.

Claude once again did the introductions. "This is Capitaine Broussard. He is from Uturoa, the main town on Raiatea, the island that shares the lagoon with Taha'a. He is the senior officer for this region. He wishes to interview each of us with regards to this tragedy."

"Thank you Captain." Turning to the assembled group he continued, "I will appreciate your assistance and I hope this matter can be quickly resolved. We, the gendarmerie, need to understand the circumstances of this event. To understand the lady who has died. I hope each of you may be able to help. Perhaps it would be best if I speak with each of you alone to learn more of this lady. It would be advisable if you did not talk to one another until I have interviewed each one of you. So I must ask you not to discuss my questions with those with whom I have not yet spoken. But first I wish to inspect the cabin of your friend. Perhaps there we will find the answer my colleague the Sous-Lieutenant Joubert may have overlooked."

Broussard and Claude returned from their inspection of the dead woman's cabin and the gendarme began his questioning of those on the boat. One by one the party joined Broussard in the saloon, answered his questions, and then moved up the stairs to the sun deck to await the next arrival.

The first to be interviewed was Ed. He explained to Broussard the reason for the gathering and some background of the others on board. Of the guests, he, perhaps more than any other, knew the most of Annette and her life, but even he had had little contact with her since the days in Hong Kong. He certainly could not shine any light on her death.

The next to meet with the gendarme was his wife. Casey could add even less to the mystery. Her husband had occasionally met Annette over the years but those meetings were infrequent and brief. She did add that Annette could be a difficult person to work with and know. There was the possibility that her past could include people who were unhappy from having come in contact with her. There was also her strange behaviour at the bar on Bora Bora. The man had certainly upset her. Maybe that was someone from her past.

Mike entered the saloon as Casey made her exit. As he did he shrugged as if the whole process was a waste of their time. He hadn't seen Annette for years. He had no idea of her friends, or enemies, or what she now did with her life. If anyone would know it would be Ed. He had been the closest of the group to her many years ago. As he left Mike squeezed Nikki's hand as she replaced him in the saloon to take her turn in the questioning.

While it was long before she had met Mike, she had only been a baby in those days, Nikki had heard stories from her partner of the time in Hong Kong. Nothing of the past that she told him seemed important to Broussard but he did learn much of the present. Nikki had seen Ana and Claude together and had heard an angry outburst from Matilde as she reproached her husband. Nor had Annette become a friend of Nikki. She had overheard an argument between Annette and Mike. Mike had never mentioned the conversation but Annette had taken pleasure in telling Nikki to watch her 'boyfriend'. She had told her "He was a bad man and no good would come from being with him." That had upset and annoyed Nikki who had defended Mike. "He's a great guy. She was just being bitchy 'cause she has problems with guys." When questioned by Broussard about specific problems Nikki had been unable to provide any details. "She just wants to boss everyone around."

The next to pass in front of the gendarme Capitaine was Pete Metcalfe. Like most of the others he had no knowledge of Annette Freidman since those earlier days. He had been surprised when an invitation to join the cruise had arrived. "It seemed like a great idea. Two weeks on a luxury boat in the South Pacific. It hasn't turned out that way." Broussard appeared to have become particularly interested in the Hong Kong days and quizzed the Australian about them. No longer were his questions of the present but only of the past. From Peter Metcalfe, Broussard learnt of the dead woman's missing husband and that there had been rumours of some affair. Rumours of which the Australian had never learnt the truth — but stories like that were common in those days. Marriages could be stressed and fall apart. His had, but then he'd met his new wife.

When it was the turn of Marly Metcalfe to meet with the policeman the line of questioning about the past ceased. She had known nothing of the earlier days and her husband rarely spoke of them. Their life was in Dubai and England. Well, her life was in England. Her husband's work was in the Emirate but she would soon escape the heat and the confinement of life in the Middle East. Of Annette she knew little; the woman had hardly spent any time with the group and when she did she was drinking. Once she had seen Ed in deep conversation with her and she had noticed Casey watching surreptitiously, unseen by either Ed or Annette.

That had seemed strange.

Only two of the guests remained to be interviewed. James was the last of those who had worked together on Project Dynasty to be questioned by Broussard. Like Mike and Pete he hadn't seen the dead woman for years. He had often wondered what had become of her. While she could be very capable in her professional work she could be a difficult person to work with. She certainly was when he knew her, and he doubted if she would have changed. She enjoyed organising people to do what she wanted. If you didn't! Well, she could be very unpleasant. Only once had he been on the receiving end, but he had seen her work others over. For her to have enemies was unsurprising. That they might want her dead? She and her husband had known some dubious characters in Hong Kong but that was many years ago. Still, even with time, people's natures don't change that much.

"What sort of dubious people would she and her husband have known?"

Paine answered Broussard's question quietly with a cautious look on his face. "There were rumours of drugs. Nothing was ever proven, or even believed with any conviction, but it was thought her husband may have been somehow involved."

"And what do you believe?"

"Nothing was ever confirmed. It was only speculation over gin and tonics in the bars. But he disappeared. That was suspicious."

"Would she have been involved with her husband in such actions?"

"Paul was bossed around by Annette. We all were really. I don't know if he would have had any secrets from his wife. Who knows? It was a long time ago."

The final guest to enter the saloon was the young Asian girl but she could add little. The first time she had met Annette was on the boat and while they had polite exchanges, the woman had preferred to spend time with the men discussing their past success. She had never become close to the woman. Only Casey was around from those days. All she really knew was the few stories her partner had told her. She had heard hints of problems in Hong Kong from James. "I gather they were all pleased when their business was concluded and they could go their own ways. I suspect it was not really the great success they claim it was and they were not a happy group when they parted."

After their interview was finished, each person went up to the sundeck to await the others. Slowly the group on the lower deck dwindled as the group gathered together near the spa pool grew. There was much chat amongst those waiting for the last to appear but it appeared most had been asked similar questions. The questions which had most intrigued the travellers were regarding Annette's health and if any of the group knew who she had been speaking with on her cellphone. They were similar questions to the ones the Sous-Lieutenant had asked the previous day. The answers that each member of the party had given were the same. Nobody knew anything about either matter, yet from the questioning suspicion began to grow that there was more to the death than they had thought.

At last the Capitaine of the Gendarmes joined the small group assembled on the sundeck and thanked them for their assistance. "From your information I have learnt a little more. It will be a start for our investigation and I thank you. Now I will speak with the crew. I hope they may be able to help understand the lady's movements on that night. I will let your Captain know what is planned."

The six crew had gathered on the bridge to await the policeman. One by one they went with Broussard onto the foredeck before returning to their duties.

Ana was the first to be interviewed. She repeated the story which she had told the first policeman of Annette disappearing down the stairs to her cabin. The lady had been speaking to someone on her mobile and had it in her hand. As she went down the steps she stumbled and fell heavily against a handrail hurting her head; the mobile had fallen from her hand.

"Did she pick it up again?"

"I think she pick it up. She bent down. That is all I saw."

"What did you think of the lady?"

Ana didn't hesitate in her answer. "She is a guest. This is an expensive boat. We must provide for their needs. We must be polite or we will not have a job if they complain."

The policeman was sympathetic. "I understand mademoiselle. It is sometimes a difficult situation. But you see much when you serve people. Did you see any disagreements or fighting? Some arguments perhaps?"

This time the young Polish woman hesitated. "I saw the dead lady and Mr Gordon talking. They were not happy but I do not know if it was an argument."

"And your Captain. He is good to work with?"

"Yes sir. He is very good to me with the work."

"And his wife?"

"She also. I do not have any complaints."

The first of the Polynesian crew to speak with Broussard was Eeva. While she quietly answered the questions put to her, it was obvious that her views were strongly held. Unlike Ana she had formed a definite opinion and decided that Annette was not a "nice lady". When questioned about this she could only say that it was the way the woman had spoken to her and spoken to others when she did leave her cabin. "That woman, she spends all her time in that cabin. She should be up in the air and sun. I think she has problems." The true nature of the problems Eeva did not specify but Broussard was left with the impression that Eeva thought they were mental problems.

Then it was the turn of Amura. The conversation took a different turn with the two men discussing questions about the boat, sailing and fishing. How did he like life living on such a beautiful boat? It would be so different to his life on his island. At last the subject returned to what activities the guests could do on a yacht such as this. Amura listed the possibilities. On the sports deck there were paddle boards and kayaks, there was a Zodiac for transport to shore or the reefs, or for water-skiing, and there was also a small dingy.

Broussard asked "Who has been down to the sports deck?"

"Mr Gordon, Mike. Mr Metcalfe, Pete. Mr James. I don't know his other name, and the older one, Mr Parker. The one they call Ed."

"Did the ladies ever come down?"

"One. Miss Nikki came once with her man. Oh, and the Chinese lady. She came once with her boyfriend. They went out on paddleboards. He could stand up, but his girl, she could not. I had many laughs but I was careful they did not see me laughing."

"And the dead lady?"

"No, I never see her near the water. Even the spa pool."

"When did you last see the dead lady?"

"It would have been when they returned from the bar on Bora Bora. I helped her onto the boat. That was the last time I saw her."

He left Broussard on the foredeck and was replaced by Tama but no new information was gathered. Their stories were very much the same. When Tama had been on watch on the bridge he had not paid any attention to the guests in the salon or on the aft deck. Later he and Amura had done a check of the boat when all the guests had gone to their cabins. Then Amura had gone to their cabin. He had done another check early in the morning when he handed over to Amura.

The last of the three women to be interviewed was Matilde, the Captain's wife. She was polite but uncommunicative. When quizzed about the dead guest she replied "I was taught never to speak ill of the dead", but did admit that the woman had been a little demanding. "It is usual for some rich people to be demanding. They pay much money and they expect everything to be perfect. It is what we must provide always."

The final person to face the policeman's questioning was the Captain of the *Ocean Rover*. He added little to what he had already told Broussard. The arrangements for the passage had been made by the agent who handled the charters. He was told to expect nine guests for two weeks of cruising wherever they wished to go. It was the usual arrangement for a charter although there was something a little different. It was as if the agent was passing on direct orders from the owner. Nothing really unusual, but just different. He had decided that, perhaps, the lady who arranged the charter knew the owner of the boat and was even a special friend.

When he had finished his interviews the gendarme asked for all on board *the Ocean Rover* to be mustered on the aft deck. This time Capitaine Broussard was the person with information.

"This is a puzzling case. At first we thought, as no doubt you all thought, that it was a sad accident. A drunken person accidentally falling overboard and drowning. Or perhaps an overdose of drugs, or a combination of the two. But it is not the situation. Her blood showed she had a high level of alcohol. It was as we expected. The test for drugs indicated some opioids but consistent with a medical condition. Perhaps she had a medical condition that required pain relief. It was not enough to be considered an overdose. But your friend did not drown."

14 A Familiar Name

There was silence around the deck. First, surprise. Then confusion. At last Mike spoke. "But she was washed up on the beach. She must have drowned."

Capitaine Broussard shook his head. "No. The lady did not drown. That is certain. There was no water in her lungs. It is impossible."

Again Mike spoke. "So what happened?"

Broussard looked around the gathered tourists. "We must consider other possibilities."

"What other possibilities?"

Broussard told the holiday travellers of a mark found on the dead woman's skull. A small bruise that would hardly come from a blow that would kill. Perhaps just a bruise from the body washing against the wooden posts of the small pier beside where it had been found.

"So perhaps she met someone on the motu who hit her?"

Broussard replied to Ed Parker's question by shrugging his shoulders. "We do not know, yet."

It was James Paine who asked the next question. "So what else could it be?"

"There are some things we do not understand Mr James. We must make more enquiries about her medical condition. I am not an expert on such things. Perhaps it may have affected her decisions. Then there are the calls on her cell phone. That is a problem. We cannot find it. Many of you made mention that she had been speaking frequently on it. We will find out to whom she was speaking but no doubt it will take much time. Also there is the man at the bar in Bora Bora. Perhaps he can assist."

"Capitaine, I am not Mr James. My name is James Paine. What do you think happened if she wasn't drowned?"

"My apology Mr Paine. That is a mystery. She was here on the boat, then she was lying on the beach, her clothes were wet but she had not swallowed any water. How did she get there is a puzzle that we must solve. You say she was not interested in the water sports. When the stewardess Ana saw her going down to her cabin she had her mobile in her hand. It was not in her room and we could not find it on the island. Perhaps it has an answer."

"Perhaps it fell out of her pocket and is at the bottom of the ocean."

"Yes, Mr Gordon, Mike is it not? That is a possibility we must consider. However if a murderer thought he, or she, could hide the evidence it was a bad plan. Eventually we will obtain a list of to whom she had spoken. Until then I must ask you to remain in French Polynesia. I will arrange a mooring for you near the marina at Uturoa. It will be convenient to the public dock for your inflatable. You will be free to leave the boat and go ashore whenever you wish.

However, I must ask that you do not leave the island."

"How long must we stay here?"

"I cannot answer that at the moment Mr Paine. It will depend on how quickly we get satisfactory replies to our enquiries in the States. Until then I regret I must interfere with your plans."

"So you are going to keep us prisoners here."

"No Ms Olson. You are not prisoners, you are assisting the gendarmes to solve the death of your friend. You are free to move around the island as you wish. The town is the main centre of the island of Raiatea and there are shops and restaurants. There is also a famous marae, Taputapuatea, that is a sacred site. It is listed with UNESCO. It is worth a visit I think. You will find much you can do on the island. The islands Sous-le-Vent are very pretty. You will only be a prisoner if you attempt to leave the island. I would not attempt to visit the airport and take a flight. I assure you, you will be free to leave as soon as it is possible."

"Sous-le-Vent. What are they?"

"My apology Ms Olson. That is the name in French. I think in English you call them the Leeward Islands. You have already visited some. Bora Bora, Huahine, and Taha'a. Now you will visit Raiatea."

"I think we would all rather fly home. This cruise has lost all its charms."

"I am sorry Madame Marlene Metcalfe. I understand your feelings but a death has occurred, perhaps even a murder committed. We must find what happened, if some person was responsible. It is a puzzling case, the sort that would interest my friend, Sidney Blaise. He is an expert in such matters of passion and evil."

"Blaise. You don't mean Sidney Blaise, the author?"

"Yes Madame Metcalfe. He is my friend. Now, he lives here in Uturoa. He is researching a new story on, I think, a French planter and his loves and his life in the South Pacific. Do you know of him?"

15   Raiatea

The two Captains left the assembled travellers and moved to the bridge. After ten minutes they emerged and Claude led the gendarmes to their boat. Within a minute it sped off to the township across the atoll. Once again a gendarme was left aboard the *Ocean Rover*.

Claude re-joined the group on the aft deck. "Capitaine Broussard will contact me when he has arranged our mooring at Uturoa. That should occur soon. Then we will leave."

Once the message was received there was immediate action on the boat as the crew prepared to weigh anchor and move to the larger island.

It was only a short passage from their anchorage, close by the motu where the body had been found, to a mooring near the public boat harbour of Uturoa. As they sailed away from the tiny islet a feeling of relief, of escape, settled over those on the *Ocean Rover*. It was as if putting distance between themselves and the site of their companion's death somehow made it less real; a bad dream that had never happened.

The sun was commencing its slow golden decline over the green-clad slopes of Raiatea as once again Matilde and Ana moved around the guests with drinks and canapes for the usual evening gathering. Tonight however the chat amongst the group was subdued, and any laughter that was heard faded quickly, unlike the noise and laughter of the first few nights. Broussard's information that it was not a drowning had come as a surprise. The initial thought of an accidental drowning now had to be discarded. But if it wasn't an accident what other reason could there be? Suicide? Suicide was unlikely. Especially with Annette. But what other explanation was there? There was an unspoken agreement within the group to move on from that consideration.

Instead, the subject was about the gendarme and his questioning. It appeared that not all had been open about the gendarme's questions when they had waited on the sun deck earlier in the day.

"I felt really nervous. I didn't like it. It was as if he thought we were to blame."

"I didn't feel like that Nikki. I thought he was just trying to understand what might have happened. He didn't give me that impression."

"It's alright for you Gaby," Pete replied. "He didn't quiz you about your past. Not that Marly and I have anything to hide. And he did get very personal with me about our relationship."

"You too? He asked Mike if anyone was having an affair with Annette. As if!"

"It's alright Nikki. He's a Frenchman."

"But Mike?"

"That must have been a common question. He asked Casey if I had had an affair with Annette," confided Ed.

"I said no, not my Ted."

"If any funny stuff is going on I reckon it might be Ana and Claude. I saw them together and I would be worried if she was like that with my Mike. I think Matilde knows." From the lack of disagreement from the other women present it was apparent that others beside Nikki had noticed the behaviour of Claude towards the young Polish woman.

"What do you think Broussard will do next?"

While Gaby's question was directed to all in the group it was Ed who answered. "I've no idea Gaby. We will just have to wait."

"What is the difference between the gendarmes and the police. I saw police cars in Papeete?"

At that moment Matilde appeared with a tray carrying another cocktail for Nikki, beers for Ed and James and champagne for Marly and Gaby. She answered Casey's question. "It is the French way, madame. Gendarmes are part of the armed forces. They are responsible for small towns and rural areas. The Police Nationale, they are a civil force. They are responsible for Paris and the bigger urban areas. However each has similar duties but also they have special duties. Even we French people find it confusing. Sometimes even the Gendarmes and Police Nationale argue over who is in charge."

Marly was more interested in the discovery that the author of the book they had all read was living on the nearby island. When she sighted Claude walking through the saloon she stopped him and asked if he had learnt anything more about Blaise during his conversations with the gendarme.

"Yes, madame. After Capitaine Broussard mentioned the name I asked about him. It seems he has become quite a celebrity on the island. The lovers of literature all want to entertain him at soirees and the rest of the community want to tell him of their many loves and the adventures in their lives. Some of it may be true, but much I suspect is false. Perhaps they see themselves as the heroes in his next story."

"What is Blaise like?"

"Broussard tells me he enjoys his company. I gather they spend time together discussing crime."

"But what is he like as a man?"

"Ah, Madame Metcalfe. That I cannot answer. I understand from Broussard that he enjoys a glass of good French red wine. I think they may share many. Also that he is interesting to talk with."

"What does he look like?"

"I have never seen him on my voyages but Broussard tells me he always wears a large straw hat when he is out during the daytime. His taste in clothing is.... I understand from the gendarme that they are most unusual. At night his hair is quite white and wild. He also has a small limp when he walks. The locals say it is from a wound in a fight in a casbah in Algeria but I do not know if that is true. Many stories circulate on these islands and not all are true."

Tied to the town wharf at Uturoa was a large and beautiful white sailing boat. It dwarfed the *Ocean Rover*, both in length and with its four tall masts towering over the low buildings beside the wharf.

"Wow, what's that boat?"

It was Ana who answered Nikki's question. "That is *the Windspirit*. It is a sailing boat that cruises the islands here in French Polynesia. It is very beautiful when it has the sails up. Also you will see it later when the lights are lit, but in the morning it will be gone. Every time I see it I think it such a beautiful boat. I see it many times since I work here in French Polynesia and for me it is always so beautiful. Can I offer you a canape and Eeva can refill your glasses if you wish?"

The sight of the beautiful yacht, and the people boarding it moved the conversation away from the discussion of the death of their friend, and the sudden discovery of the writer, to what it would be like to sail away from a port as the huge white sails unfurled. As dusk settled over the island the lights outlining the rigging of the yacht became brighter, and on the rear deck of the sailing boat people could be seen enjoying evening drinks before moving to take their seats at candlelit tables.

The happy relaxed atmosphere of the carefree tourists dining at candlelit tables only made the mystery of the death on their own yacht more troubling. It was a worrying concern that every person on the *Ocean Rover* was suppressing, but it was a fear that could not be suppressed forever.

The thought returned. "If it wasn't an accident, and it wasn't suicide, it must have been murder. But why, and who?"

16 Discoveries

It was mid-morning, the day after their arrival at their new mooring close by the township of Uturoa. Another day of clear blue skies. Of sunshine and warm breezes. Of multitude shades of pristine blue waters and of white waves breaking on low distant reefs. Small boats constantly arrived and departed from the town marina. Onshore the locals could be seen going about their daily activities.

When the nine members of the party had boarded the *Ocean Rover* to celebrate their venture in Hong Kong the cruise had seemed like a dream; a wonderful, unimagined escape into Paradise on a boat that they had only ever seen in magazines featuring the lives of the rich and famous. Now, their travels in Paradise had ceased. They were being forced to remain at some remote island in the vastness of the South Pacific. An island they had never heard of until a few days ago. The magnificent luxury yacht a prison, a gilded prison.

"It is possible for you to go ashore. Capitaine Broussard allows. It is only that you must not leave the island."

Broussard's prohibition had been discussed the previous night but it was only after Claude's remark that any of those on board really considered the possibility of going ashore.

There was a sense of relief amongst the group, at least some freedom was available, and soon the first four were aboard the inflatable with Amura heading to the dock. The inflatable returned to take two more couples.

Once onshore the four couples separated to each go their own way. There was an unspoken need to escape to a personal space, to have a privacy that they could not feel even in their own cabins on board the yacht.

It was early afternoon when the first of the travellers came together again. It was at a small café near the public marina. Pete and Marly, and Mike and Nikki were sitting around a table enjoying coffees and patisseries and watching the local ferries and fishing boats arrive and depart from the marina. It was as if each of them was trying to delay the time when they would need to signal a crewman on the *Ocean Rover* to come to take them back to their confinement. Meanwhile families came and went in small runabouts, sometimes carrying produce, or school children, or their purchases from the local supermarket.

The people in the street and at other tables at the café were a mix of old and young, Polynesian and European. By their clothing a few were obviously tourists. The dress of the locals was also varied. The older women in bright colourful dresses, the younger ones in jeans or shorts with a variety of tops showing the image of a favourite pop star, or perhaps some cause they wished to identify with. For many girls it was an opportunity to show off their perceived beauty to potential partners. The men were usually less colourfully dressed. Most wore shorts, some clean and some grubby, often with singlets. Others, perhaps the more extroverted, teamed the shorts with tropical flower-patterned shirts left casually unbuttoned to capture a passing breeze. Some wore neither singlet nor shirt. Only a few were more formally attired, if formal meant long trousers and an open necked shirt for men and a more stylish dress or slacks for the women.

"Look at that shirt. I think it's the same pattern as this plastic tablecloth, and that hat!"

Nikki's comment could only be about one man. The shirt did appear to have the same printed pattern of brightly colored parrots as the plastic sheet covering the table that held their coffees.

The man was of an indeterminate age. The hair poking out from under the broad-brimmed straw hat was white in colour, and his gait also suggested an older man, yet there was something in his manner that suggested youth. From his position on the wharf he appeared to be closely inspecting the *Ocean Rover*.

"I think that's Blaise. Claude said Broussard told him that he had white hair and a strange taste in clothes."

"Can you see if he limps? Broussard said he had a slight limp."

Just then the man moved a few steps, but from the distance and the angle it was impossible to answer Marly's question about the limp, however there was no doubting Nikki's comments on the clothing and the hair.

"Quick, go and ask him. Invite him over for a coffee."

"You come with me. I don't want to go accosting a strange man in a strange place on my own."

Together the two women approached the man. From their seats at the café their partners watched as the three chatted for a few minutes before walking back to the café.

"It is Mr Blaise. I've invited him to join us for a coffee. He accepted." Mike found another chair and the group shuffled their chairs to make room for the newcomer. Marly continued. "He has heard of our misfortune and was looking at the boat."

"Everyone on the island has heard of the tragedy. My condolences to you all. It must have been a great shock." The newcomer spoke quietly. His voice was well modulated and he spoke with a precise pronunciation of the words. While it was obvious that he had a slight accent it was impossible to place what it was.

Marly took charge of the introductions. Blaise bowed slightly to the two women before taking their proffered hands, with the men it was a firmer handshake. It was a formal greeting yet he instantly shed the formality. "Please call me Sidney, Mr is far too serious on such a happy island."

Over the aroma of freshly brewed coffee the four travellers quizzed Blaise about the island and himself. His answers were always polite and informative. While the four learnt much of island life, for Blaise was obviously a keen observer, they learnt little of the man himself, or the reason for him being on such a remote and unknown island. There was a sense, not so much of vagueness, but of discretion and privacy in his answers.

The subject moved to his book. On this Blaise was more forthcoming. "Ah, my latest. Did you enjoy?"

The two women were eager to tell Blaise their opinions, to

which he listened with interest, alternatively nodding or shaking his head as he agreed or disagreed with their appraisals.

"It is not my best book I feel, and there are many who agree. These days the reader wants a different story. I am afraid the days of gentle murders and polite manners are past. I tried to write a story with energy and excitement and passion but I fear it did not really work. Perhaps I do not have the experience of those ways. I live a life that is too quiet and unexciting."

Of the four, the two women had read the book in full while the men had only read a few of the more explicit sections and had been told of other happenings. All were unsure of Blaise's failure to write of energy and passion. Indeed the general opinion was the passion and excitement, while interesting, had been too much to take seriously.

"I am afraid the world these days is more interested in matters of depression, gender identity and dispossession. I cannot write of such things. I prefer that we have a life of opportunity and hope. Of sunshine. Of caring for our fellow man."

"Yes. I can see your caring for mankind, women in particular, in the book."

"Murder is different Mr Gordon. That world, in my books, is not real. Unfortunately it may be real for you from what Capitaine Broussard has said."

"What did Broussard tell you?"

"Very little Mrs Metcalfe. May I call you Marlene. The gendarme is very discreet and says little but I can read his manner."

"You may. So you think it was murder?"

"Marlene, with so little information I cannot say for sure, but I believe Broussard is suspicious."

"But who?"

"Again I could not say without investigating and talking to each person present on the boat."

"But why would you find out if Broussard can't?"

"My friend Broussard is a policeman, Mr Gordon. May I call you Michael? I think he is a very good policeman. But they like facts and straight lines. I am sure that eventually he will find the perpetrator. I am a novelist. My thoughts are more creative. I can imagine what he cannot see."

"Would you investigate? That would be so cool. To see you at work."

"Ms Olson, I would be most interested but I can make no promises. Also it may prove a problem for some of you. Matters best left buried may rise to the surface."

"Sidney, I have nothing to hide. Do we Mike? And please call me Nikki. You make me feel so old and stuffy."

"Yes Sidney. Do investigate. It may make for a good story in your next novel."

"Marlene. My stories are fiction. This is real. It may not lead where you wish."

"Blaise is right. I think we should leave it to Broussard. We don't want two people falling over each other in an investigation. We all just want to get away from this island and go home."

"Mike's right. I think we should leave it to Broussard."

The opinion of the two men carried no weight with their partners and soon it was decided that Blaise would visit the boat as a guest and speak with any of the passengers who agreed to speak with him. Whether he would speak with Claude and the staff remained undecided.

"What about the gendarme, Broussard? Won't he get upset?"

"I don't think that will be a problem Marlene. We have often discussed old cases. Provided I discuss my thoughts with him and do not interfere in official matters I think he will be agreeable."

The group parted; the two couples to return to the yacht to tell the others of their invitation. The novelist remained standing alone on the quay for a long time after their departure for the *Ocean Rover*. As he stood looking at the boat, one hand clasping and then rubbing the other, he hardly moved. His mind was busy preparing questions for his visit to the boat at nine the following morning. At last, as the dusk deepened, he moved off down the empty street and vanished into the growing darkness of the evening.

17 The Visit

The news of Blaise's invitation was not well received by some on the *Ocean Rover*.

In particular, Ed had been very vocal in describing the invitation as unwise. In this he was supported by his wife. James and Gaby sided with Nikki and Marly. Their view was that if Broussard was agreeable then it could do no harm, and may lead to a quicker resolution. The split was five/three, with Nikki, Marly and Pete supported by Gaby and James in favour of the visit. The boat's captain was also unimpressed by the invitation but felt he must not interfere with his guests' decision. Matilde had been overheard making her disapproval of the plan known to the Polynesian crew. That evening the usual chat over drinks before the evening dinner, and later around the table, had a subdued tone reflecting the divergence of views on the boat.

It was a few minutes past nine the following morning when an inflatable arrived with Blaise. His dress was no less colourful than on the first meeting. In fact he was even more colourful: his shirt displayed flights of tropical birds in reds and yellows and blues amid green palm trees, while his shorts, which were long and reached below his knees, were waves of bright blue with a wide green trim around the waist. He wore the same wide-brimmed straw hat as the previous day, but today he added a pair of large round dark sunglasses which gave his face the appearance of some trapped nocturnal animal peering out from under a clump of dry thatch, unable to escape from the bright light.

The novelist immediately took an unexpected command of the situation. Within minutes the party found themselves sitting around a table on the aft deck answering his questions. Many of the questions were the same as the police had already asked them and when irritation surfaced from Mike and Ed it was quickly calmed by the novelist who apologised. "I appreciate your irritation, but I also need to fully understand what happened. What people saw? Sometimes there are little matters that we overlook but remember later. They can be very important. So often we see what we expect to see, or worse, what we want to see. We must take care to see what is actually there."

Nevertheless little new information came from the group gathered around the table and it appeared Blaise was already aware of all that Broussard had gathered.

Next he arranged to chat with each woman individually. One by one the four women sat with him in the saloon and then moved back to the aft deck to join the others. When he had finished his interview with each woman he called them together and he and the four women talked for another half an hour. Their chatter was only broken by Matilde calling them to lunch.

After lunch it was the turn of the men. The same pattern of interrogation applied but with the men the conversations were brief. It was only with Ed that the questioning lasted a little longer. As they waited for James, the last to be interviewed, they discussed Blaise's questioning. All were puzzled by his method.

"Why did he spend so much time with the women? None of them, apart from Casey, even knew Annette before this trip and she didn't have much to do with them when she was on the boat anyway. I think he just likes chatting up women." There was a nod of male heads around the table agreeing with Mike's comment.

"You men are always the same. Perhaps we were more helpful." This time the heads nodding to Nikki's riposte were female.

Finally Blaise called them all together. "Thank you for your cooperation. You have been very helpful, especially the ladies."

"So what did they tell you that we men didn't?"

"Men are straightforward. You say what you see, but the ladies are much more sensitive to feelings and emotion. You men say the deceased spoke with you, or did not, but the ladies can tell me how the conversation was received. For example, you Ed spoke with the lady quietly. But was it because you did not wish to be overheard or because there was no need to speak loudly? You were observed and I learnt from that what you were feeling."

"Well I never said we didn't talk, we talked a lot about the past."

"Yes, I am sure you did. And James, you also spoke with the lady and I believe you were not happy?"

"I told you that she raked up an old disagreement. It was unnecessary. You didn't need to speak with the girls to learn that."

"That is true, but you see your ladies are much more attune to relationships. Between yourselves, and between the others on the boat. Now I must speak with those others, the crew that make your holiday so wonderful. I suspect they may have perhaps seen occurrences which to them are unimportant, but may offer clues to what happened and why."

The process was repeated with the Captain and his wife, then with the Polish girl, Ana, and finally with the three Polynesians, Tama, Amura and Eeva. Each spoke with Blaise alone, and then he called them together and he spoke briefly with the group before they dispersed. It was only Blaise and Ana who walked to the foredeck deep in discussion.

It was late afternoon when Blaise made a vague wave of farewell to those present and boarded the Zodiac to take him back to the marina. Nikki called out to him "Ask your friend when can we get out of here? This island is so small. We all want to go home."

"Ah, Ms Olson. I believe Broussard has some new information. He hasn't told me what it is. However, I suspect you may have to remain in Raiatea for longer. I believe he wants more information from the States on the lady's past. It is so difficult when the crime is in one country but the possible cause may be in a different country."

18 Births, Deaths and Automobiles

As the last of the sun's rays disappeared behind the green-clad peaks of the island, the remaining eight holiday-makers were again gathered together for the first of their pre-dinner drinks. Tonight they had come up to the deck later than usual. Perhaps seeking to extend their privacy and to minimise their time together, yet not wanting to be seen to be avoiding their fellow travellers.

They'd drifted into two groups. The women, a quieter group, were seated around a low table on the rear deck while the men stood chatting near the saloon. Occasionally the men's talk was punctuated by bursts of quiet laughter in response to some story, but it quickly faded. Ana and Eeva moved silently among the groups refreshing drinks and offering savouries.

The subject with the women was families. Of the four only Casey was a mother, the other three women were childless. The eldest of Casey's children, a boy, had been a baby in Hong Kong and their youngest, their daughter, had been born after their return to the States.

"It must have been different after you arrived back in the States. I expect you would have had an amah to help with your baby when you were in Hong Kong?"

Casey nodded her head in answer to Gaby's question. "It sure was a shock. I didn't realise the demands of children, and then I had two, a baby and a young boy, both demanding attention. I hadn't realized how much our Lili had helped. It was quite a shock."

"Mike has two daughters. I've seen some photos but I've never met them. They stayed with their mother. Mike only sees one of them occasionally. She's only five years younger than me. That's a scream, imagine me as her stepmother! We could be sort of like sisters, my little sister, well not really."

Gaby turned to speak to Nikki. "Have you got any brothers or sisters?"

"Yeah, two brothers, they're a bit younger than me. One's in the army and the other's a plumber. I've got a little sister too. She's just a little kid. She's nine and I love her heaps." Nikki's eyes went misty and a momentary look of sadness passed across them, then it was gone. "She's very special. What about you?"

"I'm an only child. I have some older cousins on my father's side but I'm really only close to one of them. I have a cousin, the daughter of my Mum's sister in Singapore. She's lovely."

"What about James's kids?

"No. James hasn't got any children. When I first met him he was very against a family but he has softened. Unfortunately there are still ...," she paused, "Things haven't worked out."

Nikki continued her questioning. "What about you Marly?"

"Two sisters, in England."

"What about kids?"

Marly's two word reply to Nikki's question told the group it was a subject best not pursued.

The conversation with the men was of their time together twenty-five years earlier, and cars. "When we were in Hong Kong you were always saying you wanted to get an old Mustang. Did you ever get one?"

Ed smiled as he replied to Pete's question. "Yep. I had to wait a few years, quite a few years, but eventually I convinced Casey that I needed it."

"What did you get?"

"A '68 coupe. 289ci 2V V8."

"What colour?"

"Gulfstream Aqua, it's a beautiful blue with black vinyl top and interior. When I got it the aircon wasn't working. I soon got that fixed!"

Casey had heard her name and the word 'Mustang' and left the women to join the men. "That's not the only one!"

"What? There's more?"

"Yes. He bought an old T-bird."

"What's that one?" Pete was intrigued.

"It's a little older. Even older than me. A '65 convertible. It's got a bigger motor. It's the V8 with the 390ci engine."

Casey continued. "And it's red. Just like the one his father had."

"Red exterior and red interior with a white top."

Nikki had followed Casey over to join the men. "Those cars are even older than my Pa. I love Italian cars. Especially red ones. I was hoping Mike would get me a Porsche but he hasn't". She looked across to him, "but I'm still hoping."

"Porsches are German, not Italian."

"I know James, but they're still red and a sports car. They're so cute."

Marly joined the conversation. "That reminds me of that Janis Joplin song. How did it go? It was about Porches and Mercedes Benzes?"

Casey provided the words for the song Marly was trying to recall. "My friends all drive Porsches, I must make amends. So Lord won't you buy me a Mercedes Benz."

Marly shared Nikki's desires. "Go girl. You stick with your dream. Pete has a Porsche. I've only got a Mazda."

The mention of Mercedes triggered a recollection in Mike. "Annette had a Benz. A fancy white convertible. She told me the night she died that she had just sold it."

Ed was unsurprised by her choice. "She always liked fancy cars. She thought it made an impression on people."

Nor was Casey. "That would be Annette. There could

never be too much bling for that woman."

"It was an SLC300 convertible. It's a lovely car."

Mike nodded in agreement to Ed's description of the car. He continued "I was surprised she sold it. She said she'd only had it six months."

"What did she replace it with?"

Mike answered Ed's question. "I don't think she did. Said who needs a car with Uber. She'd rather have the money. It seemed a strange thing to do. Buy an expensive car then change your mind and sell it so quickly. She would have lost a lot of money on it."

"Perhaps she needed the money?"

"Why buy it in the first place?"

Pete brought the subject back to Ed's cars. "What gearbox does the Mustang have?"

"They're both automatics with the three speed Cruise-O-Matic."

"Didn't Steve McQueen drive a 68 Mustang in that movie?"

"In *Bullitt*, yes, but not like mine. His was a 390 GT, same age but a lot more grunt. I'm a fortunate man with a caring wife who indulges me. She realises boys need their toys. I guess some of us never really grow up."

Casey nodded. "I think Ed caught the disease from his father. He had a brand new Thunderbird when Ed was a baby."

"So which is best. The pony car or the T-bird?"

"Pete, that's a bit like asking which is your favourite kid. They're different, but both are fun."

Gaby turned to Casey. "You must be very understanding if he has two old cars. James and I share one old Japanese sedan, but it's not that old. Maybe one day we will get a nice four-wheel-drive wagon."

James joined the conversation. "I think Gaby dreams of one day going bush in Australia, driving off into the red sunset in the empty Northern Territory. Setting up a camp somewhere remote and smelling the gum leaves and the dust."

"Well I don't want to have a four wheel drive just to do the school pick up, not that we have any kids to pick up yet. I don't see it as a Double Bay tractor, or a Balmain bulldozer!"

The expressions had puzzled Nikki. "My Pa's got a pickup. He used to take us to school in that. What's a Double Bay tractor?"

"Double Bay is a posh suburb in Sydney. Lots of parents drive big fancy four wheel drives to collect their kids from expensive private schools. It's a bit of a disparaging term."

"And a Balmain bulldozer?"

"Same thing, it's just a different expensive suburb in Sydney."

Marly was unimpressed. "I don't think I would want to do that. It would be too hot, Dubai is bad enough. I would much prefer a nice little village in England with a pub with lots of character, somewhere close to London and the

Eurostar so I could get to the Continent, not someplace at the other end of the world."

Gaby prickled at the description of her homeland. "Australia's not that bad. There are lots of lovely places to live and heaps to do. You would enjoy it once you got to know it."

"I doubt it! Too many flies. Pete is always talking about the '*Aussie salute*' to shoo them away. I don't think Australia is the place for me."

Once again the topic of conversation changed. This time it moved to questionable business practices and stories came out of dubious investment scams that the men had seen in their lives.

It was a subject that touched Nikki. "A big city man came to Walker, Minnesota and convinced Pa and some friends to put their savings into this scheme that would make 'em all rich. Folks in Walker trust people. You treat 'em fair and they treat you fair. Not like in big cities. The only one who got rich from this scheme was the man who came to town. It really broke my Pa. He lost all that he had worked for. It was hard on my Ma too. I hate people who do that. I didn't know her but from what I've heard from Mike I think Annette was a lot like that."

The men demurred out of loyalty to their friend but each harboured a suspicion that perhaps Nikki was correct in her character summation. Perhaps it was linked to her death.

19 Sidney Blaise

It was later that evening and the eight members of the party were still seated around the mahogany dining table of the *Ocean Rover*. Tama had purchased two mahi mahi from a passing local fisherman and Matilde's meal of the fish served with a creamy vanilla sauce followed by a coconut custard pie had been appreciated by all.

"The sauce was beautiful. I loved the aroma and flavour of the vanilla but there was also a sweetness. What was that?"

Matilde answered Gaby's question. "I use a dark rum to give a caramel flavour with the vanilla. Also coconut milk with the cream."

While most had enjoyed Ed's selection of two bottles of chablis from the cellar on the boat, it had not been enjoyed by Nikki.

"It's too bitter, tart or something for me. I like my drinks sweeter. Ana, can I have another one of your Tropic Sunsets?"

Ana quickly returned with the requested cocktail. The French white had not been the only alcohol drunk during the evening. In fact a great deal of alcohol had been consumed by all, especially Marly. She and Pete had been the last to arrive for evening drinks and it was obvious that a tension existed between them.

Nor had Blaise's parting comment, that they may have to remain moored at the island even longer than initially thought, been well received by several couples. Since Blaise's departure Ed and Casey had talked with Claude about what could be done to speed up matters. Marly had also approached Claude about moving to a hotel in town.

During the evening there had been discussion around the table about what the information from the States could be. What was it in Annette's past that interested Broussard? Various possibilities were suggested. Some, more fanciful than others, were made by Nikki, but all were pure speculation and added nothing to an understanding of Annette's death. Marly had made some comment about Annette's remark of everybody having secrets and pointedly looked at Pete, then James, and finally Ed and Mike.

The subject moved to their visitor earlier in the day.

"What do you think of Blaise?" Casey's question started a round of conversation amongst the group. Opinions varied.

Nikki was the first to offer her comment. "He's a funny old man, he asks weird questions."

"Why?'

"Because he wanted to know if I had done drugs with Annette. I don't do drugs, well not the hard stuff, and I've never talked to her about any of that stuff."

The conversation briefly turned to drugs and the

likelihood of Annette using but the subject quickly returned to Sidney Blaise.

Next to comment was Ed. "He's an interesting man. I'm not sure what to make of him. I think he was testing us. Looking for differences in our stories. I reckon he's smart, but I don't know what he will find. Anyway I think it is all a waste of time and we should leave it to the gendarmes. I just hope he doesn't complicate things and leave us hanging around here longer."

Casey followed her husband. "He was certainly not what I expected from the book and he is definitely not from the States. Gaby, you are the one with an interest in accents. What nationality do you think he is?"

"I can't place him. I was certainly wrong to think of him having an African background. Maybe the words he wrote gave me that impression, but his speech isn't indicative of a Anglo-African. And I was definitely wrong to think he was a woman. I agree with Ed. I think he is very observant. Perhaps he will find out what happened to Annette."

"I was surprised that he spent so much time talking to you girls." Mike continued, "I thought he would be more interested in those of us who knew Annette from the old days. Gaby and Marly and Nikki hardly knew her."

Ed added, "He also spent a lot of time with Claude and the two boys, and Ana and Matilde. What do you think Pete?"

"He's a strange coot. I was never sure what he was thinking. I got the feeling that when he asked a question his mind was somewhere else."

Ed continued. "Could he be Australian?"

"No. It's definitely not an Australian accent."

"How can you be so sure? There are lots of different Australian accents. What about me?"

Pete turned to face the Chinese girl. "Gaby, you don't have an Australian accent." Gaby remained silent but exchanged a look with her partner as Pete continued, "So James, you're English. Is he English?"

"Well it's not BBC, although that has changed over the years. Once it was the approved form but these days you hear anything on the television. It's certainly not posh, nor is it a distinct regional accent that would place him. He certainly speaks well but I don't know if English is his original language. Could he be French? The islanders seem to have claimed him as one."

It was Gaby who answered. "No. I heard him talking to Claude and his French is too good for a Frenchman. Too correct and formal. I asked Claude and he agrees. Blaise speaks very good French but he isn't a Frenchman."

Perhaps he's foreign, something else? Learnt English and French at school. Lots of Europeans do that."

"No." Gaby was insistent that Sidney Blaise was a native speaker of English.

"What about Canada?" Marly's contribution led to a discussion of the various accents of Canada, and whether there was a slight French influence in his speech. "That could explain why he was here in a French-speaking part of the world. And it's warmer than Canada. Lots of Canadians move south for winter."

Mike was unimpressed with that idea. "But Marly, this is

summer in Canada."

Pete rose to the defence of his wife. "Perhaps he came and fell in love with the islands and stayed. He looks as if he could be going feral."

"Come on Pete. He is hardly one of your Australian ferals."

The general consensus around the table was that Mike's reply to Pete was correct but the question of Blaise's nationality was still unanswered when the group moved onto his appearance.

"That guy sure has a strange sense of dressing. Did you see those shorts and that shirt? And that hat." It was obvious that Nikki had found Blaise's attire, as well as his questions, a little peculiar.

"Well the hat is probably sensible in the tropics with all this sun but I admit the colours and the patterns on his shorts and shirt did clash a bit." Marly went on with her fashion appraisal. "Maybe they are just his holiday clothes. What he wears when he relaxes." She flashed an angry look at her husband.

"Mike would never dress like that, even when we were on holidays. Would you sweetheart?"

Mike turned to Nikki before he replied. "Would you still love me sweetheart?"

"When men never take off a hat like his, I don't know whether they are bald or have hair. Without the hat they can look very different. When Blaise took off his hat I was surprised. I know we were told he had wild white hair but I wasn't expecting that." Casey continued, "If he had a haircut and wore a suit I probably wouldn't recognise him. He might even look like an old-fashioned banker like my dad."

"I think your dad was taller, and he kept his hair short and grey, although I did wonder about the white hair. Does anyone know how long Blaise has been out here in Polynesia?" No one could answer Ed's question. No one had asked that question and Blaise had not proffered information on the subject. "So what is he doing here? On Raiatea?"

"He did say to me that he was having a break after his last novel but Broussard told Claude he was researching a new story set in the South Pacific."

"Did he tell you anything else Gaby?"

"No Marly, that was all he said. Did he say anything to you? I saw the two of you chatting after he'd interviewed Claude."

"Not really. He said something about how relaxing it was here on Raiatea and how peaceful to be away from all the rush and bother of crowds. He didn't say where the crowds were. I guess he must have been referring to a big city somewhere."

"He told Ana that his life was full of violence, crime and murder, but when I questioned him about it, he laughed and said it was only in the books he wrote. 'Surely our lives are not like that, Michael' was his parting comment to me."

Sidney Blaise had been invited to solve a mystery but the man himself remained a mystery.

"I think Blaise reckons one of us is involved." The question of Annette Freidman's death was ever present. Mostly unspoken, but always there and Mike's remark had raised the subject again.

"I don't see how, or why."

"Well maybe Edward you should. And you too Mike and James." Marly, who by now had drunk too many glasses of wine, was bitter in her comment. "You men have a lot to answer for. She told me all about you."

"Marly, don't..." but Pete was cut off as she continued. "Shut up Peter. She told me you weren't any good then and you aren't now. And you Mike! All I can say to you Nikki is watch out. He's not the guy you think he is. What he did in Hong Kong. And Gaby, your boyfriend knows some bad people. She told me what he did to her husband. As for you Ed, she warned me about you. You're not the good guy you make out. You are lucky Casey still backs you up. I wouldn't."

It was Casey who first spoke after Marly's outburst. "Marly, don't believe everything Annette says. I know her. She says whatever suits her at the time. I don't know why or what, but she was up to something and the truth wouldn't matter."

"It's alright for you but she's dead."

"Yes. So what did she tell you?"

"Only to watch you. I was going to ask her more about what she meant when she was sober, but by the morning she was dead. You all have secrets you don't want spread. I don't want to be here with you, any of you. Particularly you Peter." With that she left the group around the table and climbed the stairs to the sundeck and stood alone near the plunge pool.

There was silence until it was broken by Pete. "Maybe that'll be another overboard."

"Pete, don't even think it!" No one else around the table spoke, but all agreed with Casey.

20 Girl Talk, Man Talk

Movement on the *Ocean Rover* had commenced later than usual. Couples had drifted into the dining room to help themselves to breakfast, or a strong coffee, both served by Eeva, and then disappeared back to their cabins. It was around eleven when three of the women met by the spa pool. Casey was enjoying the surging warm bubbles massaging her body. Nikki lay stretched out on a sun lounge facing the pool and basking in the sun. Gaby lay on another sun lounge, also facing Casey, but under the shade of a large umbrella. There was no sign of Marly.

"I think I've had enough of the bubbles. I'm just going to lie here and let all my troubles soak away."

"I didn't think you had troubles."

"I think I had too many drinks last night Gaby. Ted and I didn't surface too well this morning."

"I think we all did." Nikki rolled on to her side and adjusted the straps and top of her bikini. "I don't want to get marks. Why are you in the shade Gaby? The sun is beautiful? It's great for a tan."

"Old habits." Gaby was wearing a stylish colourful bikini.

However, while fashionable, it was far more modest than the four small triangles favoured by Nikki, where the knotted thin side cords of the lower half only partially obscured a small red devil tattooed high on her thigh. "I guess it's my mother's Chinese influence. Girls were brought up to be modest and discreet. I never rebelled."

"I can understand that." Casey had favoured a smart one-piece. "Besides, at my age, a bit of coverage is an advantage."

"I love your little red devil. I could never do that. Besides I don't think James would approve if I had a tattoo. He can be very old-fashioned in some ways."

"It sure attracts guys' attention. I like that. It worked with Mike. He's got a tattoo. I want him to have some work on his arm, but he says the one on his left calf is quite enough for him. I think he would be so cool."

Casey had been intrigued by another tattoo on Nikki. "What's the one on your inner arm? I can read it but it doesn't make sense to me."

" '*Livet er for a leve*'. It means life is for living. My family originally came from Norway. Way back. It's Norwegian. It's kinda nice to remember where we came from, the old folks who came out to the States. It must have been hard for them." Gaby and Casey smiled. The tattoo seemed so appropriate for Nikki and her life. "I love being tanned and it's so much nicer when it's for real and not sprayed on."

Gaby's smile grew wider. "I guess my mother had the old idea that to be brown meant you were a peasant and worked in the fields. Rich people didn't need to be out in the sun all day. Now it's the opposite. Rich people can lie in the sun on holidays and the poor work in offices and factories and are pale. It's not only tans that have changed but our body shapes as well. Once the rich were fat and the poor were skinny and starving. Now the rich spend a fortune at the gym and on diets to stay slim and the poor eat fatty food and lots of sugar and put on weight."

"Like those Rubenesque women. Some of them were on the cuddly side."

"Do you know Rubens?" asked Casey, surprised at Nikki's comment.

Nikki replied. "He was a painter. They say his women were generously proportioned. There's lots around like them in some places. They sure didn't have a good BMI. Not what you see in a gym. Well, not the finished product anyway."

"I've always loved the putti in art. All those fat, chubby little putti in Renaissance paintings and sculpture."

"Putti? What are they Gaby?"

"You see them in some old paintings Nikki. They're the fat babies, a bit like angels. Some people think of them as 'cupids' because they often have bows and arrows. They had various meanings in painting depending on the period and the artist, but in those days so many children died young. To have a fat, healthy baby must have seemed like a miracle. Families lost so many. It's a bit like parts of Africa today. So tragic."

At that moment Ana appeared with a tray asking if anyone had any wishes. The three women all shook their heads and Casey acted as spokeswoman in thanking her and asking her to return later. Ana quietly vanished down the steps to the saloon.

"Ana has no problem with her BMI. What about Annette. She looked fit and slim. Did she work out?"

Casey replied to Gaby's question with a shrug. "I don't remember her working out in Hong Kong. Perhaps she does, did. I don't know."

"Did she have many friends?"

"I don't know about good friends. She certainly had friends. Well she knew lots of people. Annette did have one very good friend. Her 'bestie' I suppose we'd say now. She was a young German woman. They must have had a disagreement because the friendship broke up, but that was over twenty-five years ago."

"Do you think there was more to it? I saw the way she was talking to Ana at Huahine. I think Ana was suspicious about her sexuality."

Casey responded to Nikki's question. "I doubt it. Heaven help us if it's just because you have a female best friend. We'd all be considered lesbians. She and Paul still shared an apartment. I don't know if they shared a bed. Probably unlikely I suspect." She went on: "After her husband disappeared Annette had a string of yachties in her life. Young, tanned, bleached hair and fit. They didn't seem to mind that Annette was older, provided she paid the bills at the bars and nightclubs. She even tried it on Mike a few times but he turned her down. She didn't take refusal well."

"Mike told me. It was after he and his wife had separated."

"Yes. Stacey hated Hong Kong. She went back to the States but Mike stayed on. They'd had one baby, and there was another on the way when she left. Mike used to visit her when he could but it didn't really work out. He liked his job, she liked the money but not the life."

"Mike told me it didn't work. He said he strayed but so did his wife."

Casey nodded. "Yes. It wasn't a good idea to leave a man like Mike alone in Hong Kong."

"I'd never leave Mike alone like that. He might not be there when you wanted him."

"I wouldn't leave my Ted alone either." Casey half-smiled at the thought of her husband being left alone. "What about you Gaby?"

"There's temptation everywhere. James has talked about it. I think he was hurt badly when his wife died. He was a bit of a recluse as far as women were concerned when I met him."

"What happened, what did he tell you Gaby?"

"I know that his wife left him. He said she had a drug problem. That she died."

Casey provided more of the story. "Yes. He'd introduced her to the man who supplied her with drugs. I don't think James used but Jane certainly did. Then she left him and moved in with her supplier. It was a bad move. She overdosed. I think James felt responsible."

"He told me he almost left Hong Kong after that but ended up staying."

"Yes. He withdrew quite a bit but by then the job was almost finished and Ted and I left for the States. We lost touch with him after that."

"James and I have been together now for thirteen years. I don't know much about the intervening years after his wife died and before we met."

"How did you meet?"

"It was just work and mutual friends Nikki. At first we didn't hit it off. He was very brusque, and I was getting over a bad romance so I wasn't wanting a new relationship either. Then eventually we both realised we actually enjoyed being together and things warmed up. We realised it was more than just work. I've never heard much about Pete's first wife. Did you know her Casey?"

Casey shook her head. There was little she could add. Julianne was an Australian like Pete. They had come to Hong Kong and Pete had worked with Mike. She was a bright happy woman, and seemed to fit into the expatriate life well. They had gone back to Australia when Project Dynasty had finished and that was all she knew. "I never really got to know her very well. She didn't mix with the group much, had her own circle of friends. They must have broken up at some stage, I think Pete and Marly have been together for about eight years."

"What about Marly?" Has she been married before? I guess at our age we all have exes of some sort."

Before Casey could answer Gaby's question Nikki raised her hand to silence her.

Marly came up the steps and joined the three women by the plunge pool. "I must apologise for last night. I'd had a bad day and drunk too much wine."

Casey acknowledged the apology and invited her to join them. "We were discussing last night. We think we all had too much. We were all very slow this morning.'

"I'm sorry. You may have picked up that Peter and I have a few problems. He wanted to come on this trip hoping things would change but they won't. We have to realise that and move on."

As the oldest of the women Casey had become the de facto mother of the four. "What are you going to do?"

"When we get away from this boat we will go our separate ways. I'm going back to England. I can't stand Dubai any longer. I miss the green. I'll find a nice village in the countryside close to London and settle there."

"That sounds real cute. Near a little English pub?"

"Of course Nikki, no village is complete without a pub. It's strange. What I really miss is a pot of tea, scones and mirabelle jam."

Apart from Marly none of those present knew mirabelle jam. She explained it was a special type of plum. "It's a memory of visiting my grandmother when I was a little girl. She had a tree with lovely yellow fruit and used to make jam. It was always at summertime. It's those old memories that come back and haunt us."

That morning the four men had met with Tama and Amura on the Sport's Deck at the rear of the yacht. It was decided that Amura would take Ed and Mike fishing in the lagoon. Soon the three men were equipped with life vests and fishing rods, then launched three kayaks and quietly paddled away. Pete and James watched them depart while Tama climbed the steps to the saloon. He returned with an icebox of beers. Then he discreetly disappeared leaving the two men alone.

"How do you like Dubai?"

Pete shrugged and replied to James' question. "It's a strange place. It's been good to me. I'm happy with my job and it pays well. You can always get away for a break if you wish. It is so central to everywhere with flights. It's hot, but everything is air-conditioned. So how's Hong Kong these days?"

"It's changed. Quite a lot. Have you been back?"

"No."

You wouldn't recognise it now. More apartments, more reclaimed land. More people, but it really changed after the handover in ninety-seven and the British left. At first the Mainland didn't interfere much but gradually they are exerting their power more and more. It still has the energy that I love but there's now also an anxiety."

"What will happen?"

"Who knows. Beijing obviously wants to exert more influence and fully control the place. Hong Kongers will be expected to behave like Mainlanders. Whether that will happen? I don't know. There's a lot of young people who have different ideas and are prepared to protest. What that means for business is uncertain."

"Will you stay on?"

"I don't think so. At some stage Gaby and I will leave. Perhaps sooner than later. We just don't know when, or where we'll go, and that affects our other plans."

"You have a plan?"

"Well, not a business plan. Gaby and I want a family. We've been trying but it hasn't happened. Time is running out. We plan to try IVF but first we want to settle somewhere and get married."

"Any ideas where?"

James explained that they were considering Australia and Singapore. After living overseas for so long he didn't feel he could settle back in Britain. It also depended on what work was available. While he had experience, he would lose all the contacts he had built up over the years. It would almost be starting from scratch again.

"What about Gaby?"

"She came to Hong Kong when she worked for a travel company. She eventually ran that end of the business. I think her skills are more transferable than mine. If all goes well she would be happy working a few days a week and motherhood. That would be easier in Singapore but her family is in Sydney. What's it like working in Dubai?"

"Business is business. I'm now involved in trading precious metals. Gold, so that's always interesting. You get a variety of characters coming through, not all of them likeable, or reputable. I guess there's always some place in the world that services such people. You do have to be careful. You don't want to upset the local powers-that-be, and they don't like to be on the wrong end of a deal. If that happens take a plane out and don't come back. The ones I feel sorry for are the labourers. Emiratis don't do hard labour and they treat the poor workers from India and other places pretty rough. Their accommodation is very basic and they have few rights. There have been cases where they don't even get paid the money they're owed."

"How does Marly like it out there?"

"She hates it. All she talks about is green England. I don't think I pick my wives very well."

"Julianne was lovely."

"We were young. Hong Kong was exciting. All was good. Then we went home to Australia. We found we just started going separate ways. I got a job based in Darwin. That was interesting. Guess I must like warm climates! Her family was in Brisbane and her father had a few health issues so she spent a lot of time down there. Anyway we just drifted apart and decided to divorce and start again. At least there were no children."

"Where did you meet Marly?"

"In Dubai. She came out to visit a girlfriend and we met. Then we got together. I think she thought she'd like the lifestyle and the money, but it wasn't quite what she expected. The locals can turn a blind eye to many things, but then they can also suddenly become very righteous. Anyway she keeps wanting to return to England, and I don't. Won't!"

"That must make it difficult?"

"You've probably noticed things aren't good with us. Last night wasn't unusual. We were going to separate months ago but then she learnt about this trip and insisted we come and add a stay on Bora Bora. Foolishly I thought things might change, but no. She keeps talking about a little English village but what she has her eye on is becoming lady of the manor."

127

"A real Lady?'

"No, the man she has her eye on is only a mister, but he has a manor house, and money, lots of it. That's what she likes."

"So what happens now?"

"When we get off this boat we part. Then it will be lawyers at ten paces. She will want as much as she can get out of me."

"She and Annette would have got on well. Annette liked money. I'm surprised she didn't find some wealthy American husband, once she got over those toy boys she used to have after her husband disappeared."

Pete took another swig of his beer. "Perhaps she hitched up with the owner of this boat. I've never heard her mention anyone, but Ed might know more. He seems to have kept in contact with her."

"Yes. I gather they used to run into each other at times."

"Talking of yachties, that Ana is a looker, and Mike's girlfriend is quite a hot chick. Did you see that red devil on her thigh?"

James had also noticed. "I agree with you. They are two attractive women. Your marriage might be on the rocks but you still have an eye for the ladies! I don't think Mike would like competition, and I think Ana may have her own ideas. Besides, the last thing you need at the moment is female complications and divorce lawyers. What are the prospects for jobs in Dubai like these days?"

The conversation continued between the two men, one looking for a new career, the other for a new single life until the three kayaks returned.

"That was great." Ed put his arm around Amura's shoulder. "This man really knows where to find fish. I've never had as much fun with a line since I was a little kid and my Dad took me out on the lake when we were on holiday."

Mike also held up his catch whose scales sparkled in the bright sunlight. "Amura says he will give them to Matilde. We might have them tonight. That's what I call fresh."

The two newcomers reached into the icebox for a beer and the four men continued discussing the morning's outing, until the gong rang for lunch and Tama appeared to invite them to the table.

21 The Women

While the men were lounging on the sports deck drinking beer or fishing with Amura the woman continued their conversation beside the pool.

As is often the case the subject eventually returned to their partners and families. Casey, the oldest of the women, had two children. Her son had trained as a pilot, moved on to jets, and was flying for an organisation doing medical evacuations and transfers. He had two sons, the eldest called Teddie after his grandfather and the youngest Walt after Casey's father. Her daughter was still single. As Casey put it, "some boyfriends, some more serious than others but no Mr Right. Fortunately no Mr Wrong either." Like many women her age her daughter held high expectations of what she wanted from life, and from a partner in particular, but Casey felt she was unrealistic in the give and take required to make a long-term relationship work.

Gaby nodded in agreement. "I see it in some of my friends. They are so immersed in their careers and having a great lifestyle travelling and being with their friends that they don't have a place for a man. When they do find one they like they want him to conform to their demands, and then get upset when he has his own plans."

"Well, what about you?"

Gaby rolled over from her position on the shaded sun lounge to answer Marly. "I was like that so I can understand their attitude but eventually I realised that I liked being with James. It took a while and it wasn't all plain sailing at first. We still have our disagreements but we both realise the benefits of being together."

"So why aren't you married?"

Again Gaby answered Marly's question. "At first it didn't seem important. What mattered was our relationship and our commitment. For us that's still the main thing, but marriage is one more step of commitment and we want to marry before we have kids. I guess deep down we are both old-fashioned and think that stability is better for raising kids."

"Do you want kids?"

This time Gaby answered Nikki's question. "Yes. James and I would like to have a family. We've been trying but it hasn't happened." Gaby's voice became quieter. "I'm worried that we may not have a baby before my time runs out."

"You've got years left."

"We have been trying for quite a few years Nikki, I don't know how many are left. I don't want to be one of those mothers having a baby at sixty."

"That's really weird. Having babies at that age I mean. But you don't want to have them too young. You need to grow up yourself before you can look after a kid. You're still only a kid yourself. It's just not right to bring a kid into this world if you can't look after it properly." Once again a sadness clouded Nikki's face. "So how do you know when it's the right guy? When did you and James decide you two were right?"

"At first James didn't want children. I guess he still had the scars of his marriage. I didn't either. I was like some of my girlfriends. But then, things changed. We were settled in our relationship and I guess my 'motherhood' hormones kicked in. Fortunately by then James had also relaxed. It just hasn't worked and we are going to try IVF. But first we need to decide where our lives will take us. We have to sort out our jobs and where we will live."

"Do you have any plans?"

"Nothing definite Casey. Perhaps Singapore or Sydney. James doesn't want to return to England and I would like to be near my parents. They're getting older."

"I remember growing up at home in Walker, my ma and pa always disagreed. Fought. That was another reason I wanted to get away. Then they would get all lovey dovey. Guess that's the time when I came along, and my brothers. But they stuck together. Then there was little Angie. She was so cute and beautiful."

"You have a little sister?"

Nikki paused before replying to Gaby. "Yes. Angela. She really is my angel."

Once again it was Gaby who moved the conversation on. "What about Annette's husband?"

Casey was the only person present who had known Annette's husband. "Paul was a very proper Englishman.

Very correct. Annette never spoke much of him, or her family, but I suspect her family didn't have much money and Paul offered an entry to a different world. She was very good at mimicking accents and manners and style so she could fit into a wealthier society. She worked hard at it."

Marly understood. "You see it in Dubai too. Smarties that you wouldn't want to know at home get jobs in the Middle East. Their partners! Some of them adopt a certain pretence, others say 'Up You', keep their accents and flash their money. It's gross!"

Nikki also understood what Casey had meant. "So Paul was a great handbag?" It's not just us girls who decorate a guy's arm. I've seen rich women go for guys just 'cause they look good. They treat them like another handbag, change them each season. Some women snigger 'cause a guy likes an attractive partner but they can be just the same. Those who aren't just after the money."

"So Paul became surplus. She no longer needed him."

"I'm not sure I'd put it quite like that Marly."

"Did she have him bumped off?"

Casey laughed at Nikki's suggestion. "That's a bit melodramatic, even for Hong Kong. She didn't have to do that. They could have just separated. It happened all the time."

"Perhaps he just wanted a clean break? A new life?"

Casey shrugged her shoulders at Gaby's suggestion. "Perhaps. It would be easy to leave HK unofficially but you would need a new identity and passport to get into another country legally. Still I'm sure that could be arranged.

James, and Mike knew lots of people who would know someone who could do it."

The subject returned to marriage. "Well I don't think marriage and children are all that important." Marly was very definite in expressing her opinion.

Nikki was curious. "But you've been married before."

"Yes, twice. Next time I will be more selective. It won't be another Pete or someone like my first husband either. This time I won't jump in just because it looks good."

"What about kids? I know Mike is fond of his daughters, even the one he doesn't see. I think he would like some more but he is frightened what might happen."

"Pete wanted kids, I didn't. It was an issue. I took very good care to make sure it didn't happen. I have two sisters. They don't have brats either. Our father was a difficult man. He bossed our mother and made her life a misery. Never considered her opinion. We weren't going to put up with that from any man. Maybe that's why I liked Annette."

"I'm not sure Annette would be a good role model for anyone."

"I disagree with you Casey. I think she was a woman who knew what she wanted and went for it."

"But Marly, her marriage didn't work. She was just a user. Not just of her husband but anyone who could benefit her."

"Well you should know Casey, from what she told me about your marriage."

"Don't believe everything she told you. She would match her story to her target. She would probably have wanted something from you if she hadn't died."

"Well she told me about you and Ed. I don't think your marriage was as good as you like to make out."

"We had our tough times. That's no secret. Every marriage has a few rough patches. Annette tried her charms on a few men, Ted included, and Mike. I know Mike knocked her back."

"That's why she hated my Mike. She told me he was a bad man. It was vengeance because she didn't get what she wanted. Mike told me."

Marely wasn't to be stopped and pushed the matter further, claiming that Annette had spoken of a more recent affair. Then she added some advice for Nikki. "You should get smart and dump that boyfriend of yours. Annette told me all about him. He might give you a good time but he'll dump you. Move on, you can do better. Become more assertive and if he doesn't like it tell him it's 'bye bye baby'."

Casey was about to respond angrily to Marly's allegation when Gaby intervened. "So what are your plans?"

When the group was finally allowed to leave the boat Marly would catch the first available flight to Heathrow. She had already arranged to spend a few days with her sister in London and would then move to a cottage in a small village outside London. A friend in Dubai would arrange for her clothes and personal treasures to be sent to her in the UK. For her, her marriage was over. It was something she should have done years ago.

"So do you have a new man in your life?"

"No." There was something about the way that she

answered that caused Nikki not to believe her. "Well how are you going to manage in some little cottage in the backwoods of England? That doesn't seem your style."

"I'll do fine. I'll have some money. It won't be a problem. You need to plan ahead. You should know."

The comment aroused Nikki's anger. "I might have a boyfriend who likes to spend money but I don't take it off him. That's ..." Nikki struggled but could not find the word she wanted to describe Marly's barb.

Casey came to Nikki's rescue. "That's cruel Marly. Nikki didn't deserve that."

Just then a gong rang out. For Nikki, it triggered the memory of hearing a similar sound at the end of a round at a boxing match. It was at a private club that she and Mike had visited as guests of one of Mike's business associates. She'd hated the sight of muscly young men bashing away at each other. Mike had not liked it either, and they'd never accepted another invitation to attend. What had surprised her were the woman watching the fight. They seemed to enjoy the aggression. Perhaps Annette and Marly were like them. But then, sometimes you had to fight for what you believed in, for what was important or precious.

This time however, it was Matilde inviting them to lunch at the buffet set out on a table on the aft deck.

The gong sounded a second time. Round two.

22 More Questions

It was early that afternoon when a small runabout pulled alongside *Ocean Rover*. Amura assisted Sidney Blaise to step across onto the larger boat. He was wearing the same clothing as the previous day and from the look of the shirt and shorts he may have slept in them. He was greeted by the captain.

"Your message. It was most interesting. I thought it best I come straight away. I could not sleep last night. There are questions that have troubled me and they have continued to worry me all morning. I realised that there were things said to me that I did not understand and they may be matters of importance. I would like to speak to several people if I may. They may be able to add more to what they have already told me."

"With whom do you wish to speak?"

"If I may Claude, I would like to speak again with Tama. What he told you is very puzzling. Also with Amura and Marlene Metcalfe if possible. As well I also realise I know so little about the lady who died. I should have asked more about her past. It may hold the clue I am seeking."

"Tama and Amura are no problem but Marlene, she and her husband are not content. A problem marital, I think."

"I suspected such, but hopefully the lady can still give me another piece of the puzzle. I am missing so many pieces."

In turn Tama and Amura joined Blaise on the foredeck. The first was Tama and the two men stood talking for ten minutes. Occasionally they laughed but mostly stood looking quietly back in the direction of the distant motu. Twice Tama closed his hands as if he was gripping something with both hands. Then it was the turn of Amura. Again they stood looking towards the motu but there was no laughter with the younger man. Once they looked towards the bridge where Claude and Matilde stood watching them.

As the couples drifted into the saloon curious about the unexpected return of the writer, Blaise, his enquiries with the two Polynesians concluded, joined them to take a refreshment. He was on his third cup of dark black coffee when Ed Parker joined the group.

"So what did you learn yesterday, Sidney?"

"Edward, you were all very helpful. I thank you, but I realised that I need to know more. That is why I returned today."

"So what have you learnt today?"

"Much that is interesting. Unfortunately each piece of the puzzle only raises another puzzle. From Tama, I heard the lady told him she could not swim. From both Tama and Amura, that they heard no boats while they were on duty. I believe you visited Tama on the bridge while he was on watch. He told me you brought him a coffee. Did you see anyone else moving around the boat when you visited him?"

"No. No one, only Tama. I thought he would appreciate a coffee. It must be a long boring night sitting in the bridge alone."

"Yes. Tama told me he plays games on his cell phone and also listens to music, but still the watch must be long. I would certainly find it boring. I think I would want to sleep but Claude says the man on watch must be alert at all times. There are those criminals onshore who want to board the boat and steal from rich foreigners."

"Well Tama was certainly awake when I left him."

"What time was that Edward?"

"About one o'clock. No, maybe later, I couldn't sleep. Pete had reminded me of an unpleasant experience we had with a client in Hong Kong and it unsettled me. Casey and I talked about it for a long time. We went for a walk around the boat to try to settle down. Eventually Casey decided to take some sleeping tablets. I still couldn't settle so I went for another walk. That's when I saw Tama. I went and made two coffees and sat and talked with him for a while."

"So how long did you talk?"

"About half an hour."

"And you didn't see the lady?"

"Annette? No. She would have been in her cabin."

"But Edward, can we be sure? Just because you didn't see her we cannot know for certainty."

""Yes Sidney, I suppose you are right."

"I am Edward, but I hope you may be able to assist me by providing more information. The lady's past? I need to know more. Did she have enemies? Who were her friends? Did she have a special romance?"

"Well I don't know that any of us can really help you. Most of us only knew her from all those years ago. So much must have happened since then. She could also be very private. She only told you what she wanted you to know, and I suspect that was not always completely true."

"We all try to present a better view to the world and those we meet. I am not innocent myself of that. It is hardly a crime, is it Edward?"

"Hardly a crime. I suppose of anyone here I would have had the most to do with her. We had met a number of times since Hong Kong, but I would hardly claim to know her well anymore, or who was important in her life these days. Annette could be difficult at times. That could cause friction."

"More than friction. She could be very bossy, it always had to be her way and she could put on a turn if she didn't get it."

"You speak from experience, Peter?"

"Yes. I suffered her tantrums several times in Hong Kong. I didn't enjoy her outbursts at all. Believe me Sidney, she could be very unpleasant."

"Pete, we shouldn't speak ill of the dead."

"Casey, the woman is dead. At least she deserves for us to

find out what happened. The truth. You must admit she was not your favourite person. Not the way she used to latch onto Ed whenever it suited her."

"I had no problem with that. I know how Ted felt. That was just Annette."

"There is a question I cannot answer. It puzzles me. Why did she invite you all on this cruise? The impression I have is that she did not do things without a reason. What was the reason for your invitations?"

James answered. "That puzzled me too Sidney. I was only the local contact in the project in Hong Kong. Annette hardly had anything to do with me. Most of the work I did was with Pete and Mike."

"That's hardly true Jimmy. You were the man who knew everyone in Honkers. Whatever anyone wanted, you knew who to see. Annette used you when she had a problem."

"A couple of times, that was all. You were the one closer to her Pete. You and Ed."

Blaise persisted with his questioning. "That still does not help my enquiries. Did she have enemies in Hong Kong, or did she have enemies after she left?"

It was Ed who answered. "We can't help you Sidney. We don't know. In Hong Kong we did our business, then we parted. She could be difficult but not enough to wish her dead. After that? Who knows? I can't help you, and James, Pete and Mike know even less."

It was obvious that nothing further could be found from that particular line of questioning and Blaise invited Marly to accompany him to the foredeck where he had previously chatted with the two crewmen. They were away for fifteen minutes before they returned to the others.

"Have you solved your puzzle yet Sidney?"

Blaise shook his head in reply to James' question. "Not yet, but Marlene was of great help. It is another small piece, but I must still find where it fits."

"So how will you solve Annette's death?"

"Mike, in a crime story we must have a means, a method and a motive. But, at present, I do not have the complete answer for any of these things."

"So how did it happen?"

"The means. Well Marlene, we know the lady was here on this boat. Edward drank coffee with Tama and left about one-thirty or a little later. It is thought she was in her cabin at that time. But in the morning she was on the motu. Her clothes were wet. She was found in the water but had not drowned. I have been told she never went in the water, a scare from when she was a little girl. Also, she was wearing a long red dress when she was found. It was the dress she was wearing when Ana last saw her. You would not go swimming in such a dress. She had a swimsuit in her cabin but it was dry. So if she did not swim, how did she get to the motu? Did she fall overboard, or was she pushed? There was no water in her lungs so she did not drown and float there. Did she struggle and swim to the motu? She told Tama she could not swim. So did she go by some water craft? Did someone come and meet her here on the boat to take her to the island? But why? Tama, and later Amura, who were on watch, tell me they heard no noise from a boat. Claude tells me they are good men. It is possible then that she could have used the paddle board or the dingy, or perhaps a kayak. They would be silent. But then, how did the paddle board or dingy return to the boat? There would need to be two people involved. The lady and one other to go to the motu and only one return. But why?"

"And who?"

"Yes, another very good question Gabrielle. When you write a detective story you must have a motive. For a novelist like me, when we write our stories, it is usually passion or revenge. They are the best. Sometimes it is for ego or status, or money, perhaps to remove a competitor and gain some advantage. I suspect Broussard believes he has a lead but he will not tell me because he wants the glory of solving this mystery. Yet I cannot see the reason here. Last night I realised I must look, not just to the present, but also to the past. To know more of the lady's past. That is why I hoped you could help me and you have. Thank you."

"So who do you think did it?"

"Edward, neither Broussard nor I can yet say. He, because he must be sure before he can make any charges. Me, because I must also be sure and have sufficient knowledge to speak confidently."

"So you don't know?"

"I have my suspicions Miss Olson, but suspicions are not proof."

"So you think one of the men on the boat did the deed? Which one, Ed, Pete, James? It wasn't my Mike. We were in bed all the time."

"Why do you say it is a 'he' Miss Olson? Surely, in these

days of equality, we must also consider the ladies. Indeed, we should always consider the ladies."

"So you don't really have any means and you are still looking for a motive. You have only a suspicion about who. What about the method?"

"The method. How did the lady die? Yes, Marlene, that is also a puzzle. I learnt much yesterday, and today, but nothing of the method. I do not yet have an answer. I hope Broussard may solve that problem. I believe he has asked the doctor for a further examination."

23 The Man

"I saw the man! The Man at Bloody Mary's."

After Blaise's visit Marly had gone ashore alone. The mood on the boat was still sombre. Partly because of the death, and partly because the boat remained confined to its mooring at Raiatea, unable to continue with the planned cruise. The differences that had started to arise between some of the remaining eight guests were becoming especially noticeable, particularly between several of the women. Even the crewmembers were affected by the atmosphere. The tension between Marly and Pete had become obvious to all. While no one commented publicly, all had discussed the relationship in the privacy of their cabins. Most of the guests and crew had taken any opportunity for a break from the boat. Some had gone ashore alone, others in pairs.

On her return Marly was full of news and excitement. "I saw the man! The Man at Bloody Mary's. I was sitting in the boulangerie near the marina having a coffee and watching the fishermen and the local ferries when I looked across the street and saw him going into a supermarket. There was a woman with him."

"Did you see him leave?"

"No. a group of tourists stood in front of me and I couldn't see. By the time I paid my bill and could go and check the store he wasn't there."

"Are you sure it was him?"

"Definitely Casey, although this time he was wearing sandals and a hat, and he was with a woman, older than you with long grey hair."

A group decision was made that the information should be passed to the police and Ed and Claude were nominated to go ashore and give the news to Capitaine Broussard.

When they returned Ed reported. "Broussard says he will look into it. I don't know what that will mean. I guess we will have to wait and see. Claude is confident that it will happen so here's hoping."

"Did you see The Man?"

"No, but we did see Blaise. Claude told him the news as well."

"Did he say anything?"

"Not much, Marly. Just 'Very interesting'."

"That was all?"

"Yes. He said he would make some enquiries."

It was sunset when a local runabout brought Blaise from the marina at Uturoa to visit the *Ocean Rover* for the second time that day. The guests were gathered on the upper deck, once again enjoying the sunset over Taha'a but, as beautiful as it was, paradise had lost much of its charm. He had news of The Man.

"I have made enquiries and the man you saw and his wife are on a yacht in the marina of Apooiti further around the coast."

"Then he could have killed Annette?"

"No Michael. That is very unlikely. He only arrived last night. Your friend was already dead."

"Are you sure? He could have killed her and then timed his arrival for later."

"He says he left Bora Bora yesterday morning and arrived in Raiatea last evening. That is possible. The marina confirms his arrival. He says he didn't know that the *Ocean Rover* would be here, although he wasn't surprised. Bora Bora to Raiatea or the reverse is a common passage."

"But is it possible he left earlier and was here before we arrived?"

"I doubt it. I think he was telling the truth. The gendarmes will check his story."

"Perhaps he flew here. That would be possible. There is an airstrip on Bora Bora and I saw an aircraft taking off from this island so there is an airstrip here. Then returned to get his yacht."

"Yes, that may be possible. But Michael, it leaves so many unanswered questions."

"Did he know Annette?"

"Yes, very definitely. He was no friend of that lady."

"Well Sidney, tell us more."

"Edward, I will tell you what he told me. After years of hard struggle your Man had had enough of bankers, lawyers and demanding customers. He and his wife decided to sell their business and follow a dream, buy a yacht and sail off into the setting sun. Ten years ago he employed your friend to assist in selling his business to a large company. She was well paid for her services but he later found out that she had a secret agreement with the purchaser to receive twenty-five percent of any reduction in price she could negotiate. As well, she talked the vendor into accepting two conditions that he thought would offer him more money in the long term. The purchaser avoided both conditions. It cost the man and his wife a great deal of money. He was not happy with your friend."

"So he had a reason to kill her?"

"Not everyone kills because they are unhappy Michael."

"But he had a motive?"

"Perhaps, but he had no idea that she would be in the bar that day. At first he wasn't even sure that it was her. I gather she had changed her hairstyle since he knew her. It was only when he heard her voice that he was sure it was the woman who had cost him so much. He was surprised and irritated to find the woman who had been the cause of his unhappy experience sitting in a bar on an island in the South Pacific."

"But Annette must have recognised him?"

"Because he was watching her so intently. Eventually she saw behind the beard and the unkempt hair. That was when she went to him and told him she would call the police, that she would tell them he was harassing her."

"That story explains Annette's remark 'The past has a way of finding you'."

"I think so Edward."

"Perhaps it was a spur of the moment decision. He wanted revenge."

"No Ms Olson, that ignores the fact he was not present when Ms Friedman died. I am confident Broussard will confirm his story."

"Sidney, when I was coming back to the boat with Claude he told me that Tama had wanted to speak with you and that was the reason for the visit this morning. Was it about the death?"

"Yes Edward. It is difficult to say. Perhaps it is of no importance."

"What was it?"

"It was after you left for your fishing. Some equipment. But I don't think it will be of concern to you."

"What was it?"

"Tama discovered a problem with some equipment. However I do not yet see how it would involve this matter. I think it is, perhaps, just an unrelated coincidence."

"So what happens now?"

Blaise answered Ed's query. "We must keep looking for the truth."

"Do you have any faith in the police?"

"Capitaine Broussard and I have often spent time discussing crime and criminals. He is very thorough and astute. I am very confident that he will solve the case," Blaise looked around the gathered group, "but perhaps the person with the answer is here with us now."

24 Project Dynasty

"You are very fortunate to be on such a beautiful boat with a cook like Matilde. Her meal was superb. The wine also. I envy you your holiday."

Blaise had accepted the invitation from Claude to remain on board and join the group for dinner. With the meal finished some had drifted back to their cabins, Ed and Casey had remained at the table chatting with Claude, and Matilde had joined them to discuss her cooking with Casey. Pete Metcalfe had walked up the steps to the sundeck and stood leaning over the rail at the bow of the boat. Below him, the water silently broke against the hull as the boat rocked gently in the low wash of a passing ferry. Blaise had joined him.

"I don't think I would call it fortunate. This trip has become a bit of a nightmare. For Annette, for me. An accident? Suicide? Murder? What else could it be? The first two seem so unlikely."

Blaise nodded his head. "Tell me about Project Dynasty."

"Do you think it's important? It was so long ago."

Blaise shrugged, opening the palms of his hands towards Metcalfe. "Perhaps, perhaps not. It may help us find out what happened. The mindset of the lady."

Metcalfe began the story. "We were a team put together to set up investments for an American fund. We were to buy a small Hong Kong business that managed investments for shareholders and then grow it. Our US owner, a company that created investment funds, would access money from clients to grow the business opportunities that we identified in Hong Kong and on mainland China."

"It was successful?"

"We did our job. We purchased the company, set up all the structures needed. We had all the right symbols, red and yellow colours, an auspicious name. The Chinese love to think of families and dynasties. We made the necessary contacts. Identified great opportunities. Then there was a change in the States."

"What happened?"

"The top man was replaced. The new man had different ideas. It happens; out with your predecessor's ideas, in with yours. We no longer were part of the plan."

"What did you do?"

"We undid all that we'd put in place. Sold off businesses, backed out of deals. Eventually even sold the original company we had begun with. It was all over in a few years."

"That must have been difficult for you?"

"We were well paid while it was happening, and I got a great redundancy. Plus the experience, especially working with Mike. That made it worthwhile. It was a pity. We were in the right place at the right time and the big bosses in New

York blew it. We could have been a great success."

"I thought Edward would be in charge?"

"He was the legal expert. His job was to make sure everything was OK with US and Hong Kong laws. He actually worked for the US company, not Dynasty. Mike was the man who had to make things happen."

"What did you do?"

"I was the accountant. The bookkeeper. CFO was too grand a term. So I worked very closely with Mike. I learnt a lot. It came in handy later when I moved to Dubai."

"And James? What was his role in the business?"

"James was already in Hong Kong. He knew the way things worked. He knew people, or knew people who knew people. He was up with the local gossip, where all the bodies were buried."

"Real bodies?"

"Just a saying, but perhaps some were real. There could be a dark side to Hong Kong."

"And the lady, Annette Freidman?"

"She worked for the parent company in the States, like Ed."

"What did she do?"

"Mostly caused problems for Mike. Like James she lived in Hong Kong with her husband. She had an ability to network, find rich people and become their friend. She talked her way into becoming the Asian director for the parent company; she wasn't really on the board. It was just a title but it sounded impressive. She was supposed to keep an eye on what Mike and I were doing and report back to the States. She just swanned around when something good was happening or the cameras were out. Any problem was somebody else's."

"You didn't like her?"

"I avoided her. Mike and Ed had to deal with her. You could always get her off your case if you loaded her up with problems to solve. Mike would do that. She would bitch on about something. Didn't really understand the situation. As soon as you asked for a solution, and pointed out the obvious difficulties her answer would cause, she was off. The trouble was she would get in the ear of the bosses in New York and Mike or Ed would have to sort it out."

"So if you did not like her why did you come on this cruise with her?"

"Marly liked the idea. Three weeks in French Polynesia. A luxury boat. Besides I thought it would be good to catch up with Mike and James, and Ed."

"Can you think of anyone who would wish her dead?"

"She could be a very difficult person, unpleasant at times. It was only all about her, no one else, but that is hardly enough to want her dead."

Ana appeared and asked if Pete would like another coffee, she then turned to Blaise. "And you Mr Blaise, can I get you a coffee or a drink of some type?"

"Thank you Ana, a black coffee would be most enjoyable. I have been up since an early hour, and perhaps Edward would also join us here."

Ed had come up the stairs and approached the two men. "Thanks Ana, a coffee for me please. You two were in serious discussion. I hope I am not intruding?"

"Not all all." Blaise replied. I was just asking about Project Dynasty."

"Project Dynasty. It was an interesting time."

"Did you enjoy your time?"

"Yes. Casey and I found it fascinating. Hong Kong is such an exciting city. So much energy."

"It must have been sad when the project ceased?"

"Casey and I were ready to return to the States. We'd enjoyed our time there but I needed to get back to where the real action was. I'd done what was needed. Another year and we would have left anyway."

"And do you know of anyone who would wish to harm the lady from those days?"

"Not really. There were some very unhappy people when the money didn't arrive to expand their businesses but Mike took that pain."

At that moment Ana returned bearing a tray with cups and coffee. The talk between the men halted.

Peter Metcalfe spoke first. "Quite a bit of pain from some sources. Annette would always be off somewhere else."

"Pete's right. Annette and I had to go to the States quite often. The Board wanted to know why we weren't moving fast enough. They didn't realise, or care, about the ill-feeling their decisions were causing. Mike had a very hard time. The Chinese place a lot of value on relationships and trust, particularly when it's to their advantage. They felt they'd been betrayed. It finished Mike's chances of working in the region."

Blaise sat sipping his coffee. "Ana makes excellent coffee. I must congratulate her. What of Annette Freidman's husband? What was he like?"

Ed answered. "Paul, Paul Mackie. He wasn't involved in Project Dynasty."

Pete continued. "He was English. I gather they were already married when he and Annette arrived in Hong Kong. He was very proper. The 'right sort' if you know what I mean. Fitted into the English expat community very well but never seemed to do much. Annette was the mover and shaker of the two."

"Paul had a separate interest in some sort of import/export business. I don't think it was very large or profitable but he seemed to have money."

"Ed's right. I think he may have had money from England. I doubt Annette would have married him if he was poor. He provided a respectable, socially acceptable position in society."

"A socially acceptable , what is the term, 'handbag' for an ambitious lady?" Both men nodded in agreement to Blaise's comment. "Yet the lady used her own name, not his?"

Pete nodded. "Yes."

"But what happened to her husband?"

Both men shook their heads. "Nobody knows. He just vanished. Perhaps you should ask James."

"That is strange, surely there would have been enquiries. The police? His wife?"

"There were," replied Ed. "But they found nothing. No clothes missing, no missing money. His cards weren't used. No communication and no body. Annette didn't seem too concerned. I think their marriage was over. She claimed he had been having affairs. I don't know if it was true or not. Perhaps he decided to move on to a new life."

"James was close to Paul Mackie?"

Ed replied to Blaise's question. "They were friends in the early days but something happened. James's wife was very attractive. Perhaps James thought Paul was too interested. Both marriages were … having problems."

Pete continued. "Ed's right, and Annette would have been a difficult person to live with. I can understand his desire for a change."

"So you think he ran away?"

"I don't know Sidney. I was never very close to him. Ask Ed, he knew them better than me."

Blaise turned to the tall man. "What do you think?"

"Like Pete, I just don't know. Perhaps he went off and became a beachcomber like the one we saw on Bora Bora."

"But it appears that was not him."

Pete shook his head. "No."

Ed continued. "Definitely not, Paul was always very smartly presented. Never a hair out of place. Besides he was much trimmer in build. That man was carrying too much weight."

Blaise smiled. The thought of his own figure and appearance twenty-five years earlier came to mind. But he said nothing.

"So the lady moved on."

"Yes Sidney. It all happened not long before our work was finished. She used her contacts and moved to the States. I lost contact with her. I believe Ed kept in contact."

"We would run into one another somewhere but I didn't have much to do with her."

"Did she have a new man in her life? It happens sometimes after such a loss."

Pete shook his head. "I wouldn't know."

Ed also shook his head. "She never spoke of anyone. There was no mention of any affair, either in Hong Kong or later. There were a few young men hanging around before she left but nothing serious."

"It is puzzling. So much of her life is missing."

"I heard you say you were up early today Sidney. Was it about this case?"

"No Edward. My new American-trained doctor says I must exercise more for my health. He also suggested going to a gymnasium. Even worse, he suggested I give up red wine — but he is young. I prefer my old French doctor, he is more understanding of a person's needs. However a walk in the morning is a good time to think of the current concern, like this death."

"Did you come to any conclusions?"

"Yes, many. That is the problem. Which possibility is the correct one?"

25 Gabrielle Secombe

Once again the morning arrived blue and bright. A cool gentle breeze wafted over the *Ocean Rover* but the clear cloudless sky held a promise of the heat to come.

The eight guests on the boat had decided to go ashore and explore the island and Amura had made two trips shuttling them to the nearby marina. Once there they had separated and each couple had gone their own way.

It was not long after Amura had departed that James and Gaby returned to the wharf and signalled the *Ocean Rover*. Soon the inflatable returned, this time piloted by Tama.

"I'm sorry to bother you but I forgot my camera and I would really like to get some photos of the island and the flowers. Would you mind running me back to the boat to get it? Gaby has decided to sit here and wait for me."

Tama and James had just pulled alongside the yacht when another figure appeared on the marina wharf.

"Good morning Ms Secombe. Your partner has left you?"

"Good morning Mr Blaise. It's only for a few minutes. He forgot his camera. How are you this morning?"

"After Matilde's dinner last night and an honest night's sleep I am a contented man. I thought I might enjoy an early walk before the heat increases."

"The dinner was excellent. We are lucky to have such a good cook providing for us. However I'm not sure everyone is as contented as you. The death of Annette Freidman has caused a great deal of restlessness on the boat."

Blaise used the mention of the dead woman's name to ask the questions that had been on his mind. "Did James ever talk to you about Annette?"

"No. Well, only very little. I think he decided that she was a very difficult person."

"And the men. They were good friends?"

"I think so. Although James and Mike may have had a few issues at times. Apparently Mike used to make fun of James, call him 'Jimmy Boy', 'Little Jimmy'. That really annoyed James. I gather they had a few angry moments."

"And what of your partner's wife? Did he ever speak of her?"

"A little. She'd left him long before I arrived in Hong Kong."

"I've heard that the separation was not very happy?"

"I know she left him. I know she had a drug problem and went off with some other man. James rarely talks about it. I think he was badly hurt."

"Are drugs a problem in your circle?"

"Drugs are everywhere. Always have been."

"What about James and you?"

"No. No. For my mother I was a good Chinese girl and my father was a Presbyterian! I loved them too much to get involved in drugs. Even when I was rebelling."

"I cannot imagine you as a rebel on the ramparts. And what about James? Surely the opportunity would have existed in Hong Kong?"

"I think there were some. I know James smoked pot but I don't think it went any further. When his wife got hooked it scared him and he was worried about her. When I first met him he didn't drink or smoke anything."

"But he does drink alcohol now. I saw him on the boat."

"Yes, a little. You watch, it is usually a very weak G&T. Some wine. No cigarettes and no drugs. I know him!"

"You told me you hardly knew Annette Friedman?"

"I only met her when she joined the cruise. Of course I had heard James speak of her and those times in Hong Kong. But that was many years ago, before I knew him."

"What did you think of her when you met her?"

"It had only been a few days."

"I know but we often form opinions about people very quickly."

"She liked to organise people and events to suit herself."

"I have heard others being less discreet. Bossy, difficult, self-centred. All those words have been used about her."

The woman smiled. "My father taught me never to speak

ill of the dead."

"Your father must have been a kind man."

"He was."

"And how did you come to be on this voyage?"

"I'm here because James came. As you know, he and Annette, Ed, Pete and Mike all worked together in Hong Kong years ago. Then they went their separate ways. This was to be a celebration of their first big deal. I don't think they have all been together as a group since then."

"Where did you meet James?"

"In Hong Kong. I was working there. Unlike the others, he stayed in Hong Kong."

"From watching you both you have been together for some time?"

"Yes, it's now thirteen years. Time moves on."

"How did you meet?"

"Through mutual friends. When I first met him I didn't like him. I thought he was just another expat party boy out for a good time. I think he had been once, but he'd grown up. He was divorced and his ex-wife had died by the time I met him, but I think there had been a few good-time girls along the way. I wasn't going to be one of them!"

"Yet you are with him now and have been for thirteen years. Your body language says you are both very close."

"Do you always watch people?"

"Yes. Writers are always watching. People are food for

our stories. Perhaps it makes up for what's missing in our own lives. You made a comment about expats but you are one yourself. You're not from Hong Kong."

"How do you know? I speak excellent Mandarin and Cantonese."

"It's your English. I'd say you are Australian. James is English, but his is a fake accent. I expect his family came from the north of England."

"How can you tell?"

"Years of listening to people. Words and expressions that slip into conversations. Sometimes sounds, a vowel or a consonant. Our speech can give clues to where we have been or who we are."

"You sound like Henry Higgins in My Fair Lady."

"Another clue. A girl your age probably wouldn't be interested in stage musicals unless her parents took her along and she was captivated by the magic."

"My father took my mother and me. So where in Australia do I come from?"

"Sydney."

"You're right. How did you know?"

"It was a guess. I could exclude the north and the west of the country. Most Australians live in big cities, so that leaves two, Sydney or Melbourne. Fifty/fifty chance. Have you always lived there?"

"Yes. My father was from Sydney. My mother was Singaporean. She came out as a little girl with her family. I guess I have my mother's looks and my father's nature. It confuses people. I keep getting asked when I came over from China. I always reply 'Mate, I'm an Aussie sheila, when did you come?' When I was a kid I took up Highland Dancing. I loved it, and the girls who did it were great fun but I used to get some strange looks. This Chinese girl doing Scottish dances, but my Dad's family were Scots. I had as much Scottish blood as some of the girls with red hair. Anyway, what is a Scot? They're Celts, Gaels and Picts, and Vikings, and the odd Spaniard from the Spanish Armada. Plus others. I've been in Scotland and seen Scots of Indian and Caribbean background."

"There have always been people moving around the world. Today we think mass migration is new but it is not. History tells us of waves of people that roll across the land changing lives and cultures. Sometimes violently, other times more peacefully accepted."

"You're right Sidney. I doubt if anyone is of some 'pure' stock. We are all a bit of a mix. I suspect even the most carefully manicured family tree will have had a stray shoot somewhere."

"So how do you find acceptance in China?"

""In Australia I look Chinese. In China I act like a foreigner so I still stand out. At least in Hong Kong there is such a mix I can drop right in."

"Speaking Mandarin and Cantonese must be a big advantage?"

"Yes. My father was most insistent that since my mother came from Singapore that I speak Mandarin, even if it was rarely spoken in our family. He believed that language and culture were important to maintain. Fortunately I seem to have a talent for languages. That was my speciality at university."

"Your father was a wise man."

"A special man. I may have my father's nature but I certainly tried him when I was a teenager and at university."

"I thought that was what all teenagers do?"

"Probably. I miss him. We only had a few years after that stage before he died. I have been very fortunate. My parents loved and nurtured me."

"Indeed, you are blest. So many must find their own way through the difficulties of life without that benefit. Do you know anything that might be helpful in solving this mystery?"

"No."

"When we spoke on the boat you said you heard Annette speaking on her cell phone in Chinese? According to Peter she didn't speak very much Chinese."

"She spoke in Cantonese. She was swearing in very rude terms."

"You are sure?"

"I speak very good Mandarin and Cantonese. I know all the rude swear words! She swore in Cantonese."

"You do not know who she was speaking with?"

"No. It could have been anyone."

"That's very interesting. Does anyone on the boat speak

Chinese? I suspect some do. Does James?"

"Yes, some, Ed and Pete, a little. Even Mike knows a bit, but not really enough for an intelligent conversation. More to order a drink and food. Casey too. They would all speak some Cantonese."

Blaise's brow furrowed and he shook his head. It was as if he was having a private conversation with himself rather than addressing Gabrielle Secombe. "No. No, it would not be anyone on the boat even if they spoke Chinese. There would be no need to call them by mobile, she could just have a private word with them. But why Chinese? Here, in French Polynesia French perhaps, but Chinese?"

"Another puzzle?"

"Yes, Ms Secombe, another puzzle. I think there is perhaps something that, at present, appears unimportant, insignificant. Or perhaps there is something we do not yet know or have overlooked. If you remember anything more, please let me know. Perhaps it will be helpful."

"If I do I will let you know. Here comes James. Now we can go for our walk."

"Au revoir Mademoiselle Secombe. I shall continue to work on the puzzle, however you may have given me a new thread to unravel."

26 New Information

It was the next morning when the grey boat of the gendarmerie pulled alongside the *Ocean Rover*. Broussard stepped aboard and was met by Captain Durand. Together they went to the bridge where Tama was waiting for them.

The guests were still assembled around the big table in the saloon chatting as Ana and Matilde cleared away the remains of the breakfast service. Soon Broussard joined them.

"Thank you for your patience." The police officer continued. "I realise the delay, it is inconvenient for you. I have had replies from my enquiries to the United States and they shed more light on your friend. I regret it has taken some more time than I had hoped, but for policemen in your country our concerns are not very important. I can understand. They must have so many problems of their own to deal with."

"Capitaine Broussard. We are not all Americans."

"My apologies Ms Secombe. Yes, you are not all from the United States. You are Australian as is Mr Metcalfe. Your partner, Mr Paine, and the wife of Mr Metcalfe are English. However the United States is the country of the deceased lady. She was English by birth but became a citizen American."

Although the group had known that Annette Friedman lived in the States, it came as a surprise to learn that she was an American citizen.

"So what else did you find out?"

"It appears the lady was in financial difficulties. From the report I received her business affairs were not good. She had considerable debt."

"I find that hard to believe. She arranged this boat trip. She would have had to pay up front for that even though we paid her for our share of the charter."

"Apparently no Mr Gordon. The boat is owned by an associate she once worked for, an old friend, who lent it to her at a very favourable price. He did it as a favour because he knew of her difficulties. I believe the price she charged you is much higher."

"That'd be Annette. Always number one first!"

"You are not surprised Mr Paine?"

"No. Annette was always out to make money from friend or foe. It didn't matter to her. I'm surprised though that she had financial difficulties. I thought she would have good contacts and a good income."

"It seems the income had been good but it had declined over the last several years. Unfortunately her expenses had not. Indeed they appear to have increased."

"Why?"

"The report does not say exactly. After all, there is no crime in the United States to investigate. However it hints, that is all it does, it does not say directly, that there may have been gambling involved. It seems your friend frequently enjoyed the bright lights of Las Vegas. That may have been expensive. And also a suspicion of using some drugs."

"But you found no drugs in her cabin and you would have tested the body?"

"That is correct Mr Gordon. We found nothing illegal, only some strong painkillers in her cabin, and the drug test showed no unusual levels of those. I believe we can exclude both a drowning and a drug death from our investigation."

"You say she had considerable debts. What sort, who too? She could have sold her apartment in Houston. That would have been worth serious money. I saw it last year when I was in Texas." Casey glanced towards her husband as if she had been surprised by his comment.

"It had been sold Mr Parker. The report says that she sold it several years ago. She was renting it from the new owner."

"That would have cleared her debts, surely?"

"Apparently not. The debts, some debts remained."

"So what else do you have Broussard?"

The gendarme replied to Ed Parker's second question. "I also have a report on her health. It tells me that she was in need of a medical procedure and had booked to have the operation. I do not understand your medical system in the United States but the report says she did not have the finances to pay the surgeon and the hospital."

"She would have had insurance."

"Apparently not, according to the report. She was in desperate need of money."

"I don't believe it. Annette could always round up someone to pay the bills. I can't believe she wouldn't this time."

"You may be correct Mr Paine. Perhaps she had a plan. Perhaps this voyage was part of her plan."

27 Marly Metcalfe

"What plan?"

"That I have yet to uncover Mr Metcalfe. Your Captain told me Tama had some information. That is why I came this morning. I hoped it may have been of the movements of your friend on the night she died, but it was not."

"Blaise said something about it being unimportant."

"Yes. It was of a later time. Like my friend I do not see it as being important. However Tama did notice Mrs Metcalfe and Ms Friedman often spoke together. I would like to speak again with you Mrs Metcalfe, if I may. You may be able to assist by providing some understanding of the lady and her emotional state." Broussard moved to the stairs leading down to the sports deck and indicated he would like Marly to join him.

"I doubt if I can help you. I only met her when we joined the cruise. I know nothing of her history. Peter never said much about her."

"But Tama says he often saw her talking with you."

"We were mostly as a group."

"Or as a group of women, but sometimes alone with her?"

"Well, yes. She did talk to me. Never said anything very interesting. I don't think she enjoyed the company of the other women."

"Did she indicate why that was so?"

"I think she felt she could relate to me. I don't think she thought Nikki Olson was worth her effort. She was just another of Mike's bimbos. Gaby was out of favour because she would question some of Annette's claims. I don't think that would ever go down well with Annette. As for Casey, there was a real feeling between those two. I'm not sure what it was, but I think it went way back."

Do you know what the cause was?"

Marly shook her head. "No, but possibly her husband."

"Mr Mackie?"

"No, Casey's husband, Ed. I think there could have been some, well, something back in Hong Kong."

"When you were alone with her? How did she seem?"

"What do you mean?"

"Was she relaxed, agitated, worried?"

"No. She could be a bit peculiar. The first time. I was lying on a lounge getting some sun and listening to a book on my iPhone when I felt this shadow come over me. I looked up and it was Annette. She was standing there, not saying anything. I thought it was strange. She looked sad, then her face changed and she looked angry. I thought it was a bit creepy that she had been watching me but she was actually looking at Ed and Mike. When I spoke to her, it all changed again. She started gushing on about when she had first moved to the States and how wonderful it was. I don't know where that came from. It was all about the past. That woman could sure drop names. I don't know how true it all was."

"Did she say anything else?"

"No. Only about going to the States to live. That must have been years ago."

"Did she speak of her recent time in the United States?"

"No. Just about how important her current business associates were, but she never actually named any of them. I think she was prone to exaggerating her claims."

"Did you or your husband have any friends in common with her?"

"Peter must have had some from way back, although I don't think she would have worried much about him in those days. She didn't think much of him now. I thought we may have known some people in common from England even though she was older than me. But there was nothing. She really didn't talk about her youth. It was all today, or moving to America. Not even much about Hong Kong. I think she was avoiding talking about her early years."

"Why would she do that?"

"I don't think her early years matched the image she wanted people to believe. It wasn't the private school, posh upbringing she claimed. More housing estate if you know what I mean."

"Did you like the lady?"

"Yes. She had balls. She knew what she wanted and went out to get it. I like that. That can upset a few men. They don't like a strong woman, they feel threatened. She had style too. I'm surprised by your claim she had no money. I thought she would have been loaded, having a friend with a boat like this."

"She mentioned her friend?"

"Not by name. That was one name she didn't drop. I asked about him and she just said she wasn't into sharing."

"In what way 'sharing'?"

"I don't know if it meant a wife or other girlfriends. These things can come at a price."

Tama had also told Broussard of another conversation between the two women. He had noticed they were sitting very close together and talking quietly, as if they were exchanging secrets. Marly Metcalfe laughed. "The secrets were about the other women. We discussed the dress Casey had worn the night before and Nikki's bikinis. She has a new one every day but there's never much material in them. They're crass! She also told me that James wasn't the sweet man that Gaby believed him to be. His marriage had been a disaster and he had caused trouble for her husband."

Broussard's attempt to gain additional information from Marly about the time in Hong Kong added little. However his enquiry about Annette Friedman's relationship with Peter Metcalfe did elicit a remark. "She did say to me that she had some juicy news about Peter that may be of interest.

It could be to my advantage. She told me to remind Peter about the Liu Wei deal. I don't think she thought highly of my husband."

"How would it be to your advantage?"

"She realised our marriage was on the rocks. She thought I could use some help in the divorce. She said she might tell me about it another day, but she died."

"Did you mention Liu Wei to your husband?"

"Yes. He said it was nothing. An old story Annette couldn't drop."

"What was it?"

"He didn't say."

Broussard was curious why the woman had come on the cruise if her marriage was ending. Marly's response was simple and direct. "Inspecteur, why would a woman waste such an opportunity? Wouldn't you accept?"

"Madame Metcalfe. As much as I would like the promotion to an Inspecteur I am a lowly Capitaine and my pay would never allow a cruise on a boat such as this. When you parted on that last occasion. What was her farewell?"

"All she said was I must go, and she left."

"Did she say anything else?"

"No. Oh yes. She did say something when she turned to walk away. It wasn't to me, it was more muttering to herself."

"What did she say?"

"I didn't hear it all. It wasn't much, only a few words. I didn't get the first bit but I think it ended '...the money'. "

" 'The money'? Are you sure? What money was she referring to?"

Marly shrugged in answer to Broussard's question. "I think that was what I heard, but I can't be sure. I have no idea what the money was that she was talking about."

28 Paddleboards

The holidaymakers remained around the table after Broussard departed. The news of Annette's financial problems had surprised those who knew her. Her expensive tastes were less of a surprise, especially to James.

"She was always high maintenance. I used to feel sorry for her husband when we were in Hong Kong. I wasn't surprised when he left."

"It depends how he left, Jimmy Boy"

"Mike, I've had enough of that. Call me James or shut up. I'm over your pushy bullying. You might have got away with it when I was in Hong Kong but not anymore."

Casey was puzzled by Broussard's mention of Annette and gambling. "Do you really think she was into gambling? My recollection was she preferred to spend the money on herself, not put it at risk on a table or in a machine?"

Mike agreed. "That's how I remember her. But Casey, people change. Some get caught up in the adrenaline rush of winning but then can't stop trying to recover their losses."

Casey shook her head. "I just don't see her as a gambler. I

know she liked the big income but the risks always had to be in her favour. From what I knew she was never troubled billing her clients big time. Ed used to say she could always turn a buck out of any deal. She was a big spender on having a good time, that's not in question, but it was always about her. I never thought that she would have problems."

"Casey, it is a long time since you saw her."

"True. When did you last see her Ted?"

"Oh, it was on a trip to a conference in Houston. She turned up. She invited me to her apartment for a drink."

"You went?"

"Yes, just the once."

"You never mentioned it."

"It wasn't important. The conference was boring, Annette turned up, invited me for a drink. It seemed like a polite thing to do. Then before I got home that trouble in Albuquerque blew up, and I ended up there for a week before I got back to you."

"What do you think her health problems were? Did she say anything to anyone?" There was a shaking of heads around the table to Pete's question.

Nikki answered. "The only thing she said to me was she had a big date when she got back to the States. I thought it was a man, maybe it was medical?"

"She didn't say anything else to you Nikki?"

"Nah, only she had plans to see a man at the TMC. Whatever that is?"

Casey explained. "TMC. The Texas Medical Centre in Houston, it's huge. I think it's the biggest in the country. It doesn't really help us know why she was planning to go there. Her problem could have been anything."

"Perhaps it was her heart?"

"Don't be silly Mike. Annette didn't have a heart."

"That's cruel. You shouldn't say things like that about anyone."

"It's alright Babe. Don't take Pete too seriously."

"But Mike baby, it's cruel."

"It's alright Nikki. We don't know if it was a heart problem. It could have been anything. Cancer, something else? She certainly wasn't showing any signs and it didn't affect her eating or drinking."

Ed agreed. "Casey's right. We have no way of knowing. Perhaps Broussard doesn't know either. He certainly didn't give any indication of what the problem was."

"What about drugs?"

"Don't know Casey. She looked OK to me. None of the signs of being a junkie. Broussard didn't seem concerned. All he found were prescription medication."

"Not everyone has scars on their arms or run around like weirdos. I saw lots of people doing drugs in the club and they were normal."

"But Nikki, did you see anything to say Annette could have been using?"

"No, she seemed fine to me Marly. I think her problem was booze not drugs."

Broussard's news had created discussion around the table, but no explanation for the death or the possible health concern had emerged. The conversation waned and a quiet fell over the group. At last Gaby spoke. "Well, Nikki and I will leave you to your problems. We've arranged with Ana to give us instructions on stand-up paddleboarding. I saw her doing it yesterday and it looks fun. Let's go Nikki, we'll leave the men to sort out their problems."

The young Polish girl was waiting at the sports deck with three paddleboards. From their actions it was clear that neither Nikki or Gaby had much experience standing on the boards, let alone paddling with the long paddles. At first Ana had them sit and paddle with their hands, then as their confidence grew they started to use the paddle she provided. Soon they were standing, or trying to stand and the laughter from their efforts drifted back to the boat. The young women were of a similar age, with Gaby the older of the three. Any distinction of social position disappeared with their efforts and it was just three girls out to have fun together.

"How did you get a job on a boat like this?"

"It was in the Med, Gaby. I come to Italy travelling but I must find work. I met a guy in a bar near the dock and he tell me he knows a boat that want a crew. I try, but it is not successful. They say me 'try other boat' and I do and get a job. Then that finish but this one in port. They want a crew to go to the Pacific. That is good for me. So I am here."

"What qualifications do you need to get this sort of job?

Perhaps one day if Mike dumps me it might be fun."

"For this boat you must speak English. I have problem when I leave home but I learn quickly when I travel. Also you must have a certificate. I must do a course to get certificate for first aid, fire-fighting, safety. That was expense but I am a nurse so it was not difficult. On the boat you have a bed and food and travel so you do not have much costs. Then pay, and you get tips from guests. Work hard. And look good, and fit the uniform. Not fat. They do not have large sizes for the female crew. To be blond is good, smile. I do not think you would have problem Nikki. You must always be nice to the guests."

"Whereabouts is your home?"

"It is a town in the north of Poland. It is called Gdynia but nobody knows of it so I say Gdansk because it is known."

"What's it like?"

"Nikki, it is a small town and a port. It is a good city to live in but I see many cruise liners with tourists come to the port and I say to myself 'one day I will also see the world' and now I am here."

Do you enjoy the work?"

"Yes. It is good Gaby. Depends on the people who come, and the other crew."

"Are the guests good to deal with?"

"Mostly. Some men can be a problem, but that is men. Some crew are a problem but that is not so big."

"Where do you sleep on the boat?"

"Our cabin is not like yours Nikki. It is tiny, at the front of the boat. Eeva and I share a cabin and Tama and Amura also a cabin."

"What do you do when there is no one on the boat?"

"Always we have to clean and polish, paint. Everything must be the very best for the guests."

Gradually as their confidence improved, the trio paddled further and further away from the boat. The sound of their laughter drifted back across the water to those watching on the boat.

"You are very good. When do you go out paddle boarding? I've only seen you the once."

Ana turned and smiled at Gaby. "In the early morning before the guests come to their meals. If I am not on duty Claude allows me. If it my turn to serve at breakfast I cannot do it."

"Did you go out the day Annette died?"

"No, that morning I must be in the galley with Eeva. Claude said Matilde was not well. We should both be on duty."

"Did you have much to do with the lady who died?"

"No, only when I serve drinks and at the meal table. It was Eeva who had her cabin to attend to."

"Was she a good person to work for?"

"I cannot say. I had little to do with her. That is good."

"Why do you say that Ana?" The young woman's answer

interested Gaby.

"I think she is a different woman. Eeva says she could be demanding, but that is usual for some guests. I think she spent much time in her cabin. She was always asking for me, not Eeva."

"Was that usual?"

"No. she should ask for Eeva."

"Why did she want you?"

"I do not know. But always I was uncomfortable with her. With Eeva it was not a problem."

"Did she try to hit on you?" asked Nikki.

"Hit on me. No. Never she was angry. Always nice to me."

"Too nice, she was attracted to you?" Ana lowered her eyes at Gaby's question.

"Yes, I feel she wanted more but I am not like that."

"You prefer men?"

"Yes Miss Nikki. I prefer boys." Ana smiled. This time the memory of some past man or boy flitted across her face.

"What about Claude? I've seen him watching you."

"He is my boss. His wife is very watchful, she sees all that happens on this boat. Claude is nice but it would be trouble. I do not want problems."

"A beautiful girl like you must have a man somewhere. Do you have a boyfriend?"

"I had boyfriend in Poland but we argued so I left to find the world. Now I do not want to be tied to a man but I can have friends."

"With your looks and on a boat like this I'm sure you could find some rich friends."

"Yes, it would be possible but I do not want that. I want to travel and discover the world. I do not want to depend on the favour of some rich fat man."

"You could still do that. They don't have to be fat. You could take your pick."

"Nikki, no. I do not want to be dependent on a man, even if he is very generous to me."

The three young women were paddling back to the yacht when the four men drifted down to the sports deck to await their return.

"Which one do you want?"

"I thought you'd made your decision Mike."

"Nikki certainly looks great but that Ana is a real stunner. I wouldn't mind getting to know her better, if you know what I mean."

"You had better be careful. If Nikki hears you she will have your balls for breakfast!"

"So James. Is that what happens with an Aussie girlfriend?"

"That depends. I would be careful with Nikki."

"Don't you worry Jimmy. She's not a problem. I have her under control."

"I told you to forget the Jimmy! We're not in Hong Kong anymore and I don't have to put up with your behaviour. Anyway, I don't know you're really man enough to handle Ana. I think it might be one tough woman in that little red bikini."

Ed stepped in to calm the tension with an observation. "I think you might have the pick James. The looks and the brains. Your Gaby is a very smart woman. Where did you find her?"

Ed's appraisal focused four sets of eyes on the girl with long dark hair. The two blondes were tanned, slim and attractive, one with long blonde curls and a tiny pink bikini that displayed a fulsome bosom, the other in the red bikini had her hair in a long ponytail. While not as ostentatious, the swimsuit had obviously been picked by the wearer to attract male attention. The dark-haired Chinese girl also wore her hair in a ponytail but there was a style in her costume and deportment that set her apart from the two blondes.

"I met her in Hong Kong. She was working for a travel company and we got to know each other. Then we became an item and now it's thirteen years."

The girls were still giggling as they paddled their way back to the boat. Occasionally their boards bumped against each other and Nikki or Gaby would overbalance and splash into the water. At last they reached the Ocean Rover and were helped aboard by the waiting men.

"That was great fun. You guys should try it. Ana's a great teacher."

"Nikki's right, you should try it James. You'd love it. Next time we can go out together with Ana."

From the upper deck Claude looked down on the group. Ana noticed him and her manner changed. Her laughter ceased and once again she became the polite and formal crew member. "I must go to work now. Matilde will need me in the galley." She turned to the two girls that moments earlier she had been laughing with. "Thank you. It has been a pleasure to assist." With that, she headed to her cabin low in the bow of the boat. Tama and Amura were left to stow the boards away.

As she walked away Gaby waved to her and called out "Thank you Ana, that was fun, and you gave me something new to think about."

29 Accusations

That night the dinner discussion once again turned to the death of Annette Friedman. However tonight, even with the allowed occasional trips ashore, the sense of confinement had resulted in a barely suppressed tension within the group. Casey and Ed, Nikki, Mike, James, Marly and Pete: all were ready to take offence at any small slight or disagreement of opinion. Only Gaby remained unruffled by the atmosphere.

A feeling of unease had crept into their conversations. If it wasn't an accident, and no one around the table considered suicide a possibility, then it must be murder. It was the thought that kept returning; a thought no one could avoid. Why had the death occurred? Who could be responsible? The man seen on Bora Bora was out of contention after Blaise's report. The thought silently came to each one of them that the culprit must be on board the *Ocean Rover*. But who? Which one, and what could be the reason for such an act?

Gaby raised the question of Annette's parting comment on her final evening.

"What did Annette mean when she said 'We all have

secrets? You have to pay for the past'? Was she talking about herself, or did she mean someone else? Perhaps she was thinking of the man on Bora Bora. You men were in her past, what do you think she meant?"

"It was the night before we arrived in Bora Bora that she said that. She wouldn't have known the man was there."

"Pete's right. She may have carried a feeling of guilt about the way she treated some people, but I doubt it. She certainly had secrets. I doubt she ever paid for them. She didn't believe in paying for anything if she could get someone else to pay." No one present disagreed with Mike's opinion. "I still don't think any of that would cause someone to kill her."

"It depends on the secret."

"Well do you have a secret that you would kill for?" Pete shook his head in response to Mike's question. Pete continued. "We all have things we would rather forget but even when Annette tried to make a big deal out of them they weren't that bad. Certainly never as serious as she tried to make out."

Gaby was quick to see the implications of the remark. "Annette's comment almost sounds like possible extortion. Did she try to get money out of any of you men?" The lack of any answers only increased the suspicion that Gaby had identified a possibility. "Did she want money?"

Ed was first to answer. "No. Definitely not. She had no reason."

"No reason to ask for money, or no reason to be paid?"

Ed replied firmly to Gaby's question. "No to both. She

had no reason to blackmail me, and no, I did not pay her money. We just talked about old times."

Mike was unconvinced. "Really? You and Annette had a past. I don't think it was as far back as you make out. Did she threaten to tell Casey unless you came good with some money, or did she want to renew the old arrangement?"

"I said I've seen her since Hong Kong, but it was only on business."

"Like the business in Hong Kong? Casey wasn't very happy then and I don't think she would be happy now."

"Ed has told me he has only seen her once or twice since then and I believe my husband."

"Very commendable, but you don't really believe him do you? Nikki told me about your outburst."

"Nikki, that was in confidence."

"I'm sorry Casey but I thought you would understand that Mike and I share. You have good reason to hate that woman. Mike told me how she used to treat you like dirt."

"You may think you share but how much has he told you about his time in Hong Kong? Maybe we should have a little chat about your boyfriend and what he's done. Then you will get to know him a bit better."

"You're too late. Annette took me aside and really tried to blacken Mike's reputation. She was such a nasty bitch. She just did it for pleasure. I can understand why someone would want to bump her off."

Mike explained his actions. "She came to me and told me she would go to Nikki and say that I'd had lots of lovers and couldn't be trusted. She wanted money to stay quiet. I refused and she went to Nikki."

"She was a total bitch. She really got pleasure out of dumping on Mike. I know he's not an angel but she made him out real bad. I guess I'm not Little Miss Innocence myself but I'm smart enough to know guys and make my own decisions."

"But Mike, why did she want money? I'm surprised, I thought she would've had plenty."

"I don't know Gaby. Perhaps Broussard's right and she was broke. She was always ready to touch the clients for as much as she could get away with charging but she's never tried this caper before."

The admission that Annette had sought money from Mike opened the gate to other experiences. James had been approached with a similar demand. "She tried the same thing with me. Said she would tell Gaby about my wife. Gaby already knew about Jane and our break up, and her death, and the drugs, so it was a waste of Annette's time. God knows why she thought it was worth the effort. She must have been desperate to think I would fall for it. But then she always had it in for me."

"Why would anyone hate you Jimmy?"

"You know damn well, and stop that 'Jimmy'. I'm over the 'Our Jimmy', 'Little Jimmy' 'Jimmy Boy' bit. She knew that I knew she was a fraud. She passed herself off as some la-de-dah pom but she was just like me. She came from a rough part of a tough town in the middle of England and I knew it. She used to call me a barrow boy but she was just the same, trying to get away from her past. She just fooled you into thinking she was posh. So Pete , did she try it on you too?"

"I don't think Annette had any money. I think she was skint. Don't know why."

James pushed his question to Pete again. "So did she try to touch you up for some money?"

"No point."

"So Annette didn't threaten to tell Marly about your adventures with her husband before he disappeared?"

"Nothing to tell."

"That's not true and you know it. I know things you wouldn't want made public. You didn't decide to bump her off to keep that particular story quiet?"

Pete reacted violently to the accusation and it was only Mike's quick actions that prevented a physical altercation between Pete and James. After both had settled, Pete spoke. "It was a long time ago. Everyone had moved on and there was no need to bring it up again. I wanted it forgotten but she wouldn't listen."

"Did she tell Marly?"

"That wouldn't matter. Marly couldn't care less. In fact I think it would suit her if it all came out. Might even help her in a divorce."

"She didn't tell me anything." Marly paused, then she continued. "She said she had some stories that would interest me but she would tell me after breakfast. She said she had news about some of the men on the boat, more than they thought she knew. There would be a few surprises and some very unhappy men. Then in the morning, she was dead."

"She didn't say which men?"

"No Gaby."

"Well that seems to put us women in the clear. It sounds as though one of you men is the suspect party."

"Hang on. There are more possibilities. What about Claude?"

By now too much alcohol had flowed too freely and the theories were becoming more and more fanciful. The interest Claude was displaying in Ana had been noticed by all on the boat. The behaviour of Matilde and the tension between her and her husband was obvious. Still, the general view was that the Captain of the *Ocean Rover* would hardly mistake Annette for Matilde if he had planned to throw his wife overboard to drown. Nikki and Gaby who had had the most to do with the young Polish girl both thought it unlikely that Ana would be behind such a plot. Even Matilde became a suspect: planning to punish her husband by pushing Ana overboard to drown but mistakenly pushing Annette instead. Only the three Polynesians, Tama, Amura and Eeva, remained innocent.

It was midnight when Ana came around offering coffee to those who remained on the stern deck enjoying the gentle waft of the breeze and the star-lit night. With the lateness of the hour and a new-found chill in the air Nikki and Mike had retired to their cabin but emotions amongst those who remained were still tender. Ana moved silently among the group offering coffees and refreshing drinks. As she passed by Ed he quietly murmured something to her. At once her manner changed, she looked startled, then an expression of anger came over her face. She immediately rushed from the travellers on the open deck and returned to the saloon. Eeva took over her duties and Ana was not seen again that night.

The unusual behaviour was noticed but few were close enough to actually hear what Ed had said.

"What did you say to upset Ana?"

"Nothing. I just asked for a fresh cup of coffee. God knows what's got into that girl."

"She looked frightened."

"Come on James, I'm hardly likely to threaten anyone, especially her. She must have some emotional problems. Perhaps it is Claude."

The strange behaviour of Ana was quickly forgotten when Casey asked about the next day's plans and it was Gaby who provided the answer. "I believe tomorrow evening Claude is trying to arrange dinner for us at a little restaurant on the island. It's further around the island than we have been, and he says it will be an interesting drive. He says the food is excellent. Perhaps he wants to give us a break from Matilde's cooking, or perhaps he wants to give Matilde a night off. He was very enthusiastic about the food. I think it might be his favourite place on Raiatea."

"Well, after tonight I hope you all will be in a more agreeable mood tomorrow night, and you will stop throwing false accusations around like confetti."

The sharp private rebuke Casey gave Ed as they went down the stairs to their cabin suggested that his night might not become more agreeable. Whether his comment of false accusations referred to Annette or Ana, or some other matter remained unknown, but it was certain that he may have further questions to answer.

30 Peter Metcalfe

The day had not yet begun to warm when the inflatable from the *Ocean Rover* pulled alongside the quay at Uturoa.

Already a figure was standing partly hidden behind a tree watching the activity as local fishermen and islanders arrived and departed in a varied collection of boats. Blaise was no longer wearing the bright colourful clothes of previous days but was instead clad in a dull mottled green, yellow and brown shirt and khaki shorts: a sort of mufti in a camouflage style sometimes favoured by younger people.

He waited until the man had jumped from the inflatable and started to walk towards the main street of the town. It was only then that he moved, unusually quickly for him and overtook the walker.

"Good morning Peter. You are an early riser to come ashore at this hour. I thought you would all be enjoying the comfort and peace of your boat."

"Peace is not the word Blaise. There was no peace last night."

"No peace. I am sorry. There was a problem?"

"I think we are all having a few problems. There are some unhappy people on that boat."

"I am sorry. Perhaps your confinement will soon be over."

"I hope so. We all need to get away. I thought a walk on my own would be good."

"I'm sorry if I interfere with your plans. I understand Claude has arranged an outing this evening. That may be a pleasant diversion."

"I don't think any outing will be enough. We just need to move on."

"I can understand. It is a difficult time."

"More so after last night."

"There were problems?"

"Not so much problems as ..."

"I have been observing you and your wife. It is a difficult situation?"

"No. We're fine. Everything is good."

"I think not. I have watched many people. I see a tension between you and your wife. Gabrielle and James are close. Edward and Casey have a familiarity of a long time together through good and bad. Mike and Nikki are like two people with a favourite toy, but perhaps one day they may have a need for new toys. But with you and Marly there is a tension."

"Is it that obvious? Yes. We have both been foolish and done things we should not have done. That's why I agreed to go to the resort on Bora Bora. We, well me, I hoped that we would find the old relationship."

"But you did not?"

"Your problems don't disappear just because you go to a new place or start a new life. We still haven't decided. Marly wants to return to England. I want to stay in Dubai. We've both been foolish. I guess too much of the good life, too much easy money, and too much temptation, for both of us."

"Perhaps I can help you if you can help me?"

"How?

"I am puzzled by a remark that you made to me the other day?"

"What did I say?"

"You told me that on the night she died the dead lady had acted strangely. In what way?"

"I don't know how you would describe it. It was as if she just...she stopped, there was nothing. You know the expression 'lights on but no one home'. It was as if her mind stopped working. It was only for an instant. It happened several times. She was also a bit unsteady on her feet. She stumbled going down the steps but that was the alcohol. She'd been having quite a few of Ana's cocktails."

"I understand she spent a great deal of time on her cell phone. Did she say anything to you about to whom she had been speaking?"

"No. All the women do. They need to check their social media all the time. Marly gets tense when she doesn't know what her friends are doing. Nikki is worse. Once we get too far away from some of the islands they lose the signal. Then they have withdrawals. It's like an addiction for some of them."

"And for Ms Freidman?"

"I don't know Sidney. She spent a lot of time on her mobile, but I don't know if it was social media or if she was messaging."

"But I believe she also spoke. Do you know with whom Annette Freidman was speaking? I believe she spoke in Chinese."

"No idea."

"Those of you who worked in Hong Kong speak Chinese?"

"A little, but not much. Most of the business was conducted in English. James speaks some. Gaby would know more than any of us. Ed probably would have picked up a bit but I don't know how much he's retained. If you don't use it you lose it."

"What about Michael?"

"Maybe. He used to have an active social life with the local ladies. They say that helps but it was probably a limited vocabulary. I have a question for you Sidney. That night Annette made a remark. She said 'We all have secrets. The past has a way of finding us.' Do you know what that was about?"

Blaise shook his head. "At present that is a mystery. Perhaps when the puzzle is solved the answer to your question will seem so obvious, but this is not yet the time. I have another question for you Peter."

"Yes."

""It is about your marriage."

"Yes."

"Did Annette Freidman cause problems for you with your wife?"

"No. Our problems are quite separate. She did say she would tell Marly about my first marriage unless I paid her money. That was a waste of her time. I had already told Marly years ago. There was nothing she could say that would cause me to pay her blackmail. Marly was already planning to leave me anyway."

"But the past, you did have a grudge against the woman?"

"Yes. She was partly responsible for wrecking my first marriage."

"So you had a grudge?"

"Yes, but twenty-five years is a long time to carry a grudge and even a grudge doesn't lead to murder."

"Peter, you say Annette Freidman wanted money. I thought she would be wealthy, or at least have a good income."

"I expect Broussard told you she had financial problems. It now makes sense. I don't think she had as much as we thought. She'd always lived an expensive lifestyle. She liked the trappings of success and the designer names. I was surprised by the look of some of her handbags and the clothes she was wearing. They were showing signs of being out of date. That was not like the Annette of old, she always wanted the latest fashions."

"Do you know any reason why she may have died, or wanted to take her own life?"

Pete thought for a moment before answering. "No. No reason for either, but last night after the meal there was something that was strange. When we were on the rear deck, we were discussing Annette's death. Ana was serving us drinks. Ed looked at her and said he'd seen her that night. Ana went pale and almost ran back into the saloon but as she went past me I think I heard her say 'It was not me. I didn't do it.' She said it very quietly, maybe Ed heard it. Maybe I misheard. I didn't know what to make of it. It was strange."

"Certainly strange, but very interesting."

31 Ed Parker

It was mid-afternoon as two couples waited at the marina for the tender from the *Ocean Rover* to return. The restriction on the yacht's departure, while not an actual confinement, was causing cabin fever. Lying on a sun lounge beside the plunge pool, reading in the cabin, playing games in the saloon, or even doing short walks around the boat had soon become tedious. At least going ashore provided a welcome diversion and so, in ones and twos or fours, the travellers had visited the island to discover its charms, or at least its freedoms.

Pete had returned to the island with Marly and together with Ed and Casey, they had worked their way through the tourist shops set up near the main quay. They had then sat drinking coffee and sampling patisseries in a café while watching the local activities. The relationship between the Metcalfes was cool but polite: the tensions of the previous night submerged by the forced necessity of remaining together, at least until they could leave the island.

Just as they reached the quay to return to the boat a familiar figure appeared.

"Good afternoon ladies and gentlemen. It is such a lovely

morning I decided to take a walk and now I meet you. It is so fortunate."

The four greeted Blaise, although some did so with more enthusiasm than others.

"Where are you off to Sidney?"

Blaise's answer to Marly's question was vague on detail but effusive in manner. Similarly, his reply to Casey's enquiry about his activities that day was also vague. It was obvious that he had something else on his mind.

"I see Tama comes with the inflatable. You are returning to the *Ocean Rover*?"

Ed replied, rather tersely. "Yes. It is coming for us now."

"Then Edward, may I ask a favour? Perhaps the ladies and Peter could go with Tama but would you do me the favour of spending some time with me? I am sure Tama would not object to returning for you later. I would much appreciate it."

Ed's reply was even more terse. "I'd rather go back with the others now."

"I understand, but I need your help. It is important and I would not like to delay your friends unnecessarily. I know a quiet place where we could chat without distraction. Perhaps you might also like to try the local beer. It is very well received."

The acceptance was grudging but made, and the two men waved to Tama and the three travellers as they made their way back to the yacht.

Blaise led the way to a small bar and purchased two Hinanos and the men settled at a table.

"Well, what do you want?"

Blaise took a sip of beer before answering. "I need to understand the events surrounding the death of the lady."

"I told you all I know when you asked your questions before. There is nothing more to say."

"I am grateful for your information but that was more about you and your involvement. There is still much missing that I do not understand. You, of all those who knew her, knew her best."

"Yes, probably. We worked closely at the time. It's true I was probably the one who had the most to do with her. The others were in the team but it was Annette and I who worked to make sure it happened without any problems to come back and bite us later on."

"And Peter? Did he work closely with the lady?"

"Not particularly. He was responsible for researching the real estate market. In those days that was his field. He's changed business since he went to Dubai. Now he's in gold trading and storage. Probably a good place to be."

"And Annette Friedman's husband?"

"Paul Mackie? Not much to say. Never knew him very well. I don't think he and Annette were very close anymore. Then he disappeared. I told you all that."

"Yes. I appreciate that, but each time we tell a story a little extra comes out. A story that is unchanging is not to be believed. It is too rehearsed to be true."

"There were rumours about his activities but I don't know how true."

"With drugs."

"Yes. You should ask James about that. Not me."

"And Peter's wife? It was not the present lady?"

"No. Back then it was Julianne. They separated after they left Hong Kong. It happens. I'd never met Marly until this trip."

"And the separation. Was it amicable?"

"Are they ever? I don't know. I've seen lots of divorces, very few of them are, as you say, amicable, even when both parties can't stand the sight of the other and both want to get out of the marriage. I'm a lawyer, there's always the money, the house, or the kids, or the dog. Or something."

"Yes. I understand. And what of Michael?"

"He doesn't have that problem. He never marries. I don't know how he manages it but he seems to move on without too many problems. I wish I knew his secret."

"The same will happen to Miss Olson?"

"Probably. She's had a good run. I expect she knows it. She'll find a new boyfriend. She's no sweet innocent."

"Are any of us truly 'innocents'? I expect not. We all have our pasts."

"Well mine is unblemished."

"You are a fortunate man. I have another question about James."

"Yes?"

"What was his role in Hong Kong?"

"James was there when we moved to Hong Kong. He knew people. He was our 'go to' man for local information or to arrange meetings. Some of the English would say 'There's a bit of barrow-boy in Our Jimmy'."

"He was not the correct class?"

"There was some snobbery. He dressed the part and spoke with the correct accent but for some of the English lads he lacked the family name and didn't go to the right school."

"I understand."

"He was actually very good. He was there to work and make money, not swan around enjoying himself until he went back to England."

"But his marriage also had problems?"

"Yes. His wife enjoyed the party life, and found drugs. That was a problem. Eventually she left him to live with her dealer. That was a disaster, still he wasn't blameless."

"Why?"

"Because if you wanted to find drugs, or anything, James was the man to see."

"He was a dealer?"

"No, but he knew who was. That was his job, to know who to see for anything, business, pleasure, legal or illegal. He knew people."

32 Nikki and Marly

It was after Ed's return from his conversation and beer with Blaise. He had gone down to join Casey in their cabin for a rest. James and Gaby were lazing on the foredeck reading. Mike or Pete were nowhere to be seen. Nikki and Marly were sitting by the plunge pool and enjoying the sun.

It was a chance for some private girl talk without interruption from the men.

Marly raised the question. "Do you really think it was Annette who was supposed to be murdered?"

Nikki turned in surprise. "What do you mean?"

"Perhaps it was supposed to be Matilde."

"Matilde?"

"Have you seen the way Claude ogles Ana? I think he has the hots for her."

Nikki, with her experience in clubs, was unfazed. "I think most men would have the hots for that chick but I don't see Claude as a murderer."

"Well it's one way to avoid a divorce. Push the wife

overboard and let her drown. I don't think their relationship is very happy at the moment."

"I don't plan to push Mike overboard just because we have a few issues. Beside I'm sure Matilde could swim. She's been around boats for years."

"Maybe Ana did it to get rid of the competition and take her place?"

"You're not serious. I don't see Ana murdering anyone either. With her looks, she could just wave a finger and most men would fall for it."

Just then Ana appeared to refresh their drinks and offer canapes. Unlike the two women sitting on the pool edge in their bikinis and gauzy shifts, their carefully painted toenails dangling in the water, Ana was dressed in a simple blouse with the logo of the boat and neatly pressed shorts. The ponytail of her hair contrasted with the carefully coiffed hairstyles of the paying guests. She returned with their drinks. "I have already seen James and Gaby. Do you know where I will find Peter and Michael to offer them refreshments?"

There was a short silence before Nikki replied. "I think you will find them down on the sports deck. They were talking of going paddling like we did. It might be best not to give them any more beer. I don't want any accidents."

Marly nodded. "They will be alright. Don't bother about them."

Both women smiled as Ana nodded and left.

Nikki laughed. "There's no need to put them under extra pressure but I have to admit she has it. No make-up, no hair, just shorts and a blouse and she still looks a million dollars. I wish I could do it. No wonder the guys get excited. I have to work hard to keep Mike happy."

"What's she like when you get her alone? She's always so polite and correct, yet every now and again she gets a troubled look, then it vanishes behind the mask."

"Gaby and I had a great time when we went paddling with her. She's good fun. She's really sweet and natural, it's just a bitch she is so good-looking and doesn't even have to work at it."

"Why bother? I'm over that. Pete can just accept what he has. Not that he will have it for much longer."

"What do you mean?"

"We've had our problems. Our days are numbered."

"But I thought you had a romantic time on Bora Bora. I want Mike to take me there when we get off this boat."

"It was great but our romance is over. Has been for some time. That was Pete's last chance and it didn't work."

"What are you going to do?"

"I want to go back to the UK. I miss the gentle grey days and the green of England."

"Don't you like Dubai? It sounds exciting."

"Too much sun and heat for this girl. After a while you get tired of the restrictions, even if you avoid the worst. Besides, Dubai will have problems if tourists ever stop coming, or it stops being the safe haven for crooks and dodgy politicians and businessmen to park their money. If the Bangladeshis and Filipinos left, and the expats leave, there would only be a few locals left."

"I thought all those skyscrapers and big resorts would be great."

"If they aren't careful the sand will blow in and the city will become a ghost town buried in the desert. Besides, I've got a guy in England that will console me."

"What about Pete?"

"He'll be OK. He has a friend who's just waiting to get her hands on him again. If you play your cards right I'm sure you could get to Dubai instead of her."

"So it really is over?"

"Yes. It has been for some time. We've both moved on. We're just going through the motions really. Not that his motions were all that great. A girl needs a bit of satisfaction. Anyway, who would turn down a holiday and a cruise like this one was supposed to be?"

"Did you have problems in the bedroom? I just didn't see that with you."

"Sweetheart, why confine yourself to the bedroom. Life is full of opportunity in other places. I'm sure you would agree. I don't see Mike as a shy retiring lover."

"My problem is to keep him from straying. I don't mind if he looks but he'd better not wander off."

"Darling, I'm sure you could find another."

"Yeah, but Mike is good to me. Good men are hard to find. There are a lot of douchebags out there. I know."

"Well if you need one try Pete. You'll get to live in Dubai. The money's good and the sex isn't really that bad."

Further conversation on the merits of men was halted by the approach of Gaby. "James's gone ashore for a run but I'm staying put. I've been reading but I need a break."

"What are you reading?"

Gaby answered Marly's question holding the cover of her book so the two women could see it. "I started out on a Booker Award winner I found on a shelf in the saloon. It won the award about twenty years ago. I thought it would be interesting, but with this sun and the blue of the ocean and this lovely breeze and the space of the South Pacific, I just couldn't get in the mood for it."

"What was it about?"

"It was set in India about fraternal twins. Perhaps another time. Now just isn't the time and place. I found another book, an old Agatha Christie detective story. It's a great, light, fun read. Much better suited to my mood at present."

"Not Poirot?"

"No Marly, this is a Miss Marple. *'Sleeping Murder'*. The book is different to what I remember seeing on TV. I loved the shows with Geradine McEwan, she was such a sweet, frail little old lady who always solved the mystery. Perhaps we need her here. She might enjoy a holiday in the South Pacific."

"Who's this Poirot and Maple?"

"Don't worry Nikki. They're old TV shows before your

time and they're very English, all these old houses and gardens. They're gorgeous."

"Marly's planning to go back to England. She's splitting with Pete."

"Shush, that's not common knowledge just yet."

Gaby looked surprised. "I'm sorry. I didn't realise the problem was that serious."

Marly's response was quick. "Don't bother, but just don't spread it."

"Well you had better watch out. Those quaint English villages are full of television murderers. Between Poirot and Miss Maple and Midsomer Murders there mustn't be anyone left."

"I think we could use another detective here for this murder. Broussard, or Blaise, neither seems to have any answers."

"Give them time, Marly. I'm sure one of them will find an answer."

"Yes, but will it be the right answer? Maybe they will just hush it up. Call it an accident. I don't care, I just want to get out of here. This holiday has become a disaster."

It was a little later in the afternoon when Mike joined the three women sitting beside the pool.

"What have you been up to Babe? Did you go paddling?"

"No, we just sat and had a few beers. Ana came down and

asked us what we wanted. She said you told her not to bother but Claude would expect her to check. She's a great girl. Looks good too."

"Yeah, well just remember who you're with Babe. None of your messing around."

"Relax honey. I thought I'd come and get you. Let's go down." He turned to Marly. "Pete's already gone down to your cabin."

"I think I'll stay here with Gaby."

"Where's James?"

Gaby explained he'd gone ashore for a run. "Cabin fever's getting to him I think. He wanted to get away from everything."

Murder on the Motu

33 James Paine

Blaise was sitting quietly on a bench near the marina watching the *Ocean Rover*. He had settled himself there in the shade of a tamanu tree after the departure of Ed and Tama to the yacht. He sat for hours, waiting, hoping, but gave no indication of what he was expecting. At last the tender from the *Ocean Rover* again left the boat. As it drew near the marina, Blaise could make out the figures of Amura and James Paine. James stepped onto the dock.

Blaise moved to greet him. "Good afternoon. You look as if you are planning to run."

"Yes. I needed to get off the boat and get some exercise now that it's cooler. A workout in the gym isn't my preferred activity. I like to get some fresh air and feel some real dirt beneath my feet."

"I understand, but physical exercise is not so important to me. That may be why I am less than perfect in my weight, but then I find wine and food are much more interesting."

"I enjoy them too, but I need to burn off the effects or I can't indulge."

"I admire your willpower. Your lady is not with you?"

"No, Gaby decided to stay near the pool and read a good book. She sometimes jogs with me but not today."

"You are very fortunate, you have a very intelligent and beautiful companion."

"I know. Second time I got it right."

"Yes. I have heard that you had some sadness."

"There was too much temptation in the East, for all of us I'm afraid."

"It must have been very different to your life in England?"

"From Manchester. Yes. I expect you know that my accent isn't real. Manchurians don't speak the way I do now."

"You have adapted very well. Only an expert would notice the remnants of your youth."

"It isn't just accents, there are other indications that some people pick up."

"The British can still be very class conscious."

"Yes, for some I will always be a working class boy from Manchester, 'Our Jimmy'. The Far East can be very exotic but for some expats the old ways of home still apply."

"When did you move to Hong Kong? I understand you still live there."

"Yes. When I finished university I managed to get a job out there. It's a great life and I've done well. I've had opportunities I wouldn't have had at home, but if I return to England I would return to the past. I'm not sure what the future holds for me but I hope it is with Gaby somewhere. Maybe we will go to Australia or Singapore."

"I understand. I would also be an outsider in Great Britain. My education was in places where my father's work took him. Some was in English. What was it like when you first went to Hong Kong?"

"It was a great life. Exciting, different. Perhaps too much booze and parties. I probably did things I shouldn't have done but we were young."

"And drugs?"

"You know don't you? I guess it was the times. They're no better now, just different. Probably worse. We all tried, some more than others. It was common, but for some it became serious. For my wife it was very serious. She died. I was the one who introduced her to marijuana. Then she..."

"And you hold yourself responsible?"

"Well I was."

"We each have to accept responsibility for our actions. She was a grown woman. She made her own decisions."

"But once the drugs take hold you lose any control."

"Unfortunately that's true. However sometimes there is nothing another person can do to resolve the problem. Ultimately, the only person who can save themselves is themselves. Until they really want to change, nothing will change their behaviour."

"What do you think happened to Annette?"

"Let us sit over there." The two men moved to the bench

in the shade where Blaise had sat waiting. He continued. "What can you tell me about Edward."

"You don't think he was involved?"

"I name no one. However I would like to learn more of him and the others who were in Hong Kong at the time. Possibly the cause is in the past but the result is in the present."

"I guess in some ways he and Casey were my mentors. He was a hot-shot American lawyer for a big investment fund. I learnt a lot from him. Casey took me under her wing as well. They were good to me."

"What about Annette Freidman?"

"I wouldn't say she was a good role model but I learnt a great deal from her."

"What do you mean?"

"Annette was..., well she used people, and treated them badly if they weren't of any use to her. However she was also very good at putting deals together. Getting people on side. You could always count on her coming out on top."

"And was it always legal?"

"Yes, legal. That was Ed's job, but ethical, that was sometimes questionable."

"And were Edward and the lady close?"

"Yes I suppose so. They worked together quite well. It could be intense at times."

"Their relationship?"

"That too. They were very friendly."

"What did his wife think?"

"I think Casey was troubled at times but they're still together. Unlike the rest of us."

"Ms Friedman wasn't from the States?"

"No, she was English like me, but she had worked in the USA. Apparently became a US citizen. Tell me Sidney, where is your home? It's a topic of conversation on the boat."

"I consider myself a citizen of the world, but I hold several passports. That can be convenient. However it also means I have nowhere that I really call my home. That is a loss."

"Annette said the same thing. She called herself 'a member of the Global Community'. I'm not sure that she was a good member of that community. She was very selfish."

"What can you tell me of Michael?"

"He was also from the States like Ed. He knew how to party. I guess he hasn't changed by the look of Nikki."

"Yes, the gorgeous Miss Olson."

"She's really quite a nice girl when you get to know her. Gaby thinks she's great and Gaby is a good judge of people. She thinks Nikki's too good to waste her life as eye candy with Mike."

"There is certainly some 'eye candy', as you call it, on your boat. Your girlfriend is also very attractive, as is the crewmember Ana."

"Would you say three different flavours of candy, Sidney? They are all very attractive women but so different in nature and experience. Some of us prefer just the one flavour."

"Why did you come on this trip?"

"Why wouldn't you? Two weeks cruising the South Pacific on a glamorous yacht. A chance to meet up with people you once worked with. No pressure, no demands. It should have been a dream holiday. But it's not. A woman died. Do you know who did it?"

"Tell me, what do you know of Peter Metcalfe?"

"He'd come to Hong Kong from Australia with his wife about the same time I moved there. That marriage didn't work out either. I think both of them found too many temptations in Hong Kong. Later they returned to Australia. I thought their marriage was a bit rocky. I wasn't surprised when Julianne left him a few years after that."

"Do you know what happened to them after they left Hong Kong?"

"Nothing about Julianne. Never heard anything more about her. Pete never mentions her. I believe he stayed in Australia for a few years then he moved to Dubai. Probably a good move. I think he met Marly there."

"Why do you say 'a good move'?"

"Hong Kong is changing now that Mainland China is exerting its muscle. Pete was in real estate then, that was the place to be, but it's all changing. Companies now deal directly with China and no longer need a rep in Hong Kong. The real estate markets have changed too with more Asian money. He wanted a new start. The action had moved to

Dubai."

"I have visited Hong Kong on a number of occasions. At one time I planned to write a story based in the Colony, but I could never get it to develop and the characters to become real for a reader. I remember the throb from the motors of the boats moving on the harbour, and at night the lights of the city reflecting on the water. For me, those sights and sounds reflected the energy of the people."

"The energy of the people is certainly being tried now with the protests in the streets. Especially with the young."

"What do you think will happen?"

"I don't know Sidney. Gaby thinks it will eventually settle down but she is always an optimist. I'm less sure. I think Hong Kong will shrivel and become less important. Already the international businesses are planning their moves, factories to Vietnam or elsewhere, even the States, Asian offices to Singapore. Gaby and I will move."

"When he was in Hong Kong, was Peter Metcalfe close to Ms Freidman?"

"No. I don't think he had a lot to do with her. Probably more with Ed. I don't think she liked him very much. Never knew why. Perhaps she thought he was an upstart colonial. She could be a snob although she had no reason. She was a bit like me, pulled herself up by her own efforts, not family connections. Although she was good at using contacts and she could bat her eyelashes when it suited her."

"She used men?"

"Annette used everyone, men and women. It made no difference to her. Do you have any more questions? I think I will give the run a miss and return to the boat."

Together they walked back to the marina and James waved to the *Ocean Rover*. Someone was watching from the boat because almost immediately the inflatable was motoring to the quay. Blaise and James Paine shook hands and the inflatable pulled away from the quay.

Blaise returned to his bench under the shade of a tree and sat deep in thought. Eventually the silence was broken by the sounds of the opening chords of "Ombra Mai Fu' from his cell phone. Blaise smiled, the thought of Xerxes of Persia in his mind as he answered the call.

34 Appearances and Disappearances

"I didn't expect to see you again so soon Sidney." James Paine had been surprised by the sudden appearance of Sidney Blaise arriving on the *Ocean Rover* so soon after their quayside chat at Uturoa.

"Nor I. However I had a call from your captain who tells me that Tama had given some new information to Capitaine Broussard. He thought I would also be interested."

"And are you?"

"I have yet to speak with Tama but I hope it will be useful. It appears my friend Broussard is keeping some information from me. Perhaps he wishes the glory of solving the mystery first. Claude has also invited me to stay for dinner. I could not refuse such an invitation to Matilde's cooking. I am sorry to say my skills have never lain in that area, no matter how much I enjoy the results."

"Did he say what Tama's story was?"

"He gave no details, only that Tama spoke with Capitaine Broussard after he ferried some of you ashore".

"Claude didn't think Broussard thought that it was very

important."

"Perhaps not, but Claude thought I would want to hear the story as well. Tama remembers something new and he wants to tell me. Something that happened on the night your friend disappeared. I have yet to speak with him. Soon I will find out if it is important."

Claude Duval and Tamahere were waiting on the bridge when Blaise arrived. The three men chatted briefly in French until Blaise asked if they could use English. "French is a beautiful language but I am afraid when it comes to understanding problems my mind works in English. Perhaps it is because I lack romance."

Duval replied it was not a problem for him and Tama was competent in English. Besides, what he had to say were straightforward facts. Tama had been troubled by the disappearance of the guest. He felt responsible as he had been on watch that night but had not seen Ms Freidman.

Blaise asked "Did you see anyone after the guests left for their cabins?"

Tama replied yes.

"Who did you see?"

"Mr Parker, Edward, came to the bridge. He could not sleep. He brought me a cup of coffee. We talked. He told me of life in America. Also Ana. She came for a swim. The Captain allows. I saw her but she did not look up to me."

"You told me of Mr Parker earlier. Anyone else?"

"No."

"Were you on the bridge all night?"

"No. I made my checks around the boat as I am told. It is boring when we are away from port. There is nothing to see. It is a long night. I was sleepy when Amura came to relieve me."

"And you saw no sign of the lady who died?"

The Polynesian crewman shook his head. "No."

But it was another matter which was concerning Tama. A paddleboard had gone missing from the sports deck.

Blaise's attention rose. "That is interesting. Perhaps that is how the lady reached the motu. It could explain why there was no water in her lungs from drowning."

Claude Duval had given Tama's information some thought while waiting for Blaise's arrival. "Perhaps she planned to meet someone on the island."

"It is possible Claude, but from what I have learnt the lady did not participate in water sports." He turned to Tama. "Did you ever see her on the sports deck with the boards or canoes?"

Tama shook his head.

"There's also another puzzle for you Sidney." The captain explained that although the board was missing, all the paddles were accounted for. "I suppose she could have paddled out to the motu that night using her hands."

"No. It is not possible." Tama spoke. "The board was there when the police came and searched the boat. It did not disappear the night the guest died."

"Tama has discovered that a paddleboard is missing."

There was silence among the group as each member thought of what Blaise's new information from Tama may mean. Then Ed spoke. "So Annette could have taken it and paddled across to the motu?"

"I suppose that would be possible, but I think unlikely." Blaise was not convinced

Again it was Ed who responded to Blaise's answer. "But she could have. She could have paddled across to meet someone, and then, after the blow to the head that killed her, the board floated away somewhere with the current."

"It is one possibility."

Pete shrugged. "It explains the death. She met someone and was killed."

Blaise nodded. "Perhaps. I have already spoken with Amura. Taha'a is his home island; he has canoed these waters and knows the tides and currents. He says it is possible."

"So we need to look for someone who arranged to meet her on the motu. Perhaps one of the calls she made on her cell phone?"

"Perhaps Edward, but the police have not found her cell phone. Besides, several of you have pointed out the lady did not participate in water sports. Tama tells me that the lady had told him she could not swim. In fact you, Michael, told Capitaine Broussard the closest she ever went to water was a lounge by a swimming pool, and you, Marlene, told me

Annette Freidman was afraid of water. Also she was wearing the red dress she had worn when she retired. That is hardly the costume of someone planning an excursion."

"So Sidney, should we be looking for someone she planned to meet on the motu, someone not from the *Ocean Rover*?"

"Yes Marlene, I suspect that was the idea. However, there is a problem with such a theory. Amura and Tama are most insistent that the paddleboard was there when the gendarmes searched the boat looking for the missing woman. They maintain it was in its rack the day the body was found. It vanished the night after Annette Friedman died."

The news of the timing of the paddleboard's disappearance caused a brief silence, then James Paine spoke. "So someone on the boat must have thrown it over the side and let it drift away?"

Blaise nodded. "Yes."

35 Conversations over Dinner

That evening Matilde excelled herself with the dinner. It was an inspired mix of Polynesian ingredients and French flair. Fresh island seafood caught that morning by Amura was served with locally grown vegetables purchased by Matilde from island stalls. The dessert was classic French, as were the cheeses. Claude had enjoyed many similar meals prepared by his wife and suggested wines from the boat's wine cellar that matched the food and his understanding of the tastes of the diners. Not that the diners added to the mood of the evening. Ed and Casey were withdrawn adding little to the chatter around the table. An unusual quietness seemed to have settled over Nikki and Mike, but that was nothing compared to the coolness between Marly and Pete. Of the eight voyagers, it was only Gaby and James who were relaxed and happy in enjoying the banquet placed before them. Yet even their happy banter could not lift the subdued mood of the other diners.

After his discussions with the crewman Sidney Blaise had remained chatting with the Captain for a long time. At last, Casey, rather impatiently, had asked him if he intended to stay for dinner. Blaise nodded, "Your Captain has asked me to join you." It was obvious the invitation was not universally approved, but Blaise made no acknowledgement of the disapproval and joined them, sitting quietly, enjoying the meal, listening to the limited conversation but adding little when asked any questions. His major contribution to the talk around the table was to compliment Matilde on her evening's presentation.

For Ana and Eeva it was a busy night serving at the table with the constant demands to refill or replace glasses as more and more drinks were requested. It was noticeable that whenever Ana approached Mike he flirted with her. Nikki's annoyance grew during the evening and her eventual coolness turned to a deep chill. Those seated around the table soon noticed that it was Eeva who took over serving Mike. Ana carefully kept her distance.

When the meal concluded four of the group moved away to the stern deck to enjoy the star-lit night. However tonight, even the occasional sounds drifting across the water from the nearby township were muted as if the township could sense the mood on the boat. Ed and Casey, Marly and Pete, and Blaise remained seated around the table. It was then that the discussion returned to the death of Annette Friedman.

Blaise raised the subject. "I am puzzled by your friend. There is so much you have all told me. I can create an image of the lady. How she looked. How she behaved. That she could be difficult and selfish. I have learnt something of her past and of her nature, but nothing that speaks of her inner soul."

"What do you mean Sidney?"

"Well Casey, what did she think of herself? Was she content with her soul? You spoke of her enjoyment of worldly possessions but did they make her happy? Did she have a God? Did she have close friends with whom she could be who she really was? Not to have a friend like that would be a great loss. Not to have the love of a partner, or a child, parents, friends from youth. Even a dog."

"Sidney. I don't think Annette's death has anything to do with whether she had a god or a dog. It was a mistake to involve you. It would be best if you just let the police deal with this matter and stay out of it. There have been enough problems on this cruise without your interference annoying all of us!"

As Ed's wife moved to her husband and laid her hand on his arm Blaise replied. "I am sorry if my questions offend you Edward. I understand your desire to leave all this behind you and return to your lives in the States and Dubai. I hope that will soon occur. However your friend has died in unusual circumstances and I am sure you would want to allow her the respect of consideration why it happened."

"I'm sorry Sidney. My husband worked closely with Annette. He does feel grief."

"I am sure that is true Casey. Sometimes when we work very closely with another, even when there are difficulties, there is still a bond. I am reminded of the experience of my father. For many years he worked with a man with whom he constantly disagreed. They fought many battles against each other, yet when that man died a part of my father's world disappeared also."

Casey removed her hand from her husband's arm. "You may be right about Annette. I don't think she had room in her heart for either a god or a dog. I expect she was lonely. She always had people around her but I doubt if they ever really became close to her. Not even my Ted."

"Casey's right. I was probably the closest of any of us but it was always on her terms. Even then she rarely confided in me. I don't know who else she would have talked with about her personal life. She mentioned lots of names but never anyone special after her husband and he didn't count."

Blaise looked intently at each of those sitting around the table, his gaze moving slowly from one to another. "There is something else missing in this mystery. She was not a sentimental person yet she organised this voyage and brought you all together. For that she had a reason. I have some suspicions but even that does not fully explain all her actions. There is something more which I suspect you know and have not yet mentioned."

"Blaise, there is something. Annette called me the night before she died. She was rambling on. I thought she had drunk too much. She told me she was expecting confirmation of some news that would cause a lot of trouble on the boat. Something that they would want to keep hidden at any cost. Someone would be very angry because it would ruin their life. They would never forgive her."

"But Edward, why didn't you mention this before?"

"I'm sorry Sidney. I should have mentioned it earlier. At first I didn't think it was important. She was drunk as usual. She did tend to exaggerate, especially after a few drinks. You couldn't always believe what she claimed. I thought she was just making a show of herself. Besides, if I had mentioned it to the others, it may have caused problems."

Blaise's face remained unchanged but his body language showed annoyance. "Did she give any clues as to what the news could be?"

"No, only that she was hoping to hear confirmation in Raiatea."

"Was she expecting to meet someone or was she expecting a phone call?"

"I've no idea."

"Did she say who it would be?"

"No."

"What was the information?"

"I've no idea."

"But Edward, why didn't you mention this before? Why now, days after her death? After Capitaine Broussard questioned you?"

"If she was killed because someone wanted to stop her spreading the news, I certainly didn't want to be a target if they thought she had told me what the information was."

"I understand. You would feel afraid, but why mention it now?"

"Because, as you say, we owe it to her."

"And you are now no longer afraid!"

"If we all know she had something on one of us then it is no longer likely that anything will happen to me. It would be too obvious who the culprit would be. It can't be me. It must be someone else."

"So it must be Peter, or James, or even Michael. That is what you are saying is it not, Edward?"

"Well it can't be me or Casey."

"That is very interesting Edward. You have given me much to consider and it is now late, I must leave. Thank you all for your company this evening. It has been most enlightening, just as Matilde's meal was most enjoyable. Claude has invited me to join you at the restaurant tomorrow night. It should be another beautiful meal. Almost as good as tonight. I hope the storm the Weather Bureau has promised will not attend." Blaise made his farewells to those around the table in the saloon as Claude re-appeared to say that Amura was ready to return Blaise to the quay.

As he was about to step into the inflatable Blaise was hailed by James and Gaby who were lounging comfortably in chairs drinking coffee on the aft deck. "Come and join us for a minute."

Blaise joined them and sat perched awkwardly on a nearby lounge.

"Have you solved the mystery?" asked Gaby.

"No, not yet, but I am learning much. I would like to learn more about Ms Freidman, or perhaps I should call her Mrs Mackie. Perhaps you can assist?"

"I can't. I only met her when she came on board, so I didn't know her but perhaps James can help."

James replied to his partner's suggestion. "I'm not sure I will be much help. I think it's best we call her Annette Freidman. That's how she preferred to be known."

"So were you close to Ms Freidman?"

James paused before he replied. "I don't think anyone was close to Annette. She was one of those people who invent a public persona for themselves. That was what you got. I doubt anyone ever got beyond the pretence."

"So what was her public face?'

"She was confident, well-presented, well-connected. Capable, well that was a bit questionable at times. She relied on others to deliver the goods but she could be very good at connecting with people if they furthered her plans."

"What was her role in Project Dynasty?"

"Annette and I were both employed for our knowledge of Hong Kong businesses and local contacts. Annette and her husband had arrived there a little before I did. She very quickly made friends with important people. I think her husband helped there. Actually her contacts were quite limited. Unless she considered you important you didn't count. That was a problem when it involved dealing with small factory owners and managers. She just wasn't interested in them, and, for us, they were important in growing the business. That became my job!"

"I understand she could be difficult to work with. Did she have enemies, someone who would wish her harm?"

James Paine continued, explaining that Annette Freidman frequently became unpopular with some people. If you could benefit her, you would be well-treated and feted, if not, you would be ignored. Those who received such treatment quickly sought to avoid her. They certainly wouldn't mourn her death but nor would they bother to cause it.

"I suspect you may have been inconvenienced by her actions?"

"For sure! She caused me lots of trouble sorting out her messes, and then she would treat me like the junior office boy. Still, it was a good job and I enjoyed most of the work."

"Did you know her husband?"

Before answering Paine hesitated as if returning to those past years. Then he spoke. "Not really. He seemed to keep to himself. When we socialised as a group he might come along, but I think he and Annette had separate lives, even though they shared an apartment. I think he had some business interests. Never really knew exactly what they were."

"And you do not know what became of him?"

James shook his head. "As I said, nobody knows what happened to him."

"What was Ms Freidman's background? It may help me understand the behaviour of the lady."

Paine shook his head and paused again before answering. She had never spoken about her past. Like him, she had been married when she arrived in Hong Kong. Paul Mackie, her husband, appeared to have had an education at an expensive school. Nothing like Eton or Rugby, but still upmarket. Then he had gone to university. That was where he and Annette had met. He thought Mackie's family had some money. Perhaps an estate somewhere in England, or a business, but it was never exactly mentioned. Annette was different, more likely to have come from a housing estate than a landed estate, although she took great care to present a persona matching her husband's. If she got drunk a few odd vowels and words would be dropped that didn't match the image she presented. She had a talent for mimicry. Her accent had certainly changed from the posh English he knew from her time in Hong Kong. Now it was some sort of mid-Atlantic posh American style that she used. She could be very cruel at times. She would pick on Mike's first wife who had a very strong southern accent. Pete would also be mimicked for his Australian accent. It was much broader in those early days.

"And you. Did she also make fun of you?"

"Of course. I suspect I was too close to her real background so I needed to be put in my place. Distance herself from me if you like. Not that it worried me but it did upset my wife. We were having a few problems at the time and Annette's behaviour didn't help. In fact it was probably the last straw. We broke up. It was partly my fault but there were too many temptations in Hong Kong for a young man."

"But you still live in Hong Kong, has the temptation disappeared?"

"Good sense finally appeared, then Gaby, but now the time has come to make a decision whether we will stay, or go somewhere else. We were just discussing it."

"James and I decided we must make a decision while we are on this trip. Time is running out. But, back to the present. Do you know what happened?"

"Not yet Gabrielle. I wait to hear more from my friend Capitaine Broussard. He is awaiting more information. I expect he will call again on you tomorrow. I also spoke once again with Tama. Hopefully his information will help me although I am not sure how."

"This must be like one of your crime stories, bodies and suspects everywhere."

Blaise smiled at the young Asian girl. "But here, only one body! As a writer I start with the crime and the victim. I know the perpetrator and I must write the story, taking care to hide clues and red herrings, so that in the final chapter when I reveal the solution to the crime, my reader will say 'Of course, I see all the clues now. It was obvious!', but this is real life. We know the victim but not the perpetrator. Perhaps it is not even a crime but a tragic accident. I am sure the clues will be there if we can recognise them."

"So will you solve the puzzle, or will Capitaine Broussard?"

"Gabrielle. Capitaine Broussard is a policeman. He has the method and the process. I am a writer. I have the imagination."

"So will you solve the puzzle first? I think it will be a competition."

"Broussard has the advantage of knowledge gained through education and experience gained through his work. It is a formidable combination. I have the imagination to perceive what might have been and what might be."

"So who will win?"

"We shall see." The four fingers on his left hand rose from where they had been resting on his knee and Blaise smiled.

36 Broussard Returns

The day started like every other day on the cruise, but then...the change. No longer was the sky a cloudless blue. It was now a leaden grey of heavy clouds from which scuds of rain fell fitfully. The once blue ocean of gently undulating swells had become a grey-green roiling sea. No longer did the waters sparkle with gem-like flashes of light. The breakers on the reef had lost their vibrancy and had become a dirty creamy foam rather than the bright pristine white of the previous days. Even the local fishermen had decided to stay on land and the waters of the atoll were only scarred by an occasional boat moving from some coastal village to Uturoa before quickly returning to its home.

The eight guests were still at the breakfast table when the grey boat of the Gendarmerie pulled alongside. Broussard and a gendarme stepped across onto the *Ocean Rover* where Claude Duval and Amura were waiting for them.

Broussard approached the group at the table. "Good morning tout les monde. I have received some information which may be of assistance in this case. Please wait here for me as I wish to speak with you. But first I must speak with your Captain and his crew." Broussard turned to Claude Duval. "I hope you have gathered them as I requested?"

Together Claude Duval and the two gendarmes climbed the stairs leading to the bridge of the *Ocean Rover*.

It was ten minutes later when Broussard and the Captain re-joined the travellers in the saloon.

"Thank you for your patience in waiting for me. I appreciate your assistance in this sad case." Broussard went on to explain that while the search had been unable to locate Annette Freidman's cell phone the Gendarmes had obtained a list of calls made by, or to her, while she was in French Polynesia. "The lady was active in making use of her cellular. Fortunately my assistant has been very clever in identifying many of the callers. Some were made to people on this boat. Others were to international numbers. There are, perhaps, other calls we could not discover that had been made using data services."

"You mean Skype or Messenger?"

"Yes Ms Olson. That would be possible. However it would be useful if we could learn why she called people on this boat. We know she called your Captain to arrange her arrival."

"She called me several times."

"It is true Capitaine, and you Mr Parker?

"She called me once."

"Only once Mr Parker?"

"No. You are correct Broussard. There was another call."

"And did you also make a call to her?"

Ed Parker hesitated. "Yes, once. It was about the trip to Bloody Mary's."

Broussard's look feigned surprise. "But why not just speak with her? She was here with you on the boat." Again Ed Parker hesitated. "I wasn't sure if she was on deck or in her cabin. It just seemed easier to call. We had a signal."

"It was late at night, was it not?"

"One call was, yes. I was on the deck. She wasn't there so I thought she must be in her cabin. I didn't want to go there."

"It was the night she died?"

"It was late the night after we went to Bloody Mary's. I was concerned about the episode with the man at the bar. It was so unlike her. I thought she must have been worried by something. I guess she must have died sometime after my call. Anyway Broussard, none of us knew what was going to happen that night."

"Thank you. The lady also made other calls to people on the boat." Broussard paused, waiting for the answer he knew must come.

"She called me twice."

"Yes Mr Gordon. That is correct. Why did she call you?"

"She was drunk. Both times. Nikki heard the conversation, well one of them anyway. Annette went on about something in Hong Kong. I don't know what it was all about. She made no sense."

Broussard continued his questioning. "Did she speak in Chinese to you?"

"No. I wouldn't have understood her. My Chinese is not that good."

"But you lived in Hong Kong?"

"Yes, but all the business was in English. I learnt very little Chinese apart from food and booze."

"There were other numbers. Some international. Do any of you know of a company 'Golden Dreams Corporation?'" There was no recognition of the name by those sitting around the table. "GDC?" Broussard watched the faces of the gathered travellers as he mentioned the letters. "Yes Mr Gordon. You are familiar with the name?"

"I don't know anything about GDC but Annette did say those letters. She said that I would be in trouble because of them. I have no idea what she was talking about."

Broussard informed the gathering that GDC, Golden Dreams Corporation, was a company based in Mainland China with an office in Hong Kong. His assistant had investigated and learnt that it also had business interests in the United States. "It seems from their website that they have many trading interests arranging for the import of goods from China to the United States. They also have property investments and interests in computer games and apps. Annette Freidman made calls to them in America and also Hong Kong."

"There were some Chinese at the resort we stayed in on Bora Bora. Perhaps Annette knew some of them? I think I saw a couple from the resort at Bloody Mary's as well. They could have come out to the boat and taken her."

It was Gaby who replied to Marly's suggestion. "There are Chinese tourists everywhere these days. They don't normally go around kidnapping and murdering people. I expect the answer to her death will be much closer to home."

Broussard turned again to Mike. "You said she spoke twice with you. What was the second call?"

"She was drunk again. Her speech was slurred and she seemed rather out of it, but she threatened to expose me for what I was. I don't know what that was supposed to be about. I don't have any great secrets. I may not have any great successes either but there's nothing that I would kill to hide."

"And you, of GDC, nothing?"

"No Broussard, nothing. Only that she mentioned those letters."

"You do not know Li Yong?"

Mike answered. "Never heard of him."

"I might know him." All eyes turned to James who was sitting quietly beside his partner. "If it's the same person. It's a very common name. It was years ago. In Hong Kong. He had a small business. It wasn't GDC. When I knew him he was dealing in toys, he would show a sample to a US company then have an order made up on the Mainland. There was a problem with the quality and we stopped doing business with him."

"James is being too cautious. There was a suspicion that he had other dealings."

"Yes Mademoiselle Secombe. What were they?"

"He may have been..." James cut in before his partner could finish. "There was a suspicion that he may have traded in drugs. Nothing was ever reported or proven. It wasn't just the quality of the merchandise that was a problem. We didn't want the hassles if the rumours were correct when we could deal with legit businesses. It all happened after the Project Dynasty time so it would have nothing to do with anyone here."

"Apart from you?"

James shook his head. "It must have been over twenty years ago. I haven't heard of Li Yong since then and he didn't trade as GDC. I don't remember anything about computer games either."

"Computer games! Apps!" Mike Gordon's eyes opened wider and his expression changed as he spoke. "So that was what Annette was on about. It didn't make sense at the time. She was talking about 'Crappy Birds' or 'Hot Chicks' and how I had to do what she wanted or I would be in serious trouble and get a visit from some bad people."

Broussard looked confused. "Crappy birds, what are they?"

Mike explained. "This kid came to me with a game he'd written, an app for cell phones. He wanted me to help him find a company to develop it and bring it to market. I guess he'd found my name somewhere because I had dealings with those sorts of business and funds. Anyway he didn't have any money. Eventually I agreed to take him on in exchange for a share of the profits. Bad move! I found a company that was interested and we did a deal. When they got their hands on the game they found it was very buggy. Nikki knows, she tried a version."

"It was crap. It kept locking up and the graphics were real kids' stuff."

"Nikki's right. It was hopeless. It would have needed to

be completely rewritten and upgraded. The other problem was it was actually called *Cheeky Birds*. The company was worried it would be considered a rip-off of *Angry Birds* and that could cause trouble. There was another problem too. One day this other Chinese kid turned up and claimed I had stolen his game and demanded money. As if I had any. All I had was a piece of paper with a promise that was worthless."

"So what happened?"

Mike continued in reply to Broussard's question. "This second kid claimed he had written the code and had already sold it to a company in Los Angeles. I had stolen his program and the company he had sold it to wanted recompense. I told him it was worthless and he could have it."

"Did he say who he had sold the game to?"

"I can't really remember. It wasn't GDC. Hi something Entertainments, something like that."

It was Nikki who came up with the answer. "HiMe Entertainments."

Broussard nodded. "Yes Mr Gordon. Mademoiselle Olson is correct. My assistant found HiMe Entertainments is a subsidiary of GDC. But it does not explain why Ms Freidman thought you must do as she wanted."

37 News

Mike explained that when he refused to pay up over her threat to tell Nikki about his past, she probably thought she could try this other caper to get some money out of him. She threatened to tell her contacts at GDC where to find him. "Dumb move. They already knew where I lived and worked."

"What was the second kid's name?"

Mike turned to Gaby and answered. "I think it was Tony... Tony Lam. Does that help?"

James, Gaby and Broussard shook their heads.

It was Ed who spoke next. "So why did Annette think you would pay up? There must be more."

"No." Mike was definite. "That's all!"

There was general discussion around the table over the news of Annette's demand but no satisfactory explanation apart from the possibility that she had heard of the claim by HiMe Entertainments and was perhaps acting for them. That could explain the calls to the States and Hong Kong. It could also explain her conversations in Chinese.

Broussard moved to his next concern. "I have spoken

again with the crew. They are very observant of everything that occurs on the boat. Also, they are very discreet, as one would expect. In answer to my questions they say only a little, or nothing, but at times, that is more important than what they do say"

"So what did you learn?"

Broussard replied to Ed's question by explaining that while the guests had known, or had known from their partners, about the dead woman, their understanding of her behaviour was influenced by their knowledge from the past. The crew, never having had contact with her before she had joined the boat, were unaffected by such knowledge. Their judgements were based solely on their association with her. He continued, explaining that questions that were discreetly deflected could often point to the truth that was being avoided. "As my friend Monsieur Blaise would say, 'When one avoids an answer to a question, it only encourages a closer search for what is being hidden.' So it was with Ms Freidman."

"So tell us, what really happened?"

Broussard responded to Ed's challenge. "You have all said she could be a difficult woman to work alongside. The crew would agree. You also spoke of her husband and her young male friends after her husband disappeared. The crew, or several of them, would be less certain of her interests."

It was Casey who spoke. "I don't believe it. Men were her thing. I should know!"

"I do not doubt your knowledge but sometimes there is more."

"Are you saying Annette was a lesbian? Are you saying

245

she was chatting up Ana and Eeva? So which one was she into?

"Madame Metcalfe. While crews on boats such as this are discreet, their jobs demand they be so. However it is known that not all guests are so discreet. There is talk in the bars, some young ladies, and some young men, are sometimes offered, shall we say, special benefits."

This time it was Nikki who spoke. "So did someone on this boat proposition Ana?" Her glance at her partner suggested the possibility may exist and if proven would cause grief for Mike.

"No Ms Olson. Both girls report no untoward advances from any of the men. Even with Ms Freidman neither girl states a definite experience. Rather it is a feeling, an intuition if you wish. Also there is another matter. Her behaviour. We know she spent much time in her cabin. That she was on medication and she imbibed frequently and greatly. Both girls, and Amura report that she was, at times, behaving strangely. They said so to Claude as they were concerned."

Once again it was Casey who answered, agreeing that at times Annette's behaviour was strange. Others had noticed how she would stop mid-sentence and appear to lose her train of thought. Other times she would appear to stumble when walking but it was usually late at night and put down to alcohol.

"Has she given any indication of problems with her health?"

Heads were shaken around the table. Then Nikki spoke. "She did say something about the TMC but I didn't know what it meant. Casey told me it was the Texas Medical Centre."

"Thank you. Ms Olson. Does any other person know of this matter?" Again heads were shaken in reply to Broussard's question. "I am still awaiting more information regarding the health of your friend. Unfortunately the information received has only raised more questions that I must ask, and replies are not always as prompt as I hope. I am told to expect an answer this afternoon. Thank you for your patience. I understand this is a difficult time for all of you. I hope it will not be for much longer. I go now. My friend Blaise awaits as he tells me he has information which you told him yesterday that I might not know."

"Are you working together on this case?"

"Mrs Metcalfe, I am a policeman, I must obey the law regarding information and privacy. But it is important to discover the truth and sometimes assistance can come in unexpected ways. At times it needs a small encouragement."

With that Broussard and his fellow gendarme stepped into the grey boat of the police force and sped away to the shore.

38 Secrets

The young dark-haired woman sitting alone on the park bench looked as if she was anywhere but in Paradise. Her look was of concern and worry. She recognised the approaching man as the one who had visited the boat the previous day.

She smiled at the man. "It can be so beautiful here and yet.... Will you join me?"

He nodded and sat beside her. "I did not expect to find you sitting here on a day such as this."

"I just needed to get away on my own for a while. The yacht has become so claustrophobic. Anyway Sidney, you are also out on such a day."

"Yes. I have just come from talking with my friend."

"Broussard?"

"Yes, Gabrielle."

"He said he was going to see you. You know he visited the boat this morning?"

"Yes. He told me of his new information."

"And I understand you had information for him."

"Yes."

"So who will win? You, or Broussard?"

"The competition? We shall see. He has still not made his decision. I have time. I think by tonight I will know."

"You are coming with us to the dinner?"

"Yes. I hope all will be answered there."

"What do you think really happened Sidney?"

Blaise hesitated for a moment before answering her question. "I'm still not sure of all the details. It's a strange case."

"Was it a murder like Pete says?"

"There are some puzzling aspects."

"Could it have been an accident? Suicide? Surely not murder? But what else could it be?"

Again Blaise paused. "It is too soon for me to say for sure and I think we should keep an open mind until the police finish their investigations. Broussard is a very thoughtful policeman. His skills would be put to better use in Paris than on a remote island such as, this solving thefts of vanilla, crimes of passion and minor drug dealings."

"So why is he here?"

"For him, I think it is a matter of family. His family would be happier here in the South Pacific than in a big city like Paris."

"I think he will say it was an accident. Like Mike says. A drunk tourist doing stupid things. Case closed. It is the easiest solution for them."

"I doubt it. My friend Broussard is honourable. He will want to find the truth."

"But what is the truth?"

"If it was an accident, how did the woman get to the motu? She did not fall in the water and drown and float. It does not have the characteristics of a suicide. There is no note. So often a suicide seeks help. They tell of their intentions to those around them, but in this case there is nothing. Often their cry is not recognised, but here, nothing. Still, not every situation is the same. Sometimes it is unexpected. My friend Broussard spoke of health and money. Perhaps that is the answer."

"When Capitaine Broussard visited us on the boat this morning he said he had some news but needs more. Do you know what it is?"

"I know what he is seeking."

"So will you or he find the answer?"

"I hope so, for all of you. But why are you sitting here all alone?"

"There's a funny mood on the boat. I think the confinement is taking its toll. We need to go our separate ways."

"But your husband is not with you?"

"My partner. No. James and I decided to come ashore and walk to the top of that hill. To look over the atoll and the island, and out to Taha'a. When we returned the rain started so we found a café and had a coffee. Then when the rain stopped he returned to the boat. I wanted more time before returning."

"You say there is a strange mood. What is it?"

"No real trouble. Just, people are different. Ed and Casey rarely come out of their cabin, they seem very withdrawn. Nikki and Mike are bickering. Marly and Pete hardly talk to each other but that's not surprising. Even Ana. She was so much fun when we went paddle-boarding. She was so vibrant at first but now she is very reserved. Perhaps Nikki's had words with her and warned her off Mike."

"And you and your partner? You do not have a problem?"

"No. But I think we need to get away from the others. That is why I stayed here for longer. James's shoes were wet from the rain. He wanted to get back to the boat."

For a while the man and the young woman sat together in silence. As they sat, an inflatable came into the marina from a catamaran anchored off the town marina. A group of tourists and their luggage arrived by minibus from the airport and boarded the inflatable.

"I hope their holiday is not as tragic as ours."

"I doubt it will be. I'm sure most people leave the island of Raiatea with happy memories."

"We won't."

They sat in silence for a minute before the woman asked her question.

"You said everyone has a secret. Do you?"

"Yes, of course."

"What is yours?"

"If I told you it wouldn't be a secret."

"Do I have a secret?"

"That is something you would know, but I suspect you do."

"What is it?"

"Only you will know that."

"Is your name really Sidney Blaise?"

Blaise smiled. "That is how I am known."

"It still seems a little fortuitous for a writer."

"You are a very astute woman, Ms Secombe. It is the name I am known by but not the name on my passport."

"And what is the name on your passport?"

"My life with that name is very unexciting. It is best if I am Sidney Blaise."

"You really do like a sense of mystery don't you?"

"That is my business. To create mysteries and puzzles for others to solve."

Once again silence descended over the pair, broken eventually by the arrival of the tender from the *Ocean Rover*. Gaby rose and moved to greet Tama and board the inflatable. As it pulled away from the quay the girl with long black hair waved, but it was not a wave of happiness. Nor was the man who returned the wave at ease. He was sure that somewhere in their conversation lay the final clue to the death, but try as he might he couldn't see it. It was only one piece of the puzzle, but it was the piece he needed to have before the evening's meal was over.

39 The Restaurant

It was four-thirty when the inflatable made two trips to the marina. The heavy darkening grey clouds still hung low over the waters; waters which reflected the dull grey sheen of the clouds and the sky above. The atmosphere hung heavy: humid and oppressive.

Waiting on the quay were two mini-buses, their standard factory white paint hidden behind decals of large and colourful flowers. The rare white flower of the tiare plant was surrounded by red, pink and orange hibiscus flowers, the white and pink flowers of frangipani and the yellow flowers of the vanilla of Taha'a. The colourful display made a vivid contrast to the greys of the sky and water.

"Claude? Don't we have a big bus to take us to the restaurant?"

"Not on Raiatea, Nikki. On the islands popular with tourists you might have the large tourist coaches. But not here, Raiatea is not on the list of the many tourists who know of Tahiti and Bora Bora and Moorea. Here it is more private and quiet. More sailors, and not the big cruise ships. On some islands you still have 'le trucks'."

"Le trucks? What are they?"

"The first buses on these islands were trucks like you use for cartage. The locals built wooden cabins on them and fitted benches so they could carry people like a bus. They were not always comfortable seats but they were cool with the breeze because they had no windows. When it rained you would lower a curtain to stay dry. Now some remain for tourists. You might have seen one on Moorea. Also on some of the other islands. Here, because there are not so many tourists, the mini bus is more popular. I think it will also be better because tonight there will be a tempest and much rain."

As well as the eight guests from the Ocean Rover, three others had come ashore for the excursion to a restaurant. Claude, who had recommended the restaurant, had come to assist as a guide and translate if needed. Ana had asked if she could accompany the group as she had heard of the beautiful food they served. At the last minute Matilde had also decided to accompany her husband.

"It will need forty minutes for us to reach the restaurant in Opoa. It is at the south end of the island. The drive will be along the coast and it will be a twisted road as it follows the shore but it is very interesting to see more of the island. Please let us board." On Claude's invitation two groups formed as they moved towards the buses. First to board a small bus were Ed and Casey, followed by Pete and Marly. A younger group boarded the second bus. Finally, Claude and Matilde joined the four in the first bus.

As Claude had promised the road followed the coastline, running around tiny inlets and beside small bays, occasionally turning inland but never venturing far before returning again to the edge of the sea. On the opposite side of the road the country often rose up into hills cloaked in green whose peaks were already shrouded by cloud. In places, scattered along the roadside, were cottages with small cultivated gardens and plantations, gardens which sometimes climbed up the slopes towards the lowering clouds. At many of the cottages a family, or a just a man and a woman, sat enjoying the last fitful rays of sunshine while carefully sheltering away from the growing wind. Sometimes they were accompanied by a lazy dog that showed little interest in the passing buses. Away from the sea the predominant colour of the countryside was green: green in a myriad of hues.

As they drove further south the clouds became heavier.

"What will this weather do Claude? Will it be heavy rain?"

"I think we will have an explosion Edward. First we will have much lightning and thunder, much rain, but the forecast says it will clear later in the evening."

"Claude. What do you know about this Sidney Blaise? Is he genuine? Or is he just a sham?"

"Before this visit to Raiatea I have never met him. I only know what Capitaine Broussard has told me and other enquiries I have made since. I do not know much of his books but I understand he has lived here for a year. He is a very interesting man to talk with. I enjoy his company."

"Is he a great detective?"

"A great storyteller. Yes, I am told it is so. But a great detective? That I cannot say. Perhaps we will discover tonight. He will join us at the restaurant."

Another question came from a voice seated behind Claude. "Do you know anything of his background? That seems to be a mystery."

"That I cannot say Marlene. He speaks good French and his English is also good, although you are perhaps a better judge than I."

"Is he French or English?"

"I do not know. His French is perhaps too correct for a Frenchman, but then his English is... Je ne sais pas quoi. I am not an expert on such things. I can say if you are American or English but not from which part. I have never heard him say where he was born, or even if he has a home somewhere else. Perhaps it is a question that you may ask him yourself at the restaurant tonight."

"So he is coming tonight. Do you know why?"

"No. Only that he asked to join us."

"Did he say why?"

"He did not say Peter, only that he hoped to discover the truth. I think also he enjoys the food at this restaurant."

The conversation amongst the group on the front bus ceased. Ted and Casey were still restrained, rarely speaking to each other. Marly and Pete were even less talkative and, apart from their few questions, no one said much during the journey. Claude, who was sitting beside the driver chatted with him, but eventually even he fell silent. Matilde, alone at the rear of the bus, had not spoken during the entire journey. Whether the atmosphere on the bus was subdued by the thought of the coming storm, or from some other cause, wasn't obvious but each person seemed lost in their own thoughts and emotions.

The atmosphere on the second bus was different. The three young women chatted away noisily and the sound of laughter filled the bus. Ana, in the seat beside the driver, was constantly turning to tell the others of another humorous, or disastrous, story of her experiences backpacking around the world. With Mike and James seated at the rear of the bus, the two men had little opportunity to join in, hampered as they were by their position. Even when James leant forward and tried to exchange a few words he was drowned out by the laughter of the women.

The question of Blaise and his background was also discussed in the second bus. Once again he was a man of mystery.

The only new clue came from Gaby. "I heard him speak of the wonders of Persia and the Persian culture. It sounded as though it was special to him and he knew it well."

"But Persia disappeared long ago with the revolution against the Shah. Now it is Iran. He couldn't be old enough to have lived in Persia."

Gaby had assumed the role of historian and answered James's question. "The revolution was in seventy-nine. That's forty-one years ago. It's a bit hard to put an age on him. He could have been a child."

"I don't think he's an Arab."

Again it was Gaby who had the answer. "No Nikki, Persians are not Arabs. They're Muslim, but they're ethnically a quite different culture with a different language and a very rich ancient history. Perhaps that's what Blaise was talking about, but I don't see him as being Iranian either, although I suppose you can't judge a book by its cover, or an author by his cover either."

Sidney Blaise was already waiting at the restaurant when the two buses arrived. It appeared that he had come in a rather battered small blue Hyundai, the only car in the parking lot. It also appeared that Blaise considered the dinner a formal occasion for gone were the shorts, the hat and the dark glasses and tonight he was wearing a bright shirt in typical island fashion, long cream trousers and loafers without socks. Nevertheless his hair had obviously resisted any attempt to subdue it into a more organised style.

"Welcome to the finest food on Raiatea. Claude has done well to suggest this restaurant."

The restaurant was a large room enclosed on three sides by folding doors fitted with shutters. However this evening the doors and shutters were closed and, instead of a gentle breeze cooling guests, the fans and air conditioners were working hard to cool the room and remove the clammy moisture from the air. Outside, the sun was sinking lower in the sky and the daylight commencing to fade. The light grey and white paint scheme on the timber wall and shutters, which on a good day would have given the room a cool refreshing outlook across the garden to the small sandy beach, and beyond to a tiny island, tonight gave the room a sombre look. Even the lit candles on the table and the warm glow from the subdued wall lights couldn't dispel the feeling of the uncertain conditions outside. On a bright sunlit day the room would have probably buzzed with laughter and gaiety but tonight, with the grey of the room, the deepening grey of the sky and the sinking sun, even the three laughing women fell quiet.

"I thought there would be more people here. The place is empty. We are the only people here."

Claude replied to Nikki's observation. "I understand the weather has caused the guests of the resort to take their meals in their rooms. They are less certain of the weather than the locals."

"I hope you are right Claude."

"Be assured Michael. The storm will have passed by the time we leave."

The seating for the group had been arranged as one long table for twelve. Five on either side and one each at the head and the tail of the table. Twelve is an awkward number. Conversations, particularly quiet conversations at one end of the table rarely pass to the other end. Even those sitting in the middle who can relay the chat from one end to the other have difficulty continually monitoring and engaging in two different threads of conversation.

Ed assumed the place at the head of the table. It was as if there was an acknowledged acceptance that he was the senior member of the party. Blaise sat at the far end. The others each took a place. What became noticeable were their seating positions. Claude, in a middle position, where he could converse with either end of the table. On his right sat his wife. Directly opposite him was Gaby with her husband on one side and Nikki on the other. Blaise was joined by Ana and Pete, while Marley sat at the other end of the table on the right of Ed. Casey sat on the left of Claude and next to Pete, closer to the far end of the table and Blaise. Mike took the final seat beside Ed and far from Nikki.

"What's this thing 'lune de miel'? I saw it on a sign as we came into the restaurant."

Gaby explained to Nikki that, unlike some expressions, the French expression translated almost word for word, although in reverse. "Lune is luna, the moon, meil is honey. Honeymoon. The resort is hoping to attract romantics."

"Well that's not Mike and I at the moment. What's the 'motu or wasu' the driver mentioned? I know motu is a little island."

This time it was Blaise who answered. "*Motu aux Oiseaux*. It means Little Island of Birds. The English would probably say Bird Island. The French way sounds so much prettier."

"I always had trouble in French class with my *à* and *au* and *aux* and my *de, du* and *des*. I think it should be *island of birds* not *island at the birds*."

Again Blaise answered. "I understand your thinking Gabrielle, but each culture and language has its own thought processes we must just accept. I am always amused by Spanish. There you do not enjoy food but food enjoys you. *Me gusta la comida*. It likes me the meal"

"My favourite French expression at school was '*Je suis désole*'. It sounded much more impassioned than 'I'm sorry.'"

"*Je regrette* is another way for the French to apologise but I understand your attachment. A Spaniard would say *Lo siento*. I feel it. Languages are so interesting. Words that are polite, perhaps even complimentary in one country, can be rude and offensive in another. Even though countries may share a common language, some words can have very |

different meanings in different countries. I speak from an experience of great personal embarrassment."

"Do tell, Sidney,"

"Ah Marlene. It is an experience I wish to forget."

"Do you also know Chinese, Sidney?"

"No Gabrielle. I fear I must show my ignorance. I can neither speak nor read Mandarin or Cantonese. I have enjoyed my visits to Hong Kong but I have never learnt the language. Yet I expect many of you can from your time in Hong Kong."

"No." The rapid answer from Ed was very definite, an answer that James was equally quick to correct.

"That's not true. We all learnt a little, well those of us who were there. Annette could speak enough to make herself understood."

"It's alright for you Jimmy Boy, you made lots of Chinese friends but for the rest of us it was just enough to get a drink or a taxi." James looked angry and was about to reply to Mike when two waitresses appeared to take orders for their meals.

Claude Duval spoke with the first waitress and turned to the group explaining that tonight the house specialty was *carangues,* a type of Kingfish caught locally. The seafood on the menu also included squille and stuffed crabs cooked in the local style.

"What are squille?" asked Nikki. "I don't know that."

Casey agreed. "Me neither." It was only Blaise, Matilde and Claude who understood the term.

Blaise explained. "They are crevettes. You may know them better as shrimp or prawns depending on your local term. They are excellent. I would also recommend the Foie Gras with the pan-fried mangoes and pineapple chutney. It is my favourite."

"Do you eat here often Sidney?"

Blaise responded to Marly's question. "Unfortunately not as often as I would like. However I have tried most of the carte. For those who enjoy their seafood can I suggest the carpaccio de saint jacques with vanilla oil and green asparagus. For the lovers of chicken perhaps the pineapple chicken. The local cuisine favours the pineapple and vanilla."

Ed had already made his decision. "Well I'm going to have the foie gras. You French make a speciality of it. These days some places don't serve it."

"What's that?"

Claude Duval explained to Nikki it was the liver of a duck that had been especially fed corn.

"And what's the carpaccio thing?"

Blaise, obviously very familiar with the menu, described the dish to Nikki. "It is scallops, thinly sliced and raw, served with an oil flavoured by the local vanilla pods. Most delicious."

"Raw scallops. I think I prefer my food cooked."

"Grow up Nikki. Try it. Try something different for a change."

Nikki flashed an angry look at her partner. "I might just

do that!"

"Well I'll have the carpaccio. I like things on the raw side."

This time it was Pete who responded. "Maybe you're not the only one who likes something on the side."

With orders taken, the two waitresses left the room to report the requests to the kitchen. Soon they returned with carafes of water and to take orders for drinks. Claude took charge. "With your permission I think we should start with fine French champagne to acknowledge the tragedy of the lady who brought us all together and to celebrate our voyage. Then I will select some wines to compliment the food you have chosen"

Soon the group were standing toasting the memory of Annette Freidman. Those who knew her from the Hong Kong days stood silent and it was Marly who spoke up. "I liked her. She was a girl with balls. She knew what she wanted and went out to get it. I would have liked to have had more time with her. I hope whoever is responsible for her death gets his comeuppance." Again silence, until Ed waved to the table for all to take their seats.

Once seated, the conversation turned to Sidney Blaise.

"So Sidney. Where do you come from? Claude says you speak very good French, your English is excellent, you must know some Spanish and you have an interest in Persia, but now you live on an island in the distant parts of the South Pacific?"

"My story, Michael, is a long one and not very interesting, but I have been fortunate to have travelled far and to have met interesting people and have seen many interesting places. I envy this charming lady on my left." At his compliment Ana's face showed a slight blush beneath her tan. "For her, the world is there to be discovered and enjoyed. She is starting out on her adventure. And you Gabrielle, I think you and James have also adventures awaiting you. For me, now I move closer to my allotment of years and I must rush to fill them as best I can."

"You must still have quite an allotment to fill?"

"I hope so, but one never knows. Our lives can change so quickly. I think of your friend who is no longer with you. Perhaps it is best we do not know our future, only our past. *The moving finger writes; and, having writ, Moves on.*'"

" *'Nor all thy Piety nor Wit Shall lure it back to cancel half a Line, Nor all thy Tears wash out a Word of it.'* That's Omar Khayyam. He was Persian wasn't he?"

"Yes Gabrielle. I loved also his passage *'There was a Door to which I found no Key: There was a Veil past which I could not see: Some little Talk awhile of Me and* Thee *There seemed—and then no more of Thee and Me.'* For a great mathematician he was an interesting philosopher. Perhaps we should always live as if our futures will be brief."

"Can you see past the veil to what happened to Annette Freidman?"

"I think that veil is lifting Peter. But enough of this, the first of our food comes. Let us enjoy the benefits of this evening."

After the waitresses had placed the ordered dishes on the table a quietness settled over the gathering as the guests commenced eating. Then the conversation resumed as the women questioned Matilde about the various dishes that had been chosen.

"Claude. How do you go with your guests on the *Ocean Rover*? These days everyone seems to have 'Dietary Preferences'. It must make it difficult for Matilde if you have people who will not eat this sort of food, or that sort of food. Perhaps a gluten intolerance, or vegan?"

Claude smiled. "I am fortunate James. Matilde is very competent. But we must always try to be sure of our guests' needs before we leave the port. Still, sometimes we are troubled. Now so many are vegan or vegetarian, or no fish, no meat. I suspect for some it is, perhaps, only a fashion. The young women and the grand-mères. They are the ones most concerned with such things. For men it is the heart attack, but many soon forget when they see the beautiful meals prepared for the others. But yes, it is a problem in these islands if we are not prepared."

"And what about alcohol? The boat has a very good supply. Do you have some who do not drink?"

Claude smiled at Pete's query. "The problem there is to know all the cocktails that some ladies prefer. Ana is very good with that. The men it is not so difficult. Whisky, Scottish of course, brandy, the beers, especially the local brands. There is always curiosity and then they revert to their favourite beer."

A faraway clap of thunder sounded and a distant blue flash lit the room.

"That's getting closer, are you sure we won't have a hurricane tonight?"

Once again Claude reassured the group. "No Ed, we will have a storm, the wind and the rain, but it will not be a cyclone."

"So what's the difference between a hurricane and a cyclone?"

Claude answered Nikki's question. "Cyclones, hurricanes and typhoons are all the same. It is just where they occur. You have hurricanes in the States and the Caribbean, in the South Pacific we have cyclones and in the north-west of the Pacific you have typhoons. For us, this is not the cyclone season."

Once the main course was cleared away the waitresses moved among the group taking orders for desserts. The conversations around the table continued but now became more confined to those close to each speaker. With Ed and Mike the subject moved from football to fishing. Mike spoke of a recent week's fishing in Florida and Ed told of spending holidays as a youth with his parents in a cottage beside a lake. There he would row a small boat around the lake checking his favourite fishing spots. The talk of rowing led to the subject of Nikki. Mike confided to Ed that ever since she had gone paddling with Ana and Gaby her attitude had changed. Where once she had been eager to please, since that day she had become argumentative and demanding, often disagreeing with his wishes.

"Perhaps you should ask Gaby or Ana if they know any reason to explain the change?"

Mike was unconvinced by Ed's suggestion. "I think those women are as thick as thieves. They probably wouldn't tell me the truth anyway. But I wouldn't mind getting to know that Ana better. She is a stunner."

"You had better be careful boy. You might find your bed empty."

"I think the time is coming when that might be a good idea. Nikki's had a good run."

"Nikki's not the only one who's acting differently. Ana's changed as well. She was very strange after Annette's body was found. She went very quiet and withdrawn. It was only after she came back from paddling with the girls that she started to behave the way she was when we first came onto the boat."

At the other end of the table Ana, Gaby and Nikki were continuing their animated chatter from the bus, but their laughter was the only happy sound in the room. Blaise and Pete Metcalf appeared to be in serious conversation, while at the other end of the table, Marly, his wife, was also in deep conversation with James. She did not look happy. Claude was left to chat with Casey on his left and his wife on his right. Matilde rarely responded to his attention.

Outside the restaurant the sounds of rain and wind grew louder and louder. Suddenly the night was shattered by another violent clap of thunder. The room was lit by a blue flash, and then darkness. All the lights of the resort were extinguished. Even the candles on the table flickered and ceased, blown out by a stormy gust sneaking from some unknown opening. No one spoke. It would have been impossible to hear them anyway with the screech of the wind and the noise of the rain lashing the roof and walls of the restaurant. The group sat motionless, in silence.

40 Party Games

Almost immediately the waitresses reappeared to re-light the candles on the table. Soon the group was enclosed in tiny bubbles of soft yellow light that sent flickering shadows to play on the walls. The senior of the two Polynesian women spoke quietly to Claude who passed the message on to the group. "The patron, the manager, says all will be well. He hopes power will soon be restored. He has gone to check the other guests in their rooms and will return to speak with us. These ladies will now bring out our desserts."

"I love the menu description 'Mousse glacée aux fruits de la passion.'"

"So what is it Gaby? I decided to have the panacotta 'cause I know that."

"I guess the passion depends on the man or woman. It's not really as romantic as it sounds Nikki. It's frozen mousse with passionfruit. The pamplemousse tuile is a grapefruit biscuit thing. You'd probably call it a cookie. The classic one has a curved shape, like those old-fashioned roof tiles in Europe. Which is your favourite Sidney?"

"Ahh Gabrielle. I enjoy both. It is always a difficult

decision, but here comes the manager."

The resort manager joined the group and apologised for the lack of lighting. There was a problem at the transformer station and men were already at work. He hoped power would soon be restored. All guests were safe and the storm had done no other damage. Meanwhile there was candlelight, coffee was available, and the bar would provide any requests free of charge.

The four men moved to the bar where a waitress stood ready to meet their requests. Claude remained seated at the table chatting to the women. It was five minutes later when his cell phone rang. He answered and talked briefly in French and then returned the cell phone to his pocket. "I think we must wait longer for the storm to clear. The road to return to Uturoa is blocked by fallen trees. Workers are already on their way to remove them but it would be better to wait here than in a bus on the roadway. Perhaps another coffee or a glass of wine?"

It was Marly's suggestion to play a game to fill in the time. They would each choose a character, or a play, by Shakespeare that suited each person.

Casey made the first suggestion. "That could be fun. I think Pete should be *The Merchant of Venice*. Venice was a great trading and financial centre. Dubai now has a similar role. I can see Pete as the Merchant of Dubai."

"So what about Marly?" Pete was quick in his answer to James' question.

"The Merry Wives of Windsor."

"Why that one?"

Marley answered Gaby's question. "It's near where I grew up as a little child. I used to live in Berkshire, near Windsor Castle."

"Isn't that where the Queen of England lives?"

"Yes Nikki. Among other palaces and houses, but I used to live in a little village, it wasn't a castle but is a beautiful old house. It was lovely. I was happy there."

"So what is the *The Merry Wives of Windsor* about?"

"It's about the behaviour of wives." Pete's answer carried a note of anger that was reinforced by Marley's riposte. "And lecherous old men! I prefer *A Midsummers Night's Dream*. At least it is a comedy with fantasy and magic and love and all live happily ever after. There should be more of that in the world."

"I love *Romeo and Juliet*. It's so romantic."

"Nikki have you ever seen it?"

"No. Why Mike?"

"They both die. You can forget that. I'm not planning on dying for you or anyone!"

"Oh babe?"

"Forget it. You're more *As you like it*. That's your scene."

What's that about?"

Gaby explained the play was about confusion between lovers but in the end everyone gets the one they want and the bad guy repents his behaviour.

Nikki approved. "I like that. We should all get the lovers

we want. I think *Macbeth* would suit Matilde because she is a cook. That's the play with 'Double, double toil and trouble; Fire burn and cauldron bubble.' We did that at school."

"I don't think that would be appropriate. It's not nice to Matilde. They were witches." Gaby and Marley nodded in agreement with Casey.

"I didn't think of that."

"Grow up Nikki. Shakespeare is not your thing. Stick to the parties and clubs."

"Mike, just ..." Gaby entered the discussion and tried to ease the developing situation. "There are lots of food quotes in Shakespeare but I can't think of another cook. My favourite cooking quote is *'tis an ill cook that cannot lick his own fingers.'* It's just so much like my mother when she's cooking."

"I think *A Comedy of Errors* would be best for Gaby and me."

It was Casey who asked for an explanation. Gaby answered. "I think James thinks it sums up our first few meetings. Something always went wrong. I didn't like him when I first met him and I think he thought I was a real pain in the arse. Perhaps *All's Well That Ends Well* would be a better choice. What about you Casey?"

"I agree with Marley. I would like *A Midsummers Night's Dream*. It was the only Shakespeare I did at school and I loved the imagery and romance, and the fun. All that mistaken identity. At least true love came out in the end."

"What about Ed? Would he agree with your choice?"

"I think my husband could be Julius Caesar."

"But he gets killed too."

"True Gaby, but a great man with fatal flaws."

"I think fatal flaws is a harsh judgement on Ed. None of us are perfect but I'm sure he's not that bad."

"Well I know one play that would suit Annette if she were here." All heads turned towards Mike waiting to hear his suggestion. *"The Taming of the Shrew."*

"Mike! That's unkind. The poor woman's dead."

"Well let's face it Casey, she could be a real bitch. It was only about her. She didn't care what she did to any of us and that included her husband."

"You still shouldn't speak that way of the dead."

"Just ask anyone here. None of us will miss her."

A silence fell over the group and again it was Gaby who attempted to ease the tension. "We haven't chosen a play for Ana and Claude."

"Or Mikey! Who has a suggestion?"

Marley suggested *Measure for Measure* but when the others heard her explanation of the plot they disagreed. Nikki said nothing.

Finally Pete made a suggestion that met their approval. "I think Claude should be the captain of the ship in The Tempest. Not because he is like that Captain but just because of the weather outside."

Claude smiled. "I cannot comment. I do not know your

play but I understand the weather. The sun will again come out. The tempest will pass."

"So that leaves Ana."

This time it was Blaise who made a suggestion. "The play has already been used but I would think the character Helena, but not the Helena in *A Midsummer's Night Dream*. The Helena who is a capable woman who takes control of her life amidst many challenges."

Which play is that?"

"*All's Well That Ends Well*. The same as chosen by Gaby and James."

"Well what about you Sidney? We have to find a play or character for you."

Various options were suggested. Falstaff, or the magician in *The Tempest*. Someone from *A Midsummer's Night Dream*. All met with disapproval.

It was James who asked Blaise to nominate his own preference. "Well Sidney. What's your choice?"

Blaise smiled "No, I think I will leave that to others."

Even when Gaby pressed him to select a character, he refused. "Well if you won't choose your own what do you think of our selections for the others?"

"It is difficult. Each play has many varied characters and the title or story may not match each of you perfectly. I am impressed with your knowledge of the greatest English writer of all time but it is perhaps unfair to those whose education is in the USA. They also have great writers."

"So Sidney. Is our voyage a comedy or tragedy?"

"Peter, a lady has died. That can never be a comedy, no matter how the modern movies may treat death."

There was a distant rumble of thunder and the sky again filled with a flash of lightning, but by now the storm had moved far off out to sea. When the last noisy burst of heavy rain on the roof ceased and conversations once again became possible a silence still remained over the group. It was Ed who asked the unsaid question that was on all their minds. "Well Sidney, we are all gathered together. The storm has passed. Isn't this the time when you explain the murder and show how each one of us had a motive and the opportunity and you expose the guilty party?"

Blaise answered. "I have also seen those movies."

"Well, we are all here."

Ah, but we are not all here. There are three missing"

"Tama, Amura, and Eeva. You're not suggesting they are to blame?"

"I am suggesting nothing but they each hold a key to this puzzle."

There was a brief flicker from the wall lights and then the lights of the resort returned. A cheer went up from the group.

"I thought tonight you were going to tell us what happened to Annette. So when will we see your solution?"

There was another brief flicker from the wall lights but this time the lights did not go out.

Blaise clasped his hands together in front of his chest. "Tomorrow Edward, I promise you." He opened his hands. "Broussard will be present." Again he clasped his hands. "Tonight I have had confirmation of what I suspected. But here comes Claude. I think it is now possible for you to return to your boat."

As the two buses drove away from the restaurant a solitary figure with wild white hair stood watching them leave. A smile slowly came across his face as he walked towards the battered blue car.

41 The Day After

The darkness and ferocity of the previous night's storm had vanished, replaced by a warm gentle breeze. Torn branches and blown leaves still littered the roads and gardens but the sky had recovered the vivid blue of earlier days. Once again the waters reflected the cloud-free sky above and white breakers traced the lines of the atoll's surrounding reefs. Paradise was restored. It was only the leaves and broken branches lying beside the road and in the gardens that gave any indication of the savagery of the previous night.

Capitaine Victor Broussard and Sidney Blaise were seated at a small plastic table close by a food van selling coffees and snacks. From their uncomfortable plastic chairs they could see the *Ocean Rover* swinging quietly on its mooring.

The boat and the events of the previous evening were the subject of their discussion. Broussard also held a sheaf of papers which he passed one at a time to Blaise. "I must admit your suspicion was correct."

Blaise nodded politely at the compliment. "It was only a suspicion but it grew in intensity."

"I am very pleased that you insisted we wait until the final report of the autopsy. It changed our knowledge so much."

"Victor, it has been a very interesting case. So many people who have a reason to hate the lady, not that, perhaps, I think we should consider her as a true lady – but then we should be generous in death."

Broussard nodded. "It does no harm to be generous."

" 'We all have secrets. You have to pay for your past'. When you interviewed Peter Metcalfe he told you that Ms Freidman had said those words on her last night. There were many secrets on that boat."

The gendarme nodded. "That is true my friend. They all had secrets."

"Secrets that they hoped would remain hidden, or hopefully be forgotten. For the guests on the *Ocean Rover* the secrets only re-emerged because the group was brought together again. Sometimes our actions have unexpected consequences. Her death was surely not what Annette Freidman had expected when she arranged this voyage."

"Also the puzzle of how she died. That I could not understand, but now."

Blaise agreed. "I also. It was a great puzzle. There was much for which we needed to find explanations. Remarks and actions that once made no sense I think we now understand."

"Do you think it was her past that caused her death?"

Blaise shook his head. "I don't know if it was the past that she most assuredly had, or just... We cannot always predict our lives, some things we can control, others are maybe just chance. For Annette Freidman, she no doubt sought to control her life and the lives of those around her but the final events, and the cause, I suspect, was not in her control."

"What should we do?"

"You are the police. It is your duty to bring the matter to a close."

"But it was you who guided the enquiry that reached the conclusion. It was you who found among the stories we were told what the true events were. I think you should be the person to take the news to those on the boat. I will come later to make formal the conclusion."

They parted and Blaise moved to the marina to await the inflatable which would take him to the *Ocean Rover*.

The eight guests were already waiting and seated in the salon of the *Ocean Rover* when Blaise arrived. On his request the four crew members joined them and stood quietly at the back of the room beside their captain and his wife. It was noticeable that Marly was sitting with Casey and Ed while Pete was on the opposite side of the cabin beside Mike. After their barbs on the night of the storm a feeling of acceptance had taken hold of Marley and Pete. At least, for them, the breakdown in their marriage would not be accompanied by the ongoing bitterness and anger that blighted so many lives. Nor were there the complications and worry about children, or the financial difficulties that separation so often brings. Marley would return to her life and career in the soft grey weather and the green of the English countryside that were her comfort and home while Pete would remain in the harsh, bright sunshine of Dubai to continue his business efforts.

Each would have to make a new life for themselves in their chosen worlds.

It was also noticeable that although they sat together Nikki was no longer constantly reaching out to touch or hold Mike. Their relationship had changed during the twelve days in Paradise, and while there was now a distance between them that had not existed when they had first arrived on the boat, it was impossible to know where this change would lead each of them.

"Well, you have got us together again. Are you going to tell us who the murderer is this time, or will this be another disaster like the restaurant?"

"Do not be too anxious Edward. All will become apparent in good time. I think by the time Capitaine Broussard arrives the matter will be resolved, but perhaps not as some may wish."

"Broussard is coming?"

"Yes Edward. He has that which puts this matter beyond doubt. It will confirm my explanation."

"So who did it?"

"First we must look to why and how the lady died. That has been a puzzle until now. Initially our thoughts were to an accident. A drunken person falling overboard."

"Well we already know she didn't die of drowning."

"Yes Peter. Then there was suicide, however there was no note, a common feature, no threat of such behaviour, also a common feature, and you all thought it a most unlikely act for such a person as Annette Friedman."

"OK, so it wasn't an accident and it wasn't suicide, it must be murder."

"Do not rush ahead Michael. Yes, we had the possibility of the man she saw on Bora Bora—but he has been cleared by Broussard. He could not have been present at the time of death. He did however give an insight into the lady's nature. She could be a very difficult and demanding woman. A woman who used people for her advantage with little care for them. To understand this death we must look at the reasons for this voyage."

"So?"

"The dead lady spoke of secrets. I once told Gabrielle everyone has a secret. Sometimes we carelessly divulge those secrets, sometimes we try to hide them behind false information, and at other times, those around us give clues to the secrets we seek to hide. So it is with this case."

"OK, so it was the chance for us to have an inexpensive holiday on a luxury boat, and catch up with old friends. That's hardly a big secret."

"Yes, in part you are correct. But Michael there was another reason you were brought together. The lady who arranged it had serious problems. As a favour, a friend allowed her to use his boat to raise funds. You have told me the price she charged was very reasonable but it was still a profit for her. However, she still lacked the money she desperately needed. More importantly she got to spend time with you."

"Blaise, Broussard said Annette had money problems. So how was spending time with us going to solve her financial problems?"

"Because Michael, she thought you all had secrets you would prefer not to be disclosed."

"But we also know none of us paid up."

Blaise nodded. "So we have discovered."

"Anyway she spent most of her time in her cabin. She hardly spent any time with us. She would only turn up for meals and a drink, or drinks. That girl had a problem with the booze."

"Yes Michael. That is true. The post-mortem showed a high level of alcohol. She was also very ill and suffering with headaches from her illness. That is why the medical tests found so much medication for pain in her body. Ms Olson's remark about the Texas Medical Centre was most helpful."

"What about the phone call? Gaby says she heard Annette speaking to someone in Chinese. Annette could have arranged for someone to come to the boat and meet her?"

"That is true Peter. Unfortunately Gaby did not hear with whom she was speaking, or if it was a man or a woman. At first I thought it must be someone not on the boat. But who? Was it someone close-by? Was she planning to meet him? Or her? We must not exclude women in these days of equality. There have always been evil women such as Salome or the Hungarian noblewoman, Elizabeth Bathory, known as the 'Blood Countess'. Unfortunately in these days of equality bad behaviour has become more common in women. Although Broussard could not find the cell phone the telecommunications company was able to give the gendarmes the information about who she called. Some were to people far away."

"We've been through all that. You know she called some of us on the boat."

"Yes. Each of you has an explanation. But why call someone on the boat? It seems unnecessary. She could just walk up to them and chat. But then, perhaps the dead lady did not wish to be seen talking with a certain person on the boat. Or perhaps someone did not wish to be seen talking to her. Now we can exclude some people. Nikki and Marly do not speak Chinese, Gabrielle speaks Chinese but had little to do with Ms Friedman. You four men lived in Hong Kong for several years so you could speak the language. And you also Casey. Gabrielle, where were you when you heard Annette speak on her cell phone in Chinese?"

"Here, on deck. She was standing on her own, leaning against the rail, and looking out over the water when I walked past to ask Ana to refill my glass."

"And who else was there?"

"We all were, I think. No. Mike went down to their cabin, Nikki had asked him to get her a stole."

"Was he on the deck when Annette was speaking?"

"No. She made the call after he went down."

"I told you she called me twice. Once was when I was down in the cabin. I told you about the calls. She was a really nasty bitch saying all sorts of strange things, for some reason she kept rambling on in Chinese. God knows why. I didn't understand half of what she was talking about. She was incoherent at times, but I didn't kill her."

"You told us of the difficulty with the game for phones but there was more was there not? Why did she try to blackmail you?"

"She didn't!"

Blaise said nothing, but the focus of his sight remained fixed on Michael Gordon. All the others present turned and looked at Mike. The silence seemed to last for minutes but was only ten seconds.

"OK. She tried the scam over *Cheeky Birds* and when that didn't work she made another attempt. My biggest client is a very religious man with a hatred of drugs since the death of his grandson. Annette knew I helped finance her husband's last drug investment, the failed deal that led to his death. I tipped the drug dealers off about his purchase of an airline ticket to Thailand in exchange for the return of my money. That doesn't mean I killed her, or him."

"I believe you."

"I don't think she was too worried about her husband's disappearance anyway. She had other interests at the time."

"Yes, that is true, you hinted as much at the restaurant. There are also others with secrets. Edward, the lady no doubt tried to blackmail you for money? From my chats with you all, I learnt that you had once had an affair with her in Hong Kong. However, the news of other meetings raised suspicions with your wife. Did she plan to tell your wife of what had happened on these other occasions? A divorce can be very expensive and possibly avoided if the suspicion dies. Also she was not a woman who would take rejection well; rather she may seek vengeance in any way she saw available."

"I didn't kill her."

"Revenge can also be motive. Perhaps we should also now include the women. Protection of their love is a very strong motive. Your wife had many reasons to hate Annette Freidman. That lady perhaps hoped to reignite the affair."

"But Casey was asleep in our cabin when Annette died. She'd taken sleeping tablets."

"Yes. Therefore, she must be innocent, but then she cannot be an alibi for you. The problem is if it was somebody on the boat who killed Annette Freidman when did he, or she, have the opportunity? You all have an alibi for the time. You were all in bed with your partners. Each was the alibi for the other. There is also the possibility of lies. That one person left the cabin and met with the lady. Now, in the movies, the villain would put sleeping tablets in the partner's nightcap or coffee but that is so melodramatic and happens only in cheap movies and novels."

"So, if it is all about blackmail, who else would have a secret that they wanted to hide? What's my crime?"

"Yours James, was certainly a lesser matter. In Hong Kong you had contacts. It was you who introduced your wife to the world of drugs that led to her eventual death. It was also you who introduced Annette Freidman's husband to the drug syndicate that no doubt led to his death."

"But Sidney, James told me all that before we started living together. It's no secret between us. Blackmail wouldn't work."

"That is good Gabrielle, but Annette didn't know that, and she thought it could be used to extract money."

"James told Annette to forget any ideas of him paying her money."

"That was very wise. Paying a blackmailer only encourages them to continue to try to extract even more money once they have had a success."

"So that leaves me. Why was she blackmailing me?"

"That I have not discovered, but it is not important Peter. Perhaps it was something concerning your wife in Hong Kong." Blaise's guess must have been close to the mark because a flush came over the face of Peter Metcalfe and he fell silent. Blaise continued. "The answer to this investigation lies in the nature of the medical condition of the lady. Peter mentioned that she would, at times, act strangely. His expression was 'lights on, but no one home'. She would also occasionally stumble and be clumsy in her movements. Others spoke of her being vague, lacking in concentration and forgetting events of the past that you would think she should have remembered. This, and the pain for which she was taking medication raised my suspicions that they were symptoms of the condition Broussard discovered. She had a brain tumour that was in urgent need of surgery. Clumsiness can be a symptom of the disease. Ana told me that on the night of the death she saw the lady hit her head against the handrail as she was going down to her cabin. She appeared dazed but had recovered by the time Ana reached her. It was a heavy fall and it would have made the bruise we found on the body. The concussion would likely also have affected her brain tumour."

"That hardly puts her on the motu?"

"Yes Edward. That was the next puzzle. How did she get to the motu? Michael told me that 'the closest Annette ever got to water was to lie on a lounge beside the pool with a Daiquiri and ogle the pool boys'. Marlene said that Annette had confided in her that she never went in the water. Amura told me that Ms Friedman had told him she could not swim. So I think we must dismiss the idea that she swam to the motu. Besides she was wearing a long red dress. That is not the sort of clothing one would wear for an evening swim."

"But it was wet."

"Correct Edward, it was wet, but from her body lying in the water beside the pier where she was found. In that position the tide would have washed over her."

"So how did she get there? Did someone come to the boat and take her away?"

"That was yet another puzzle. Tama was on watch that night. Yet he did not see anyone come or go from the boat. This yacht has paddleboards and a dingy as well as the inflatable so it is possible to use one of them to go to the motu. But Ana told me that Annette Freidman had a fear of water and did not like to be alone near water. So it is unlikely she would go herself. However she would go with someone she felt secure with, someone with experience with boats and water. Someone that interested her. But why would that person take her? Perhaps because she was also being blackmailed, not for money but for fear."

"Fear?"

"Yes, Ms Friedman had made a person in this room anxious with her behaviour. That is true, is it not?" Blaise turned and looked to the crew members standing at the rear of the room. The seated guests all turned to follow his gaze to the Polish girl. "She convinced you to row her to the motu?"

"Yes. She said if I didn't she would tell Matilde I was

having an affair with our Captain. It is not true but I knew Matilde would not believe me and I would be discharged. I would not be able to get another job on a boat."

"So you rowed her to the island. What happened next?"

"When I help her from the dingy she try to grab me and hold me. I pushed her away. I am not like that. Then she started to scream abuse at me, threatening to tell Claude anyway. I was frightened. I jump back in the dingy and start to return to the boat. She stood there shouting at me then she move and slip. She fell and hit her head on the post on the pier and fell to the ground. I stopped. She seemed to be in a daze then she awoke and started screaming at me again so I left her there."

"You told no one?"

"I was frightened. I knew I would be in trouble but I could not stay there with her. Then in the morning when her body was found, I was afraid. I knew the police would think it was me. She was alive when I left her."

Blaise nodded his head. "I believe you."

The first of the group to respond to the new information was Marlene. "So Annette put the hard word on Ana. But she'd been married, and what about the tanned young sailors in Hong Kong, and Ed? Casey was very coy about their particular history."

"Marlene, that is true, but remember there was also her German lady friend in Hong Kong. It appears your friend was not exclusive in her relationships. There is one other question we must ask. Why did Tama not see Ana and Annette leave?"

"So he'd dozed off on watch. Is it important?"

"Yes James, it is very important. That was because he was asleep. It was unusual. The duty of the night watch is to make sure people do not come on board to threaten or steal from the wealthy tourists. It was most unlike him. Claude tells me he is very responsible and reliable. He was drugged, but how? The coffee. I assume you put some of your wife's sleeping tablets in Tama's coffee. Is that correct Edward?"

"That doesn't mean I killed Annette."

"Then why did you drug Tama?"

"I didn't want to be seen with Annette. She'd threaten to show Casey some messages I had sent to her cell phone unless I paid up. She told me to meet her on the fore deck at one o'clock that night."

"That hardly requires drugging poor Tama?"

"I'd had enough of her threats, her demands. There was always another demand.   This time if she was still unreasonable... I thought about it, pushing her overboard. I knew she was drunk and couldn't swim. I thought she would drown and nobody would hear her calls. Everybody would be asleep. Any enquiry would decide that she fell overboard drunk. But I didn't do it. I'm not responsible for her death."

"So Edward, what happened?"

"Annette didn't show up. That was not unusual. It was her old trick. I've seen her use it before. Turn up late or not at all and claim some problem and the need to renegotiate a deal. I didn't know she had other plans, she certainly kept that side of her life separate from me. Then I saw Ana and Annette on the sports deck. They rowed away from the stern of the boat towards the motu. Only Ana returned."

"Could you see the lady on the motu after Ana returned?"

"No. There was no moon that night. There were stars but not much light. I could see them clearly when they were leaving the boat but by the time they reached the islet I couldn't see them, only vague shadows."

"Did you hear any sounds or loud talk from the motu?"

"No, nothing. All I heard from where I was standing was a noise from the engine room. A generator or air con or something. I was surprised when I saw Ana return alone. I didn't understand that but I thought Annette would be alone on the motu. So I took the dinghy and rowed across to the island. Annette was standing on the jetty, quite still, then suddenly she fell into the water. By the time I arrived she was already dead."

"So why didn't you tell someone you had found the body? You could have told Broussard. He would have questioned Ana."

"Blaise, get smart. Nobody had seen me. Ana didn't know I'd seen her, or rowed over to the motu. Broussard would have wondered why I had gone there. I was the last person to see Annette alive. He would have thought I did it. Why else would I go to the motu?"

"So why did you go to the motu?"

"I wanted to have it finally ended with her. I admit I did have thoughts of going through with my plan but it was too late, she was already dead. When I found the body I was worried that the police would find Annette's cell phone. There were messages on it that I didn't want Casey to know about. It wouldn't look good with the police either."

"And the cell phone. She had it with her?"

"Yes. I saw her put it in a pocket of her dress when she got into the dinghy with Ana. I took it and dropped it in the ocean."

"So then you returned to the boat and pretended you knew nothing. Yet often you sought to cast suspicions on others. That in itself made me suspicious."

"So Sidney, who do we believe? Ana or Ed? There has to be someone who did it."

"Do not be so certain Ms Olson. I think we can believe both of their stories. Consider, Annette Freidman did not die of drowning. There was no sign of any physical harm, no gunshot or knife wound. There were no marks on her body, apart from the bruise on her head that she obtained falling down the stairs here on the *Ocean Rover* before she went to the motu. There were no signs of physical or sexual abuse. Nor does Broussard's report show any indications of asphyxiation. Rather his report confirms that the stories of both Ana and Edward are true."

"So what's in this report you say Broussard has?"

"The Capitaine informed me of the report from the autopsy done in Papeete. Annette Friedman died from a traumatic brain injury. She was already suffering from the effect of the tumour. That explains much of her behaviour. Then she fell going down the stairs on the boat and badly bruised her head. From her actions she was suffering concussion from that fall but recovered. Then the second fall on the jetty of the motu. Perhaps it was a delayed effect from the first fall or perhaps instability caused by the tumour. We will never know. Even a mild second concussion can lead to Second-Impact Syndrome which is often fatal. In any case the autopsy shows a fatal injury occurred."

"But people don't just die from falling over. Not like that."

"They can, and do Ms Olson. There are stories of fit young football players who suffer a severe hit. They rise and play on but suddenly die, perhaps on the field, perhaps in the locker room. There may be no visible injury but the brain swells and bleeds, the brain cells begin to die and it can be quickly fatal. For the unlucky ones it may take only a few minutes, for others an hour or longer. There was the circumstance of a famous actress who had a skiing accident. She didn't hit anything hard, another skier, a building, a tree or a rock, but fell on soft snow. She walked away from the fall and joked about it with her companions but tragically within hours died of the injury."

"So you think that was what happened?"

"Broussard's report confirms the cause of death."

"So we are all innocent?"

"Innocent? Yes Edward, through your good fortune you are innocent of the death of Annette Freidman, but not of the intent in your heart."

"So when can we get off this floating jail?"

"I believe Capitaine Broussard will arrive shortly. I expect he will no longer require your presence, and then Edward, you and your friends will be free to continue your voyage."

"I have a question for you Sidney?"

"Yes, Ms Olson."

"The paddleboard? What happened to it?"

Sidney Blaise turned again to Ed Parker. "It was you who set the paddleboard free to confuse the investigation, was it not?"   The look on Ed Parker's face confirmed Blaise's accusation. "The board was found washed up on a beach by a villager who contacted the gendarmes. He was afraid a swimmer had fallen from it and drowned."

Almost instantly the group around the table parted, drifting off to their cabins or a quiet corner of the boat to digest the news that Annette Friedman's death was not murder, or suicide, but an accident. An accident compounded by a medical condition. For the travellers, all thoughts of continuing the voyage had vanished. Each was already planning their own escape from their companions and the swiftest way to leave the memories of a now tarnished paradise behind them. Sidney Blaise was left to sit quietly on his own as he waited for his Gendarme friend to arrive. No one questioned him, or spoke with him. He was part of the past they all wanted to forget.

As arranged, it was not long until Capitaine Victor Broussard boarded the *Ocean Rover*. Broussard gathered them together once again. He thanked the group for their assistance and patience and confirmed the explanation the Blaise had given. The boat was free to sail on and he wished them well for their voyage but all each traveller wanted was a flight out of Paradise. Broussard moved to the crew and shook the hand of each one, finishing with Claude Duval. "Thank you my friend. I hope next time you visit our island it will not be such a sad time." With that he and Sidney

Blaise boarded the grey boat of the Gendarmerie and motored away to the nearby town and police wharf.

42 Epilogue

Once again the sun was shining over French Polynesia. In the sky two faint wisps of horses-tails were the only clouds to be seen, and they were quickly vanishing over the far horizon. The ocean had regained its multitudes of blues, and once more the sparkle of white diamonds had returned to dance on the calm waters, ruffled only by an occasional waft of a warm gentle breeze. The happy laughter of children playing a game around slender palm trees drifted across the water of the tiny inlet.

At the café overlooking the marina two people sat taking their coffees and watching the buzz of activity on the water. Once again boats of all types and sizes came and went. Runabouts disgorged families to do their shopping, commuters arrived and later departed for distant villages, fishermen unloaded their catch or took on more crewmembers. Backpackers, with snorkels and fins, joined excursions to dive at nearby reefs.

"Their life is so different to ours. For us it should have been a life of luxury and indulgence, where we would have no cares or worries, and yet it was a disaster."

"Perhaps Gabrielle, their lives are not so different. People are still people. They love, and hate. They have jealousies and rivalries. They share, they worry for their families. They struggle for a living. Certainly the rich have comforts that the poor do not have, but riches may not bring happiness. Happiness is something we must find in ourselves."

"Are you happy Sidney?"

"Yes. I have the world to see. Like the *Ocean Rover* I am planning my departure from here. My book is complete. Now I will find another place, another story. There are many wonderful exciting places to see. So many that maybe I will never set foot in them all, but these days we are all citizens of a small world. A world that is changing and is fascinating. Exciting, as it is frightening."

"And do you have a love in your life?"

"Ah Gabrielle, always the question of youth. But what are you going to do now?"

"Like you, we are all planning to leave. Claude is arranging for flights back to Papeete and then we will go our separate ways. James and I leave tomorrow. I think we all just want to get away from the events of the past two weeks."

"Yes, I understand. It has been a time that I think will change lives."

"What do you think will happen to Ed and Casey?"

"Edward must live with the knowledge of his plan, and his previous behaviour. Maybe they will remain together, maybe not."

"And Nikki and Mike?"

"Ms Olson is fortunate. I think she has discovered that

she can be her own person. There is more to life than parties and a boyfriend to indulge her. For Mike? Well for Mike, he thinks there can always be a new woman but one day he may realise that he is growing older and he has missed the opportunity for a deeper happiness. Perhaps he will realize the opportunity he now has."

"Pete and Marly?"

"It is sad. Sometimes these things do not work out. Marlene will return to England as she wishes. Hopefully she will find happiness. Peter to Dubai. Maybe next time they will be more fortunate in their partners."

"And the crew? Claude and Matilde?"

"I suspect they will resolve their problems and continue. He is not the first man whose gaze has been drawn to a pretty girl."

"Then Tama and Amura, and Eeva?"

"Amura told me he is homesick and wants to return to Taha'a, his island with the sweet scent of vanilla. There his girlfriend is waiting for him. Tama and Eeva were concerned that the *Ocean Rover* was cursed by a murder, but now they know it was not a murder on the motu but natural causes. They are relieved. Tama says they will stay with the boat when it goes to the Mediterranean. I think Tama wants to see the French rugby team play in France and Eeva has read magazines of movie stars partying on luxury yachts like the *Ocean Rover* and dreams of seeing them."

"How will they go in that world? It is so different."

"So true. It will be an interesting time for them but they are sensible young people, perhaps more so than some of their clients who seem to create problems in their charmed lives. And you. You are so fortunate. You have the relationship we should all hope to find. And I congratulate you on your good fortune."

"Our good fortune?"

"I think you will be great parents."

"Why do you say that? How do you know? It is too soon to know. Even I'm not sure, let alone James."

"I am a writer. We observe. What you both want is a child and I think this voyage has been the answer."

"Well we certainly have been trying. If it is a boy we shall call it Matthew Andrew."

Blaise looked surprised. "But why those names?"

"Matthew Andrew Sidney, novelist, crime and mystery, writing under the pen name of Sidney Blaise, born..."

"That is quite sufficient."

"Nationality British. Born 1959, Clavering, Essex. Educated in Tehran, Caracas, Dhahran. Studied law at the University College London. You certainly had an interesting education. It didn't say where you live."

"But how did you find out?"

"Because I too have been doing some research. It took some time before I found your story. It's no wonder we couldn't place your nationality. And you, will you sail off into the sunset to discover new exciting worlds with the beautiful Ana?"

"Gabrielle, I envy her for her youth, her energy, her enthusiasm to discover life. However your question? That is the fantasy of tellers of stories, and this is real life."

ABOUT THE AUTHOR

Valverde Maclean: *"I don't do depression, dispossession and dysphoria. Nor gratuitous violence or gratuitous sex. I guess that may restrict my appeal for some, but it still leaves a huge and interesting amount of subject matter. The relationships between people, their lives, and the world around them are fascinating, and the bonds and enmities between people provide rich material for stories. While we must not forget that there is heartache and suffering in the world, there is also great beauty, humanity and, of course, romance and intimacy."*

Valverde Maclean has travelled widely through many parts of the world and has a particular passion for Australia. He has lived and worked in both the southern and northern regions of Australia. This experience shows in the way he writes of an Australia far from the big cities.

Australian history, particularly the development of the inland, and the ramifications for the economic life of the nation form a backdrop to his early stories.

His first novel "The Disappearance of Merry" was well received by readers who enjoyed the combination of romance and mystery. This was continued in his second novel "Magenta". His third book "The Letter" combined the present and the past, of life in the big cities and the Australian Bush.

Readers of these books have the pleasure of travelling today's Australia and discovering, or for some rediscovering, an Australia they had heard of, or remembered.

However it is not only the past, or Australia, but also the present-day changes and challenges to life and culture that are apparent in his writing. He is a keen observer of human behaviour wherever it may occur.

His fourth book "Murder on the Motu" marks a change, with a mysterious death in French Polynesia. However, like his previous stories, it is more than just a detective story as it investigates the personalities of those involved and the beautiful setting of the islands of the South Pacific.

Valverde Maclean now lives in a small village in the beautiful Sunshine Coast Hinterland of Australia.

Website: **www.valverdemaclean.com**
Email: **valverdemaclean@valverdemaclean.com**

Also by Valverde Maclean

"The Disappearance of Merry"

A man and a woman meet after many years. While visiting an historic Australian gold mining city an old mystery returns. Years earlier a young woman had disappeared. At the same time her brother was killed in a car crash. It's an old mystery but someone still doesn't want questions asked. Together they must travel Australia to find the answer, avoid death, negotiate their past and decide on their future.

There are great cups of coffee, and there are some bad cups of coffee. Little did I know where this particular cup of coffee would take me.

I was looking forward to seeing her again, but somehow I didn't really expect her to come. I still half expected that she would change her mind overnight and disappear like last time. She had done that once before, and she could do it again.

The island had always been a great place to escape from the world. The gardens were beautiful, the island perfect for daydreaming of beachcombing, of white beaches and of beautiful sunsets over the sea. There the dream became the reality.

"Fire brigades were called to the scene in Bolton Avenue, Armadale at eleven thirty last night by neighbours who heard a loud explosion and found the house blazing furiously. So far the investigators have failed to locate the occupants, believed to be a man and a woman."

The legs of a policewoman viewed through the bars of the grate was the best sight I had seen for a long time.

Visit **www.valverdemaclean.com**

The second novel by Valverde Maclean

Magenta

The story follows the twists and turns of their lives and their travel adventures as Suzie Benedict and Peter Jamison seek to understand their relationship.

VALVERDE MACLEAN'S

Magenta

In a remote region a young woman's body vanishes— only to re-appear fifteen hundred kilometres away. A road trip across the North and the West of Australia brings unexpected revelations, romance, danger and uncertainty that change relationships forever.

The *follow* up to the well-received first novel
"The Disappearance of Merry."

The thoughts that had been with me on my flight from Melbourne returned. What was I doing here? Worse, at the front door there was a posy of bright red roses and a note.

As we drove up to the parking spot near the beach we could see the vehicle. It was a small van with a painting of Elvis Presley on the side, but it was empty. There was no young woman with magenta hair on one side of her head.

The airstrip was a cleared strip of graded red dirt. A sign board proudly proclaimed "Mitchell Plateau-Arrivals and Departures Lounge". Around us the rocks of the gorges carved out by the river showed a variety of colours: reds, yellows, various greys and brown.

"Where are they?" Inspector Adamson's question took us by surprise. "Where's what? What are you talking about?" "The diamonds?" Adamson ordered coffees for three and told us a story of diamonds and drugs.

Visit **www.valverdemaclean.com**

The third novel by Valverde Maclean

The Letter

A search to understand the mystery behind a faded letter written almost a hundred and forty years earlier leads a woman to distant places far from her home and family.

Her unexpected discoveries will change her life, and the lives of those around her forever.

A faded letter discovered in an old shoebox leads a woman on an Australian journey that will take her from Sydney and Melbourne to Noosa, Emerald, and to the far west of Queensland. To Bourke and the Outer Barcoo.

Her search to solve the mystery of the cryptic references in the letter written one hundred and thirty-eight years earlier will lead her to uncover family secrets—some long hidden, or perhaps even forgotten.

Her discoveries will give her, and her family, a greater understanding of events that have shaped their lives.

It's a journey that will forever change her life, and the lives of others, especially her granddaughter. She must also finally face a decision that she has long avoided.

A story of past and present relationships and of Australia as it is and as it was.

A novel for those who enjoy a present-day romance and mystery with an interesting backdrop of history.

It was the old brown cardboard box that started my search. It was a shoe box, the sort that people once used to store memories, which changed our lives.

"That was Bella. Mike has problems. Big problems. They all have."

There was a hot, dry, wind blowing across the plain, coating the mourners gathered around the freshly dug grave with a thin layer of grey dust. Outside the cemetery fence the kangaroos stood watching the activity wishing the humans would leave so they could graze on the scant grass growing between the graves.

To be standing at the place where our family journey had begun had made it even more poignant. It was as if the circle had been completed.

Visit **www.valverdemaclean.com**

www.ingramcontent.com/pod-product-compliance
Lightning Source LLC
Chambersburg PA
CBHW060950030726
47503CB00003B/816